	DATE DUE		

A
Merry Heart

Center Point
Large Print

This Large Print Book carries the
Seal of Approval of N.A.V.H.

A
Merry Heart

The Brides of Lancaster County

1

Wanda E. Brunstetter

CENTER POINT PUBLISHING
THORNDIKE, MAINE

This Center Point Large Print edition
is published in the year 2008 by arrangement with
Barbour Publishing, Inc.

All Scripture quotations are taken from the King James
Version of the Bible.

All German-Dutch words are taken from the *Revised Pennsylvania German Dictionary* found in Lancaster
County, Pennsylvania.

The text of this Large Print edition is unabridged.
In other aspects, this book may vary
from the original edition.
Printed in the United States of America.
Set in 16-point Times New Roman type.

ISBN: 978-1-60285-356-0

Library of Congress Cataloging-in-Publication Data

Brunstetter, Wanda E.
A merry heart : the brides of Lancaster County / Wanda E. Brunstetter. -- Center Point
large print ed.
p. cm. -- (Brides of Lancaster County ; 1)
ISBN 978-1-60285-356-0 (lib. bdg. : alk. paper)
1. Amish--Pennsylvania--Fiction. 2. Christian fiction. 3. Large type books. I. Title.

PS3602.R864M47 2008
813'.6--dc22

2008036548

In loving memory of my sister-in-law,
Miriam (Mim) Brunstetter,
who always had a merry heart.

A merry heart doeth good like a medicine;
but a broken spirit drieth the bones.
Proverbs 17:22

Chapter 1

"I wish our teacher wasn't so cross all the time."

"*Jah*, my brother Sam says she's just *en alt maedel* who never smiles. I think she must have a heart of stone."

Miriam Stoltzfus halted as she stepped out of the one-room schoolhouse. She recognized the voices of Sarah Jane Beachy and Andrew Sepler and noticed that they were playing on the swings nearby.

Perhaps some of the children's words were true. At the age of twenty-six, Miriam was still unmarried, and as far as she was concerned, that made her an old maid among the Old Order Amish group to which she belonged.

Miriam pursed her lips. "I'm not cross all the time, and I don't have a heart of stone." But even as she spoke the words, she wondered if they were true. She did tend to be a little snappish, but that was only when the children in her class didn't behave or whenever she suffered with one of her sick headaches.

Miriam glanced at the swings again and was glad to see that Sarah Jane and Andrew had left the school yard. She didn't want them to know she had heard their conversation, and she wasn't in the mood to hear any more talk against herself. She would be glad to leave the school day behind and get home to whatever chores awaited.

She hurried around back to the small corral where her horse was kept during school hours and soon had the mare hitched to the box-shaped buggy she had parked under a tree that morning. She wearily climbed inside, reached for the reins, and, for the first time all day, experienced a moment of solace. Speaking a few words of Pennsylvania Dutch to the mare, she guided it out of the school yard and onto the road.

A short time later, Miriam directed her horse and buggy up the long driveway leading to the plain, white farmhouse where she lived with her parents and Lewis, her only unmarried brother. She spotted her mother right away, sitting in a wicker chair on the front porch with a large bowl wedged between her knees. "Look, daughter, the first spring picking of peas from our garden," Mom called as Miriam stepped down from the buggy.

Miriam waved in response, then began the ritual of unhitching the horse. When she was finished, she led the willing mare to the barn and rubbed her down before putting her into one of the empty stalls.

"How was your day?" Mom asked when Miriam stepped onto the porch some time later.

Miriam took a seat in the chair next to her mother, her fingers kneading the folds in her dark green cotton dress. "It went well enough, I suppose, but it's good to be home."

Mom set the bowl of peas on the small table nearby and pushed a wisp of graying hair away from her face where it had fallen loose from the tight bun she wore under her stiff, white head-covering. "Problems at school?"

Miriam released a quiet moan. Her mother always seemed to know when she'd had a rough day or wasn't feeling well, and she knew if she didn't offer some word of explanation, Mom would keep prying. "It's probably not worth mentioning," she said with a sigh, "but after school let out, I overheard two of my students talking about me. They seem to think I'm cross and have a heart of stone." She clasped her hands tightly around her knees and grimaced. "Oh, Mom, do you think it's true? Am I cross all the time? Do I have a heart of stone?"

Mom's forehead wrinkled as she shook her head. "I don't believe any Christian's heart is made of stone. However, I have noticed how unhappy you are, and your tone of voice is a bit harsh sometimes. Does it have anything to do with William Graber? Are you still pining for him?"

Miriam's face heated up. "Of course not. What happened between William and me is in the past. It's been almost two years, and I'm certainly over him now."

"I hope you are, because it would do no good for you to keep fretting or dwelling on what can't be changed."

An uncomfortable yet all-too-familiar lump formed in Miriam's throat, and she found that she couldn't bring herself to look directly into her mother's brown eyes. She was afraid the hidden pain in her own eyes would betray her words.

"If your troubled spirit isn't because of your old beau, then what is the problem?" Mom asked.

Miriam shrugged. "I suppose everyone feels sad and out of sorts from time to time."

"Remember what the Bible tells us in Proverbs: 'A merry heart doeth good like a medicine: but a broken spirit drieth the bones.' Happiness and laughter are good medicine for a troubled spirit, Miriam."

"I know that, Mom. You've quoted Proverbs 17:22 to me many times. But it's not always easy to have a merry heart, especially when things aren't going so well." Miriam stood. "I'd best go to my room and change. Then I'll help you get supper started."

"Jah, okay."

Miriam hurried inside, anxious to be alone.

When the door clicked shut behind Miriam, Anna bowed her head. *Heavenly Father, I know my daughter says she is over William, but her actions say otherwise. I believe she's still pining for him and hasn't found forgiveness in her heart for what he did. Please take away Miriam's pain, and help her to find joy in life again. Show me if there's anything I can do to help her be at peace with You. And if it's within Your will, please send Miriam someone who will love her in a way that will make her forget she ever knew a man named William Graber.*

Anna felt something soft and furry rub against her

leg, and she opened her eyes. One of the calico barn cats sat at her feet, staring up at her with eyes half closed, peacefully purring. She leaned over and stroked the animal behind its ears. "I think Miriam could learn a lesson from you, Callie. She needs to take the time to relax more, enjoy each precious moment, and carefully search for the right man to love."

The cat meowed as if in agreement and promptly fell asleep. Anna reached for the bowl beside her and resumed shelling peas.

Miriam's upstairs bedroom looked even more inviting than usual. The freshly aired quilt on the bed was neat and crisp, giving the room a pleasantly clean, outdoor smell. The bare wooden floor was shiny and smooth as glass. Even the blue washing bowl sitting on the dresser across the room reassured her of the cleanliness and orderliness of her plain yet cozy room. On days like today, she wished she could hide away inside the four walls of this familiar room and shut out the world with all of its ugliness and pain.

Miriam took a seat on the comfortable bed and pulled her shoes off with a yawn. *How odd that some of the young people among my faith desire to leave this secure and peaceful life for the troublesome, hectic, modern world. I don't believe I could ever betray the Amish faith in such a way. Modern things may have their appeal, but simplicity and humility, though they separate us from the rest of the world, are a part of our culture that I treasure.*

She fluffed up her pillow and stretched out for a few moments of rest before changing her clothes. Staring at the cracks in the plaster ceiling, she reflected on the voices of the two children she had heard talking about her earlier. "How little they really know about their teacher," she whispered. "They don't understand my pain. They truly believe I have a heart of stone."

Her vision blurred as tears burned her eyes. "My heart's not stone—it's broken and shattered, and I'm afraid it always will be so."

A tear slid down Miriam's face and landed on the pillow beneath her head. She squeezed her eyes shut, refusing to allow more tears to follow, for she knew if she let her emotions take over, she might lose control and never be able to stop crying. Miriam longed to be loved and feel cherished, and she knew in her heart that she was capable—or at least had been capable—of returning that same kind of love to a man who was willing to give his whole heart to her. She thought she had found such a man in William, but after his betrayal, she was certain that no man could ever be trusted. So she would guard her heart and her emotions and never let anyone cause her that kind of pain again.

Unwillingly, Miriam allowed her mind to wander back to when she was a twelve-year-old girl attending the one-room schoolhouse where she was now the teacher. . . .

• • •

Miriam sat upright at her desk, listening attentively to the lesson being taught until a slight tug on the back of her small, white head-covering caused her to turn around.

William Graber grinned, and the look in his deep, green eyes seemed to bore into her soul as his gaze held her captive. Even at her young age, Miriam knew she wanted to marry him someday.

William handed her a crumpled note he'd taken from his shirt pocket.

Miriam took the piece of paper, turned back around, and opened it slowly, not wanting the teacher to hear any rumpling. She smiled as she silently read William's words:

Dear Miriam:

I want to walk you home after school lets out. Meet me by the apple tree out behind the schoolhouse.

Your friend,
William Graber

Miriam turned and gave William a quick nod; then she folded the note and placed it inside her desk. Impatiently, she waited for the minutes on the battery-operated wall clock to tick away. . . .

Miriam's thoughts returned to the present. Releasing a sigh, she crawled off the bed and shuffled across the room to stand in front of the open window, where she reflected on the first day she had walked home from school with William. It was the beginning of many walks home together, and over the next few years, their friendship had grown as he continued to gain her favor.

Miriam and William's eighth year in school was their final one, and they both spent the next year in vocational training at home. William was instructed in the best of Amish farming methods, and Miriam learned the more arduous homemaking skills. She was sure they would eventually marry and settle down on a farm of their own, and she wanted to be sure she could run an efficient, well-organized home.

William was given a horse and courting buggy at the age of sixteen, and a few days later, he asked if he could give Miriam a ride home after a young people's singing. That had been the beginning of their courting days and the night Miriam had known she had fallen in love.

The months melted into years, and by the time the young couple had turned twenty, they still hadn't made definite wedding plans. Though they often talked of it secretly, William said he didn't feel quite ready for the responsibilities of running a farm of his own. After working full-time for his father since the age of fifteen, he wasn't even certain that he wanted to farm. He knew it was expected of him, but he thought he might be more suited to another trade.

The opportunity William had been waiting for

arrived a short time later when he was invited to learn the painting trade from his uncle Abe, who lived in Ohio.

Miriam cried for days after William left, but he promised to write often and visit on holidays and extended weekends. It wasn't much consolation, as she had hoped that by now the two of them would be married, perhaps even starting a family.

Impatiently, she waited for the mail each day, moping around in a melancholy mood when there was no letter, and lighthearted and happy whenever she heard from William. His letters were full of enthusiastic descriptions of his new job, as he explained how he had learned the correct way to hold a paintbrush and apply paint quickly yet neatly to any surface. He told her about some of the modern buildings in town they had been contracted to paint, and he promised he would be home soon for a visit.

William's visits were frequent at first, but after he'd been gone a year, his visits came less often, as did his letters. On Miriam's twenty-fourth birthday, a letter arrived with the familiar Ohio postmark. Her heart pounded with excitement, and her hands trembled as she tore open the envelope. It was the first letter she'd had from him in several months, but William's words had shaken her to the core.

Miriam groaned at the memory as she pressed her forehead against the cold window. When the pain became unbearable, she moved away from the window. Slowly, as though she were in a daze, she made her way across the room to her dresser. She knelt on the floor and pulled open the bottom drawer with such force that it nearly fell out. As she removed the stack of letters she had received from William during his time in Ohio, a sob caught in her throat. Her hands shook as she fumbled through the envelopes until she found his final letter. In a shaky voice, she read it out loud:

Dear Miriam,

I've always thought of you as a special friend, so I wanted you to be the first to hear my good news. I've fallen in love with a wonderful Amish woman—Lydia Stutzman. I love her so much, and we plan to be married in a few months. We'll live here in Ohio, and I'll keep painting for my uncle, as I'm sure you know that I could never be happy working as a farmer.

I hope you will fall in love with someone, too—someone who will make you as happy as Lydia has made me. I'll always remember the friendship we had as children, and I wish you the best.

Your friend,
William

Even though William's final letter had come nearly two years ago, to Miriam it felt like only yesterday. Her heart ached whenever she thought of him or read one of his letters. Did he really believe she would fall in love with someone else the way he had done? She had been crushed when he'd referred to their relationship as only a friendship. Had their years together meant nothing at all?

Miriam shuddered and leaned heavily against her dresser. The bitterness she still carried created a feeling of fatigue that never allowed her to feel fully rested. Suddenly, the room felt stifling, and she wanted to race out the door and never look back. But that wouldn't solve a thing.

With a determined grunt, Miriam grabbed the stack of envelopes, marched across the room, and flopped onto her bed. As tears streamed down her cheeks, she ripped each one of William's letters to shreds and dropped the pieces into the wastepaper basket near her bed. William had left her with a heart so broken she was certain it would never mend. But at least his letters could no longer remind her of that horrible pain.

Chapter 2

In the kitchen, Miriam found her mother standing at the counter, rolling out the dough for chicken potpie.

"Are you feeling better now?" Mom asked with a cheery smile.

Miriam reached for a clean apron hanging on a nearby wall peg. "I'm fine."

"That's good to hear, because we have guests

coming for supper, and it wouldn't be good if you were gloomy all evening."

"Guests? Who's coming over?"

Mom poured the chicken broth into the kettle before answering. "Amos Hilty and his daughter, Mary Ellen."

Miriam lifted her gaze toward the ceiling. "Oh, Mom, you know I'm not interested in Amos. Why must you go and scheme behind my back?"

"Scheme? Did I hear that someone in my house is scheming?" Papa asked as he entered the kitchen.

Miriam slipped her hand through the crook of her father's arm. "Mom's trying to match me up with Amos Hilty. She's invited him and Mary Ellen to supper again, and they were just here a few weeks ago."

Papa leaned his head back and chuckled. His heavy beard, peppered generously with gray, twitched rhythmically with each new wave of laughter. "Daughter, don't you think it's high time you married and settled down with a good man? Amos would make you a fine husband, so please don't close your mind to the idea."

"I think it's her heart that is closed." Mom glanced over at Miriam and slowly shook her head. "A heart blocked off from love soon grows cold."

Miriam turned away and began setting the table.

At that moment, Miriam's youngest brother, Lewis, came in from outside, sniffing the air as he hung his straw hat on one of the wall pegs near the back door.

"Somethin' smells mighty good in here, and it's makin' me awful hungry."

"We're having company for supper, so hurry and wash up," Mom said, nodding toward the sink.

"Who's coming?"

"Amos Hilty and his daughter," Miriam answered before Mom had a chance to reply.

"Aha! I think Amos is a bit sweet on you, sister."

"Just because he's a widower and his little girl needs a mother doesn't mean I'm available. Why can't you all see that I'm content with my life as it is?" Miriam compressed her lips. "I don't need a man."

Lewis gave Mom a knowing look, and she smiled, but neither of them commented on Miriam's remark. Did they really believe she would be happier if she were married to Amos, regardless of whether she loved him or not?

Miriam clenched her teeth so hard that her jaw ached. *I won't give up my freedom to marry a man I don't love, and since I will never allow myself to fall in love again, my family will have to get used to the idea that I'm en alt maedel and will always be one.*

Amos Hilty clucked to his horse and squinted against the setting sun shining through the front window of his buggy as he and his six-year-old daughter headed for Henry and Anna Stoltzfus's place. This was their second time eating supper at the Stoltzfus home in less than a month, and Amos wondered if Anna had extended the invitations because she knew he couldn't cook well or if she simply enjoyed entertaining. He was fairly sure that Anna had no idea he had agreed to come for supper again because he wanted to spend more time with Miriam and hopefully win her hand in marriage. More than likely, Miriam's mother thought he kept accepting her invitations because he was without a wife and needed a decent meal.

He glanced over at Mary Ellen, who sat on the seat beside him with her head turned toward the side window. A little over a year ago, the child's mother had been killed in a tragic buggy accident, and even though Mary Ellen seemed placid and well-adjusted on the outside, Amos wondered if she might be keeping her feelings bottled up. He figured what his daughter needed was the hand of a woman—someone who would not only care for her needs but also share in her joys, sorrows, and hopes for the future.

That sure isn't me, he thought with regret. Mary Ellen rarely spoke of her mother or expressed her feelings about anything of a personal nature. He had a hunch she might be hiding behind her forced smiles and the pleasant words that seemed to slip so easily off her tongue. Someone like Miriam Stoltzfus, whom his daughter seemed to admire and respect, might have a better chance at getting through to Mary Ellen than he ever could. At least he hoped she would.

As the Stoltzfus place came into view, Amos drew in a deep breath for added courage. *God willing, I hope that someday I might be able to get through to Miriam, too.*

Shortly after six o'clock, a knock sounded on the back door. Since Miriam was alone in the kitchen at the moment, she went to answer it. Amos and Mary Ellen stood on the porch. He held his straw hat in one hand, and Mary Ellen, who stood beside him, held a small basket of radishes. The little girl smiled up at Miriam and handed her the basket. "These are from Pappy's garden, Teacher. I picked 'em right before we left home."

"*Danki*, Mary Ellen. I'll slice a few for supper." Miriam motioned them inside and then placed the basket on the counter.

When Miriam turned around, Amos nodded at her and smiled. "It's good to see you this evening. You're . . . uh . . . lookin' well."

Miriam didn't return the smile, nor did she make any response. Instead, she rushed over to their propane refrigerator, retrieved a bottle of goat's milk, and placed it on the table.

Amos shuffled his feet a few times and cleared his throat. "Mary Ellen tells me she's doin' pretty well in school these days. She says that's because you're such a good teacher."

"I do my best," Miriam mumbled, refusing to make eye contact with him.

Mom, Papa, and Lewis entered the kitchen from the living room just then, and Miriam sighed with relief.

At least she wouldn't be expected to carry on a conversation with Amos anymore.

"*Gut-n-owed*, Amos," Mom said with a friendly smile.

"Good evenin' to you, as well. It was nice of you to have us to supper again."

"Our *mamm* knows how important good food can be for a man," Lewis said, giving Amos a wide grin.

"That's true enough." Amos cast a glance in Miriam's direction, but she chose to ignore it.

Papa pulled out his chair at the head of the table. "I think we should eat now, before the food gets cold."

Everyone took their seats, and all heads bowed. Miriam pressed her lips tightly together as she folded her hands. She was only going through the motions of praying tonight, and she felt too frustrated over Amos being here to even think about the food set before her.

When Papa signaled that the prayer was over by clearing his throat, he helped himself to the potpie and passed it to their guests. The main dish was followed by an array of other homemade foods that included coleslaw, sweet relish, sourdough rolls, and dilled green beans.

Miriam couldn't help but notice how Mary Ellen seemed to be studying everything on the table. It made her wonder if the last time the child had been served a decent meal was when she and her father had eaten supper here a few weeks ago. *I know Amos isn't much of a cook,* she thought, *for I've seen some of the pathetic lunches he's made for Mary Ellen.*

"You forgot to put the radishes on the table, Teacher," the child announced, pulling Miriam out of her musings.

"I'll see to them now." Miriam excused herself and moved across the room to cut up the radishes, wishing she could be anywhere but here.

"Teacher's real *schee*, don't ya think so, Pappy?" Mary Ellen asked her father.

"Jah, she's quite pretty."

Amos's words had the effect of fingernails raking across the blackboard, causing Miriam to grit her teeth as she returned to the table. This meal couldn't be over quick enough to suit her.

Amos helped himself to some of the potpie. "The women of this house make a good *nachtesse*."

Lewis grabbed one of Mary Ellen's radishes from the bowl. "Jah, Mom and Miriam always put together a mighty fine supper."

"Please, have some bread," Mom offered, handing Amos the breadbasket. "Miriam made it, and it's real tasty."

"Danki." Amos grabbed two pieces of bread and slathered them with butter.

Papa chuckled. "You certainly have a hearty appetite."

"Guess that comes from eatin' too much of my own cooking." Amos smiled at Miriam, but she turned slightly sideways in her chair and focused on her plate of food, which she hadn't yet touched. She had no appetite and would have excused herself to go to her room but knew that would appear rude. Besides, she rather enjoyed Mary Ellen's company.

Miriam felt relief when supper was finally over and Papa announced that he and Amos were going to the living room to play a game of checkers. Lewis left the house a few minutes later, saying he needed some fresh air and thought he would go for a buggy ride. Miriam had a hunch he might have a date and didn't want to say so.

The women remained in the kitchen with Mary Ellen, who sat on the floor playing with Boots, one of their kittens, while Miriam and her mother did the dishes.

Miriam pulled a kettle into the sink of soapy water and began scrubbing it vigorously with a sponge, as she watched the child out of the corner of her eye. The young girl's brown hair, twisted on the sides and pulled to the back of her head in a bun, looked a bit limp, as though it might come undone at any minute. Miriam tried to visualize Amos, his large hands clumsily trying to do up his daughter's long hair and never quite getting it right. She realized how difficult it must be for him to raise the child alone, as there were so many things only a woman could do well. He did need to find another wife—but certainly not her.

Amos had a hard time keeping his mind on the game of checkers, when all he could think about was the woman in the next room who hadn't said more than a few words to him all during supper yet obviously cared for his daughter. Mary Ellen seemed to like her teacher, too, and Amos wondered if she saw something good in Miriam, the way he did—something that lay hidden deep within Miriam's heart.

After listening to Henry gloat because he had won nearly every game, Amos finally decided it was time to go. He slid his chair away from the small table that had been set up in the living room and stood. "It's about time for Mary Ellen to be in bed, so guess I'd better head for home."

"Jah, okay," Henry said, as he cleared away the checkerboard. "I'm sure my wife will have you over for supper again soon; then we can play again."

"Maybe I'd better do some practicing before then, because you've sure skunked me good this evening."

Henry chuckled. "When you're as old as me, you'll likely win every game, too."

Amos smiled and bade Miriam's father a good night, then he headed for the kitchen. He found Mary Ellen kneeling on the floor with a kitten in her lap, and Miriam and her mother at the table, drinking tea. He nodded at Anna. "Danki for havin' us over. The meal was good, and it was much appreciated."

"*Gern gschehne*—you are welcome," she replied with a smile.

He glanced over at Miriam, but she never looked his way, so he directed his focus back to his daughter. "*Kumme*, Mary Ellen, come. We must get you home and into bed now."

"Oh, Pappy, do we have to go already? I'm not even tired yet."

"You might not think so at the moment, but half an hour from now, I'm guessin' your eyes will be droopin'."

Mary Ellen released a small sigh, placed the kitten on the floor, and stood. "See you in school on *Mondaag*, Teacher."

"Jah, Monday morning," Miriam said with a nod.

Amos grabbed his hat off the wall peg where he'd hung it earlier and steered Mary Ellen toward the door. Before his fingers touched the knob, he stopped and turned toward the table. "It was . . . uh . . . good to see you again, Miriam. Maybe I'll come by the schoolhouse soon."

"I'm sure Mary Ellen would like that," she mumbled.

Amos knew that many of the scholars' parents dropped by the school during the year—some without warning; some after letting the teacher know ahead of time. Since Miriam didn't seem too friendly toward him, he wasn't sure if he should let her know when he planned to come by or if it would be better if he just stopped at the schoolhouse unannounced. Knowing he could make that decision later on, he tipped his hat and said, "*Gut nacht*, Anna. Gut nacht, Miriam."

"Good night," they said in unison.

Chapter 3

On Monday morning, a few minutes after the school bell rang, Mary Ellen entered the classroom and presented Miriam with a small pot of newly opened heartsease. "These are from Pappy," the child explained. "He said he hoped some pretty flowers might make you smile." She stared up at Miriam, her hazel-colored eyes looking ever so serious. "You always look so sad, Teacher. God doesn't want us to be sad; Pappy said so." She placed the wild pansies on the teacher's desk and hurried to her seat before Miriam had a chance to respond.

Miriam studied the delicate flowers; they were a lovely shade of purple. It was kind of Amos to send them, but she was disturbed by the fact that he could look into her heart and see her sadness. *Perhaps I do seldom smile,* she thought, *but then there needs to be a reason to smile. If God wants me to be happy, then why did He allow William to crush my heart with his deception?*

She forced her gaze away from the pot of flowers and scanned the room to see if any of the children were absent. Satisfied that everyone was in their proper seats, she said, "*Guder mariye*, boys and girls."

"Good morning, Teacher," the class replied in unison.

Miriam opened her Bible and read from Proverbs

18. "'A man that hath friends must shew himself friendly; and there is a friend that sticketh closer than a brother.'"

The passage of scripture made Miriam think about her friend Crystal, who had always been there for her. If not for Crystal's friendship, Miriam didn't know how she would have gotten through her breakup with William. Crystal never reminded her that William had married another woman or that Miriam was an old maid.

With a concentrated effort, Miriam pushed her thoughts aside, reminding herself that she had scholars to teach and knowing that it did no good to dwell on the past. "And now we shall repeat the Lord's Prayer," she said to the class.

As Amos left his blacksmith shop and headed down the road toward Jacob Zook's place to shoe a couple of horses, he thought about Miriam and wondered if she liked the pot of heartsease he had sent to school with Mary Ellen. It was the second time he'd sent Miriam flowers using someone to deliver them in his place; only this batch of wild pansies had been delivered via his daughter and not his so-called friend.

Unwillingly, Amos allowed his mind to wander back in time. Back to when he was sixteen years old and had just received his courting buggy . . .

"I'm a little *naerfich* about being here tonight," Amos told William, as they simultaneously pulled their buggies up to the Rabers' barn, where the young people's singing was to be held.

"How come you're nervous?" William asked, stepping down from his open buggy. "I thought you were looking forward to coming."

"Jah, but that was before I learned you had given Miriam the bouquet of flowers I'd asked you to deliver and then you let her think they'd come from you." Amos clenched his fists until his fingers dug into the palms of his hands. "That was a sneaky thing to do, and it made me wonder if you're really my friend."

William snickered and thumped Amos on the back. "Miriam's had her eye on me ever since we were *kinner*, and when I gave her the flowers, she just assumed they were from me."

"You could have told her otherwise."

"I didn't want to disappoint the girl." William gave Amos a wily smile as they led their horses to the corral. "You may as well accept the fact that it's me she likes and find yourself someone else, because Miriam Stoltzfus is my girlfriend now."

When a car whizzed past, the horse whinnied, snorted, and stamped his hooves, causing Amos's mind to snap back to the present. As far as he knew, Miriam had never learned that the flowers William had given her a few days before the singing had really come from Amos. As much as it had bothered him to do so, Amos had stood by and watched William lead Miriam along, allowing her to believe he planned to marry her and then leaving her in the lurch when someone he thought to be more appealing had come along.

Amos had been in love with Miriam ever since he was a boy, and William knew it. Yet that hadn't stopped him from making a play for her, and it hadn't stopped him from breaking her heart, either. When William started courting Miriam, Amos had looked the other way and made every effort to forget that he'd ever loved her. After a time, he'd met Ruth, whose parents had moved to Pennsylvania from Illinois. Soon after, they had started courting and eventually married. Even though Amos hadn't loved Ruth as intensely as he had Miriam, they'd had a good marriage, and their love had grown during their six years together. The product of that love had been a delightful baby daughter.

Amos flinched and gripped the reins a little tighter as the memory of his wedding day washed over him like a drenching rain. Ruth was a sweet woman, and he still missed her, but she was gone now, and Mary Ellen needed a mother as much as he needed a wife—maybe even more. Truth be told, Miriam needed a husband, too; she just didn't seem to know it.

"She's been gloomy ever since William jilted her," Amos muttered. He hoped maybe some colorful flowers would cheer her up and put a smile on her face. It might make her more inclined to accept his invitation when he stopped by the schoolhouse after he finished shoeing Jacob's horses, too.

Amos's buggy horse whinnied as if in response, and he chuckled. "You agree with me, Ed? Jah, well, for Mary Ellen's sake, I hope I'll be able to make Miriam see that we could all benefit if she and I were to marry. And maybe someday she will come to love me as much as I love her."

By the end of the day, a pounding headache had overtaken Miriam. Fighting waves of nausea, she leaned against the schoolhouse door, feeling a sense of relief as she watched the children file outside. She would be glad to get home again, where she could lie down and rest awhile before it was time to help Mom with supper.

Just as she was about to close the door, a horse and buggy pulled into the school yard. Amos Hilty stepped out, his large frame hovering above the little girl who ran to his side. With long strides, he made his way to the schoolhouse, meeting Miriam on the porch.

He removed his straw hat and nodded. "I came to pick up Mary Ellen, but I wanted to talk with you first."

"Is there a problem?" Miriam asked, stepping back into the schoolhouse.

When Amos and his daughter entered the room, he motioned to the flowers on Miriam's desk. "I see you got the heartsease. Do you like 'em?"

"They're very nice." Miriam, feeling a bit dizzy, sank into the chair behind the desk. "Is there a problem?" she repeated, knowing that her patience was waning fast and might not hold out much longer.

Amos shook his head. "No problem. I just came by to . . . uh . . . offer you an invitation."

"Invitation?" Miriam stiffened on the edge of her seat. She hoped he wasn't about to ask her to go somewhere with him.

"I was wondering—that is, Mary Ellen and I would like you to go on a picnic with us on Saturday afternoon. We're planning to go to the lake, and—"

"It will be a lot of fun, and we'll take sandwiches and cookies along," Mary Ellen interrupted. "Pappy said he might bring some of his homemade root beer. It's real tasty, and I know you'd like it. The cookies won't be homemade, but I'll pick out some good ones at the store. . . ." The child babbled on until Miriam thought her head would split wide open.

"I appreciate the offer, but I—I really can't go with you on Saturday," Miriam said, when she could finally get in a word edgewise. She pushed her chair aside and stood, then moved quickly toward the door, hoping Amos would take the hint and leave. "Now, if you'll excuse me, I must be going home."

At first Amos stood there with his mouth hanging slightly open, but after a few moments, he took hold of Mary Ellen's hand and went out the door.

As Miriam watched them go, she noticed the look of rejection on Mary Ellen's face. She knew she'd been rude to them and hadn't even bothered to thank Amos for the flowers, but her head hurt so much, she'd barely been able to think. Placing her hands over her forehead and leaning against the door, she prayed, *Dear Lord, please take away this headache—and if it's possible, remove the horrible pain in my heart that never seems to go away.*

Amos glanced over at Mary Ellen, who sat in the front seat of the buggy beside him, wearing a scowl on her face. The child was obviously not happy about her teacher's refusal to join them for a picnic on Saturday, and he felt bad about that. However, it was a relief to know that his daughter was still capable of frowning, since she normally smiled even when things didn't go her way.

Amos hoped Mary Ellen didn't take Miriam's unwillingness to join them in a personal way. He was sure it was him Miriam didn't care for, not his daughter.

I wonder what she would have said if I'd told her the truth about William. He shook his head. *No. I don't want to hurt her any more than she's already been hurt.*

They traveled nearly a mile before Mary Ellen spoke; then she turned to face Amos and said, "Pappy, do you think maybe Teacher don't like picnics?"

"Most people enjoy picnics, and I'm sure Miriam does, too."

"Then how come she didn't want to go with us on Saturday?"

"I can't rightly say. Maybe she's made other plans for the day."

Mary Ellen tipped her head, as her eyes squinted into tiny slits. "Then how come she didn't say so?"

"I—I don't know," Amos answered as honestly as he knew how. If he could figure Miriam out, he might have been able to get through to her by now.

"Some of the kinner at school think Teacher Mim is mean, but she's never been mean to me."

" 'Teacher Mim,' is it? When did you start calling her that?"

She shrugged her slim shoulders. "It just popped into my head this minute."

"Jah, well, you'd best not be callin' her that at school, because she might not like it."

"How come?"

Amos gritted his teeth, unable to offer his daughter a responsible explanation.

"Pappy?" the child persisted. "Why can't I call her 'Teacher Mim'?"

"She . . . uh . . . might not appreciate it, Mary Ellen."

"Would it be all right if I asked her?"

"Sure."

"And if she says it's okay, then can I call her 'Teacher Mim'?"

"It's fine by me if it's all right with her." He reached across the seat and took hold of Mary Ellen's hand. "Let's talk about something else, okay?"

She offered him one of her cheery smiles. "Can we talk about the food we'll take on the picnic?"

He grimaced, no longer in the mood for a picnic.

"How about if we go to the farmers' market on Saturday instead? I could rent a table and try to sell some of my homemade root beer."

"Can I help?"

"Jah, sure."

"Okay then."

Amos wasn't sure if Mary Ellen really wanted to go to the farmers' market or if she was merely giving in to what she thought he wanted, but he decided to leave it alone.

Anna was in the kitchen, peeling vegetables over the sink, when Miriam arrived home from school, and she felt immediate concern when she saw her daughter's face. It looked paler than goat's milk, and her eyes appeared dim. "Sit down, Miriam. You don't look so well." Anna left her job at the sink and pulled out a chair at the table. "Are you sick or just tired?"

"A little of both." Miriam placed a pot of pansies on the table and dropped into the chair with a groan. "I have another one of my sick headaches. They seem to be happening more often these days."

Anna went to the stove and removed the teakettle filled with boiling hot water. She poured some into a cup and dropped a tea bag inside, then placed it in front of Miriam. "Drink a little peppermint tea to settle your stomach, and then go upstairs and lie down awhile."

Miriam nodded. "That sounds nice, but what about supper preparations?"

"I think I can manage on my own. Anyhow, someday after you're married, I'll have to do all the cooking without your help."

Miriam released a sigh and took a sip of her herbal tea. "I have no plans to marry, Mom. Not now. Not ever."

"My, what lovely pansies," Anna said cheerfully, feeling the need to change the subject. "Did one of your students give them to you?"

"Mary Ellen Hilty brought them. She said they were a gift from her *daed*." Miriam grimaced as she made little circular motions on her forehead with her fingertips. "It was another one of his tricks to gain my approval, that's all."

"Miriam, please don't be so harsh. I'm sure Amos means no harm. I believe he likes you, and he's no doubt been lonely since Ruth died."

"I'm sure he is lonely." Miriam slowly shook her head. "He came by after school today and invited me to go on a picnic with him and Mary Ellen this Saturday. I suppose he thought the flowers would pave the way."

"Did you accept his invitation?" Anna asked hesitantly yet hopefully.

"Of course not." Miriam pushed the chair aside and stood. "All he wants is a mother for his child and someone to do his cooking and cleaning."

Anna reached out and touched Miriam's arm. "I'm sure Amos wants more than that. He needs a friend and companion, just as you do."

"No, I don't!" Miriam's voice broke, and she dashed from the room before Anna could say anything more.

Nick McCormick hurried across the parking lot of the Lancaster *Daily Express* and had almost reached his car when his cell phone rang. "McCormick here. Can I help you?" he asked after clicking it on.

"Nick, it's Pete. I was on the phone when you left your office, but I wanted to tell you about your next assignment."

"Already? I was just on my way to do a piece on the fireman who saved the kid who'd fallen in an old well, like you asked me to do."

"I still want you to cover that, but I'd like you to go to the farmers' market in Bird-in-Hand on Saturday."

"What for?"

"As I'm sure you know, tourism has started in Lancaster County, and I thought it would make a good human-interest story to have an article and a couple of pictures of the Amish and Mennonite people who shop at the market or sell things there."

"Can't you get someone else to do it?" Nick asked as he opened his car door. "I'm supposed to have Saturday off, and I'd planned to drive into Philadelphia for the day."

"Marv Freeman was going to do the piece," his boss said, "but he's come down with the flu, and it's not likely he'll feel up to working by Saturday."

Nick pulled his fingers through the back of his hair

and grimaced. Walking around the farmers' market trying to take pictures of people who probably didn't want to be photographed was not his idea of fun, but he would do it in order to stay on the good side of his boss. Pete Cramer seemed pleased with his work these days, and if he played his cards right, in the future he might be given bigger and better stories to cover. "Yeah, sure, Pete," he said in an upbeat tone. "I'd be happy to go to the farmers' market on Saturday."

Miriam stood in front of her bedroom window, trembling from head to toe. *Why doesn't Mom understand the way I feel? Why does she keep coming to Amos's defense? Can't she see that he's not interested in me as a person? He only wants a mother for Mary Ellen.*

She leaned against the window casing as she thought about the eager look she had seen on Mary Ellen's face after Amos mentioned going on a picnic. But the child's expression had quickly changed to one of disappointment when Miriam said she couldn't go.

Miriam moved away from the window and over to her bed. *I hope Mary Ellen didn't take it personally. It's not her I don't want to be with, it's her daed.* She sank to the edge of her mattress with a moan. Sooner or later, Amos was bound to realize there was no hope of them getting together. If she kept turning him away, eventually he was bound to look for someone else to be Mary Ellen's mother. At least she hoped he would.

CHAPTER 4

Early Saturday morning, Miriam and her family decided to go to the Bird-in-Hand Farmers' Market. While none of them would rent a table in order to sell their wares, they all agreed it would be fun to browse and visit with many of their neighboring Amish friends and relatives.

The sun gave promise of a warm day, and as Clarence Smoker, their Mennonite driver, drove his van into the market parking lot, Miriam wiped the perspiration from her forehead and groaned. She hoped this summer wouldn't be as hot and humid as last summer had been.

Papa climbed out of the van first, then helped Mom down. As the two of them started toward the market building, Miriam stepped down, followed by Lewis. "I'll be inside soon," he said, nudging her arm. "I want to speak with Clarence about givin' me a ride to my dental appointment in Lancaster next week."

"Jah, okay. I'll go on ahead." Miriam hurried toward the market and was halfway across the parking lot when she stumbled on a broken beer bottle someone had carelessly tossed on the ground. Her legs went out from under her, and she landed on the shattered glass. She winced and struggled to her feet, hoping no one had seen her calamity, and wondering what the nasty bottle had done to her dress and knees.

Suddenly, Miriam felt two strong arms pulling her to an upright position. She looked up and found herself staring at a tall English man. His sandy blond hair was neatly combed, and he wore a pair of sunglasses.

"Are you all right?" he asked, bending down to pick up the broken bottle.

Miriam's face heated with embarrassment. "I . . . uh . . . I'm fine, really—thank you."

He whipped off his sunglasses to reveal clear, wide-set blue eyes. "Your dress is torn, and I see blood showing through it. You'd better let me see your knees because they might be cut up pretty bad."

His resonate voice was as impressive as his looks, and Miriam had to tear her gaze away from him. "I—I appreciate your concern, but I'm fine," she stammered. There was no way she was going to lift the hem of her dress so the man could see her knees.

Miriam glanced down at her soiled skirt and rubbed her hand against it, as though in doing so it might take away the red stain and ugly tear. She took a few tentative steps and cringed but determinedly went on.

"At least let me offer you some assistance." The young man put one arm around Miriam's waist without even waiting for her reply. "I'll walk you to the building. I assume that's where you were heading before your little accident?"

"I was, but I can make it there on my own." Miriam shook herself free from his grasp.

He smiled, revealing a set of gleaming white teeth and a boyish grin. "I didn't know you Amish ladies could be so liberated. I figured you might like to have a man look after you."

"I'm not liberated, but I don't need looking after." Ignoring the sharp pain in her knee, Miriam hurried on ahead.

The man continued to walk beside her. "I'm afraid we've gotten off to a bad start. I'm sorry if I've offended you." He extended his hand. "I'm Nick McCormick. Pretty catchy name, wouldn't you say?"

Miriam made no reply, nor did she make any move to shake his hand.

"I make it my duty to rescue fair ladies in distress." He reared his head back and laughed.

Despite her best efforts, Miriam found herself unable to keep from smiling. At least she thought it was a smile. She smiled so seldom anymore that she couldn't be sure.

After a few awkward moments, she finally took his hand and gave it a quick shake. "I'm Miriam Stoltzfus, and I'm sorry if I seemed rude. Now, if you'll excuse me, I need to catch up to my family."

"You're married, then?"

She shook her head. "I was speaking of my parents." Miriam wondered why she was answering this man's personal questions. It was none of his business who she was here with or what her marital status was.

"I see. Then perhaps you wouldn't mind giving me a guided tour of the place."

"A guided tour?"

"I'm a photographer for the *Daily Express* in

Lancaster. I've come to take some pictures for a cover story about the Amish and Mennonite people who are here at the market."

Miriam eyed the camera bag hanging over his shoulder. She didn't know why she hadn't noticed it before. Her body stiffened, and the familiar frown was back on her face. "I have no intention of acting as a tour guide so you can photograph my people. And in case you aren't aware of this, we don't pose for pictures."

They had reached the market, and Nick dropped the broken bottle into a trash can and opened the door, letting Miriam step inside first. "I'm afraid it's my turn to apologize, Miriam. In spite of what you say, I am aware that a few Amish people do allow pictures to be taken, especially of their children. I can see that you have your guard up for some reason, and I've obviously offended you by asking for your assistance. Please accept my apologies."

"It's of no real consequence. I get my feelings hurt a lot these days," Miriam said with a shrug. "Good day, Mr. McCormick." She turned and limped off in the direction of the ladies' restroom.

Nick watched until Miriam disappeared; then he turned in the opposite direction. He wished she would have been willing to show him around or at least talk to him long enough so he could get some information about her. Was she here to look around? Did she work at one of the places selling hot dogs, hoagies, or pretzels?

He thought about waiting until Miriam returned from the restroom but decided against it. She'd been anything but friendly during their encounter in the parking lot, so it wasn't likely that she would be willing to tell him what he wanted to know.

Not wishing to waste more time, he made his way down the aisle closest to him. English vendors selling craft items and souvenirs ran the first two booths, so he moved on until he came to a root beer stand run by an Amish man with dark brown hair cut in a Dutch-bob. A young girl sat on the stool beside him, reading a book. When Nick stopped in front of their table, she looked up and said, "Would ya like some root beer? My pappy makes it, and it's real tasty."

"Please excuse my daughter. She thinks it's solely her job to sell our root beer." The Amish man motioned to the jugs sitting on the table.

"It looks good, and I might come back for some on my way out," Nick said, "but right now I'm on a mission."

"What's a mission?" the child questioned.

"Mary Ellen, never mind. Go on back to your reading," her father admonished.

"That's okay; I don't mind her questions." Nick pulled a notebook and pen from his shirt pocket. "I'm a reporter for the *Daily Express*, and I, too, like to ask questions."

The Amish man's forehead wrinkled. "You're here to do a story?"

Nick nodded. "I'd like to ask you a few questions."

"About the farmers' market or about the Plain People who are here today?"

"Both," Nick said. No point aggravating the man if he was opposed to him doing a story on the Amish.

"What do you want to know?"

"Well, to me and many other Englishers like myself, the Plain life is kind of a puzzle."

"In what way?"

"I've heard it said that you Amish want to live separately from the world, yet you integrate by selling your wares right along with the English here."

The Amish man nodded.

"I understand some of your men serve as volunteer firemen, working in conjunction with the English firefighters."

"Jah, that's true. We're willing to work with others outside our faith and have congenial relationships with them, but we still remain separate by the plain clothes we wear, our simple transportation and farming methods, and our restrictions on the use of media among our people."

Nick grimaced. *Ouch. That last comment was obviously directed at me.* He managed a smile. "We all have a job to do, and mine involves bringing people the news."

The man opened his mouth to say something, but an older Amish couple showed up, and he turned his attention to them. "It's good to see you both. How are you two doin'?"

"Real well," the woman replied.

The bearded Amish man who stood beside her nodded. "We were feeling kind of thirsty, so we decided to come on over and get some of your flavorsome, homemade root beer."

The little girl, who had returned to reading her book, looked up and grinned. "You think maybe Pappy and me might get another invite to your house for supper soon?"

The Amish woman nodded and reached out to pat the child's head, which was covered with a small, white cap. "We'd like that." She smiled at the child's father then. "What do you think, Amos? Would you be able to come over again soon?"

He nodded with an eager expression and poured the man and woman each a glass of root beer. "If you think this is any good I'll bring a jug whenever we do join you for supper."

The older man took a quick drink and licked his lips. "Umm . . . it's *wunderbaar*."

"Wunderbaar. That means 'wonderful,' doesn't it?" Nick asked, butting in.

"That's right," the Amish man said. "Are you from a *Deitsch* background?"

"No, but I took a few years of German in high school, so I'm able to pick up on some of your Pennsylvania Dutch lingo."

"The man's a reporter for the *Daily Express*," Amos said. "He wants to do a story about the farmers' market and the Plain People who've come here today."

"We get too much of that already." The older man grunted. "Curious tourists askin' a bunch of questions is one thing, but I've got no time for nosy reporters."

"Okay, I know when to take a hint," Nick said, slipping his notepad and pen into his pocket. "Guess I'd better find someone else to interview."

He had already started to walk away, when the little girl called out, "Aren't ya gonna try some of Pappy's root beer?"

"Maybe some other time."

After inspecting her knees, Miriam found that only the right one was bleeding, but the cut didn't appear to be too serious. She wet a paper towel and blotted the knee to stop the bleeding; then she tried unsuccessfully to get the blood off her dress. She was afraid of scrubbing too hard for fear of tearing it more, so she decided to wait until she got home to tend to it properly.

Miriam was about to leave the restroom, when the door flew open and a little girl burst into the room. It was Mary Ellen Hilty. "Teacher!" she cried excitedly. "I seen your folks a bit ago, but I didn't know you was here today."

"Actually, I've only been here a short time," Miriam responded. She was tempted to correct the child's English but decided not to mention it since this wasn't a school day and she wasn't Mary Ellen's mother.

"Pappy will be glad to see you." The child's hazel-colored eyes shone like copper pennies, and her round cheeks took on a rosy glow. "He thinks you cook real good, Teacher. He said so after we had supper at your place last time."

Miriam tried to force a smile, but inwardly, she was seething. *Of course he likes my cooking. He would like any woman's cooking.*

"Your mamm said me and Pappy could come to supper at your place again soon." Mary Ellen twisted her body from side to side like a wiggly worm.

Oh, great. That's just what I need. Miriam tried to force a smile. "Are you happy it's almost time for school to be out for the summer?" she asked, hoping the change in subject might get Mary Ellen's mind on something other than their next supper invitation.

The child offered her a wide grin. "I'll enjoy spending more time with Pappy when he lets me come in his shop, but I'll miss school—and you, Teacher Mim. Is it all right if I call you that?"

"Jah, sure," Miriam mumbled.

"Some of the kinner don't like you so much, but I think you're real smart—and pretty, too."

"Danki." Miriam moved toward the door. "I must be going now, Mary Ellen. I need to find my folks."

"They're still talkin' to Pappy over by his root beer stand. Why don't you go on over and try some? Pappy gave your folks a glass for free, and I'm sure he'd give you one, too."

Miriam only nodded in reply, but when she left the restroom she turned in the opposite direction, away from the side of the market where the refreshments were sold. The last thing she needed was another meeting with Mary Ellen's father.

She didn't have to go far before she saw a familiar face. Her sister-in-law Crystal was heading toward her, holding hands with her two-year-old twin boys, Jacob and John.

"Aunt Mimmy, *dummle*—hurry," Jacob squealed.

"Aunt Mimmy, dummle," John echoed.

Miriam knelt next to her nephews to give them a hug, but the pain in her knee caused her to wince, so she carefully stood up again.

"Miriam, what's wrong? Are you hurt?" Crystal asked with a look of concern.

"It's not serious. I fell outside in the parking lot and cut my knee a little. I embarrassed myself some, too." Miriam made no mention of the brazen young English man who had offered his assistance. Why bring more questions from Crystal?

Crystal pointed to Miriam's dress. "You've torn your skirt. Let's go find your mamm. Maybe she has something we can mend it with. Your folks are here with you, aren't they?"

"Jah. I was told they're over at Amos Hilty's root beer stand."

"Let's go find them," Crystal suggested. "Maybe after Mom fixes your dress, she'll watch the twins for me. Then we can go off by ourselves and do some shopping. It will be like old times for us."

The idea of some time alone with Crystal did sound

kind of nice, but Miriam wasn't eager to see Amos. She hesitated before answering. "Why don't you go on? I'll meet you over by the quilts. I'd like to look at some Karen Freisen has for sale."

"That's fine, but what about your dress?"

"It can wait until I go home."

"Come with us anyway, and I'll treat you to a nice cold root beer," Crystal prompted.

John tugged on Miriam's dress. "Dummle, Aunt Mimmy."

"Dummle, Aunt Mimmy," echoed Jacob.

Miriam shrugged. "Oh, all right. I can see that I'm outnumbered. Let's get ourselves some root beer."

Amos was busy pouring a glass of frothy root beer for a young English boy when Miriam showed up with Crystal and her twins. He handed the glass to the boy and offered Miriam what he hoped was a friendly smile. "It's good to see you again. Your folks were here a few minutes ago. You just missed them."

"Oh, wouldn't you know it? I wanted Anna to watch these two for me," Crystal said, nodding at her boys.

"Maybe we should try to find them," Miriam suggested.

Jacob pulled on his mother's skirt, and John pointed toward a jug of root beer.

"Jah, boys, we'll have some root beer first," promised their mother.

Amos lifted the jug that was already open and poured some root beer into four paper cups. He handed the two larger ones to the women and gave the twins smaller servings.

Frothy foam covered John's and Jacob's noses when they simultaneously took a drink. The grown-ups laughed—even Miriam. It was the first time Amos had seen her laugh in a good long while, and it sounded real nice to his ears.

After the drinks were finished and they'd engaged in some polite conversation, Miriam said they should be on their way. Amos nodded, feeling a sense of regret, and said he hoped to see her again soon and was sorry she had missed Mary Ellen, who had gone to the restroom.

"I saw her in there," Miriam said. "I'm sure she'll be back soon."

Amos shrugged. "If she doesn't run into someone she knows and gets to gabbing."

"That's the way I was when I was Mary Ellen's age," Crystal put in. "My daed said I was the most talkative child in our family."

Miriam glanced around with an anxious expression. "Well, as I said before, I really should be on my way."

"That's right," Crystal agreed. "We need to find your mamm so we can see if she's willing to watch the twins while we do some shopping."

The women headed off, and Amos, determined to get Miriam off his mind, busied himself by setting several more jugs of root beer on the table.

• • •

"Amos is definitely interested in you," Crystal whispered to Miriam as they walked away.

"Well, I'm not interested in him," Miriam replied with a firm nod. "Furthermore, it troubles me the way everyone keeps trying to match us up. Even his daughter is in on the plot."

Crystal touched Miriam's arm. "Mary Ellen's a sweet child. I'm sure no such ideas have entered her mind."

"Maybe not, but some adults, whom I won't bother to mention, are in on the scheme to marry me off to Amos." Miriam wrinkled her nose. "I'm afraid some of them might be using that poor child as an instrument of their devious ways."

Crystal laughed. "How you do exaggerate. No one's being devious or plotting against you. We just want your happiness; surely you can see that."

Miriam just kept on walking.

"Ever since we were little girls, all we talked about was how we would marry someday and have a family. We both knew how happy we'd be if God gave us good husbands and a bunch of fine kinner to raise."

"That's easy enough for you to say, because you're happily married to my brother Jonas. And you have these *lieblich* boys to fill your life," Miriam added, pointing to her adorable nephews. She touched her chest. "I, on the other hand, am an old-maid schoolteacher, and I'll always be one."

CHAPTER

That was a great story you did on the farmers' market," Pete said when Nick entered his office the next weekend.

Nick pulled out a chair and took a seat in front of his boss's desk. "Thanks. Glad you liked it."

"You must have some kind of a connection with the Amish, because the quotes you got were awesome, not to mention the pictures you included."

Nick nodded. "I took a few years of German, so I understand some of what they say when they speak Pennsylvania Dutch to each other, which is how I got some of the information included in my article."

"And the pictures? Did they willingly pose for those?"

"Only a few of the Amish kids did. The older ones don't like to have their pictures taken, so I had to get those on the sly."

Pete nodded, and a slow smile spread across his face. "You're not only good with words and pictures, but you're crafty, as well. I like that in my reporters. That's how great stories are born, you know."

Nick lifted his shoulders in an exaggerated shrug. "I do my best."

Pete's balding head bobbed up and down. "And I'm sure you'll do your best on the next piece I give you."

"What might that be?" Nick asked with interest.

"Covered bridges."

"Covered bridges?"

"Yep. There are a lot of them in the area, and some of the older ones are in the process of being restored. I think it would be good to do an article about the bridges so our readers will know where they are and how to find them."

"Do you know where they all are, Pete?"

"Nope, but that's your job to find out."

Nick felt a trickle of sweat roll down his forehead. Driving all over the countryside searching for covered bridges did not sound like an interesting assignment, and he told his boss so.

"You don't have to drive around aimlessly. I'm sure the Amish in the area know where the bridges are, so I would suggest that you stop by some of their farms and ask for directions." With that, Pete stood and motioned to the door. "Your assignment begins right now, Nick."

The morning sun beating against the windows had already warmed the kitchen when Miriam came downstairs. She squinted against the harsh light and turned away from the window. Her head felt fuzzy; another pounding migraine had sent her to bed early the night before, and the unpleasant remnants of it still remained. What she really needed was something to clear her head of the dusty cobwebs lingering from her disturbed sleep. Since today was Saturday and there was no school to teach, perhaps she would have a cup of herbal tea, wash her hair, and then go sit by the stream to dry it. Some time alone might do her some good. Papa and Lewis were already out in the fields, and Mom had gone over to her eldest son, Andrew's, place to help his wife, Sarah, with some baking, so no one would need Miriam for anything.

While she waited for the water in the kettle to heat, she cut herself a wedge of shoofly pie and took a seat at the table. She liked solitude, and the quietness of the house seemed to soothe her aching head a bit. By the time she had finished eating, the water was hot, so she poured some into a cup and added a peppermint tea bag. After drinking the tea, she went to the sink to wash her hair, using a bar of Mom's homemade lilac soap. A hint of the perfumed flower tickled Miriam's nose, and she sniffed appreciatively. She rinsed with warm water, reached for the towel she had placed on the counter, and blotted her hair, being careful not to rub too aggressively, which she knew would only aggravate her headache.

When she was satisfied that the majority of water had been absorbed from her hair into the towel, she wrapped another towel loosely around her head, picked up her hairbrush from the wall shelf nearby, and went out the back door.

Miriam found the stream behind their house to be clear and blue, so inviting. She sank to the ground, slipped off her shoes, and wiggled her toes in the sun-drenched grass. At moments like this, she wished she were still a child. Life seemed easier back then, and it wasn't nearly so painful.

She reached up and pulled the towel from her head, causing her damp hair to fall loosely about her shoulders. She shook her head several times, letting the sun warm her tresses as she closed her eyes and lifted her face toward the sky.

Oh Lord, she prayed, *why must my heart continue to hurt so? I want to be pleasing in Your sight, yet I know that most of the time I fall terribly short. How can I have a merry heart, as Mom says I should, when I'm so full of pain and regrets?* Tears squeezed from her closed eyelids, and Miriam reached up to wipe them away.

The crackling of a twig startled her, and when she turned, she spotted the lens of a camera peeking through the branches of a willow tree. When she realized it was pointed at her, she gasped and jumped to her feet.

Nick McCormick stepped out from behind the tree and smiled. "Sorry if I surprised you."

"I—I never expected to see you again."

He smiled sheepishly. "I can't believe my luck—it's the liberated Amish woman I had the privilege of helping to her feet last Saturday. And what beautiful feet they are," he said, pointing to Miriam's bare feet. "I had no idea I'd be seeing you again today, either. Especially not like this."

Miriam pulled the hairbrush from her apron pocket and began brushing her tangled hair, knowing she must look a sight. "I don't appreciate you sneaking up on me. And I don't like the fact that you were taking my picture. I told you last week—"

"Yes, yes, I already know. The Amish don't like to be photographed." His smile widened, and he moved closer to her.

Miriam's teeth snapped together with an audible *click,* and she twisted the handle of the hairbrush in her hands. Why did she feel so nervous in this man's company? "The Bible tells us in Exodus 20, verse 4, 'Thou shalt not make unto thee any graven image,' " she explained. "We believe that includes posing for photographs or displaying them for impractical reasons. We also don't want to appear prideful."

"I can see that you're well versed in the scriptures," Nick said as he took a seat on the grass. Before she could comment, he quickly added, "And for your information, I photographed several Amish children at the farmers' market the other day, and none of them put up such a fuss. Is their religion any different than yours?"

Miriam lowered herself to the grass again, making sure she was a comfortable distance from the insolent intruder. "Children haven't joined the church yet, and they don't know any better. Besides, some English folks bribe them with money or candy. They're not strong enough to say no."

Nick laughed, causing the skin around his blue eyes to crinkle. "How about you, Miss Stoltzfus? Would you allow me to photograph you for a piece of candy?"

"I wouldn't pose for a picture at any price." Miriam looked the man squarely in the eyes. "Anyway, you've already taken my picture without my knowledge or my consent. I'm sure you probably have some prize-winning shots of the silly Amish woman sitting by the stream without her head-covering in place."

Nick's face sobered. "I've offended you again, haven't I?"

"To be perfectly honest, you have."

Nick held his camera in front of her face, and as he pulled each of the pictures he'd taken of her onto the screen, he hit the DELETE button. "There. Is that better?"

Before she could open her mouth to reply, he added, "Please accept my heartfelt apology for intruding on your privacy."

Miriam's defenses dropped just a little. "Thank you, Mr. McCormick."

"Nick. Please, call me Nick." He grinned at her in a most disconcerting way. "You know what, Miriam?"

"What?"

"You're beautiful when you smile."

Miriam felt the heat of a blush stain her cheeks. She hadn't even realized that she'd given him a smile. She looked down at her hands, clasped tightly around her hairbrush, and noticed that she was trembling. "I—I don't know what to say." Her voice was strained as his gaze probed hers. How could this man's presence affect her so, and why?

"Now I've embarrassed you," he said. "I apologize for that, too."

Glancing out the corner of her eye, she admired the perfect line of his profile. He was the most handsome man she had met since William. Instantly, she halted her thoughts. How bold of her to scrutinize the Englisher like that. As much as she would have liked to get to know Nick better, she was eager for him to leave.

"What's wrong? Aren't you willing to forgive me?" he asked, his lips twitching with a flirty smile.

"Of course I am. It's just that . . . well, no one has ever called me beautiful before."

"Then they must have been wearing blinders." Nick rose to his feet. "I'd better get going. I'm on a quest to find covered bridges, and so far I've only found two." He grunted. "I thought I could get some information from people living in the area, but you're the first person I've run into, and you probably wouldn't be willing to help."

"What makes you say that?"

"You didn't want to show me around the farmers' market last week, and I've offended you twice already today, so I just assumed—"

"You assumed wrong, Mr. McCormick."

"It's Nick, remember?" He looked at Miriam in such a strange way, it made her mouth feel dry and her palms turn sweaty. Maybe she just needed something to drink. "So do you know where some covered bridges might be?" he asked.

She nodded. "There are a few not far from here, and several more throughout the county."

"Can you give me some specifics?"

"Let's see. . . . There's one near Soudersburg, just off Ronks Road. Another is close to Strasburg, off Lime Valley Road." She paused and thought a minute. "There are two south of Manheim, one north of Churchtown Road, one east of Rothsville, and another one northeast of there. Then somewhere between Reamstown and Martindale you'll find one, and I believe there's one north of Ephrata, too."

He whistled. "That's pretty impressive. You must get around quite a bit."

"Not anymore. I spend most of my time teaching school. I used to travel the area a lot when I was a teenager."

"You're a schoolteacher?"

She nodded. "I teach at the one-room schoolhouse about a mile from here."

"So the liberated Amish woman is not only beautiful, but she's smart, too."

Miriam's defenses rose once again, and she clenched the hairbrush tighter. "I am not liberated, and I wish you would quit saying that."

"Sorry."

There was an awkward pause as they stood there staring at one another. Finally Nick smiled and said, "I've heard that the Amish only go through the eighth grade. Is that correct?"

Her only reply was a quick nod.

"Then how much training does a teacher for one of your schools need?"

"Same as the other scholars—we graduate eighth grade."

"That's it? No college or other formal training?"

She shook her head. "Amish teachers are selected on the basis of their natural interest in teaching, academic ability, and Amish values."

"What kind of values?"

"Faith, sincerity, and willingness to learn from the pupils."

"Ah, I see. Very interesting facts you've given me." Nick smiled. "One of the things I enjoy most about being a newspaper reporter is learning new things when I interview people."

"My mother's a reporter, too." Miriam hadn't planned on blurting that out, but she thought maybe Nick might be interested since he also wrote for a newspaper.

"What newspaper does she write for?"

"*The Budget*. Mostly Amish and Mennonite people read it, although I understand that some Englishers subscribe to the paper, too. Have you heard of it?"

"As a matter of fact, I have. I believe it's published in Sugarcreek, Ohio. Am I right?"

She nodded. "There are Amish and Mennonite people all over the country who write columns that go into the newspaper, and my mother is one of the scribes."

"That's interesting. What kind of news does she report?"

"Oh, just the happenings in our local community—

things like weddings, funerals, those who have had recent out-of-town visitors, accidents that have occurred in the area—that type of thing."

"What's your mother's name? I might decide to pick up a copy of *The Budget* and check out her column."

"Anna Stoltzfus."

"I'd like to meet your mother sometime. Maybe we could swap stories."

Miriam wasn't sure if Nick was only kidding or if he really wanted to meet her mother, but she was pretty sure Mom wouldn't take to the idea of some fancy English reporter who toted a camera asking her a bunch of questions. So rather than comment on his last statement, she merely shrugged and said, "It's been nice talking to you, Nick, but I need to get back home now."

"Do you live near here?"

She pointed to the field behind her. "Our house is on the other side of that pasture."

"Just a stone's throw then, huh?"

"Jah, if you've got a long arm."

He chuckled and held out his hand. "It's been nice talking to you again, Miriam. I appreciate your help on the covered bridges, and I hope this won't be the last time we meet."

Miriam didn't respond to that comment, either, nor did she shake Nick's hand. The man had a way of getting under her skin, but something about him fascinated her, too, and that bothered her more than she cared to admit. "Good-bye, Nick," she murmured.

"Bye, fair lady."

As Nick walked away, Miriam pressed a hand to a heart that was beating much too fast and wondered why the thought of seeing Nick again held so much appeal.

"Oh, Sarah," Anna said, as she and her daughter-in-law sat at the kitchen table drinking a cup of tea, "I'm worried about Miriam."

"What's the problem? Is she feeling sick or something?" Sarah asked.

Anna shook her head. "My daughter's body isn't sick, but her heart seems to have been shattered, and I fear it might never be mended."

"She's not still pining over William Graber, is she?"

"I'm afraid so. She's rejected all suitors ever since William jilted her, and now Amos Hilty has shown an interest, and she's giving him the cold shoulder, too."

"Many young people have breakups with their boyfriends, but most recover after a reasonable time." Sarah clicked her tongue. "If there was only something we could do to make Miriam realize that life goes on when bad things happen. God is always there to help us through our trials; we just need to trust Him and look for the good."

"I wish she could see that." Anna released a sigh. "I really think Amos would be good for her, and from what I can tell, his daughter seems to like Miriam a lot."

"She's a good teacher; Rebekah has told me that often."

"If she can teach the scholars and make them like her, then she has what it takes to be a good mother."

Sarah's forehead wrinkled as she stared at the table. "Sorry to say this, Anna, but not all of Miriam's students like her. Some say she's an old-maid schoolteacher with a heart of stone. Rebekah told me that, too."

Anna nodded. "Miriam overheard some of the kinner saying that not long ago, and it nearly broke my heart to see how sad she looked when she told me about it."

"Maybe we need to look for some fun things we can do that will involve Miriam."

"Jah, maybe so. Although she doesn't seem open to the idea of doing many fun things anymore. I'm going to keep praying for my daughter—that the Lord will give her a merry heart and that, if it's His will, Miriam will fall in love and get married."

CHAPTER 6

By the time school had let out for the summer, the weather had become hot, and Miriam found it difficult not to complain about the stuffy, humid air. Some days, not even a tender breeze graced Lancaster County.

One evening, a summer storm finally brought wind and rain, but it only caused more humidity. That evening, Miriam sat on the front porch steps watching streaks of lightning brighten the shadowy sky.

"God's handiwork is a pretty picture, isn't it?" said a deep voice from behind her.

She turned and discovered her father standing on the porch, stroking his long, full beard. "You startled me, Papa. I didn't hear you come out."

"Sorry about that." He pointed to the sky. "God's quite the artist, wouldn't ya say?"

Miriam nodded. Papa had such a way with words and a love and understanding of God that had always astonished her. He saw the Lord's hand in everything—things others would have simply taken for granted.

"We need a good rain," Papa said as he took a seat on the step beside Miriam.

"I suppose so, but it's making the air awfully muggy."

"Jah, well, we can put up with a little mugginess when the good Lord answers our prayers and brings the rain. The fields are in need of a good soaking."

Miriam couldn't argue with that. She knew how important the crops of alfalfa, corn, and wheat were to the Amish farmers in the area. She reached for Papa's hand. "How is it that you always see the good in things?"

" 'For as he thinketh in his heart, so is he,' the Bible tells us in Proverbs 23:7."

Miriam wasn't able to dispute that, either. Perhaps the reason she was so unhappy was because she thought unhappy thoughts. But how could she make herself think pleasant thoughts?

She shuddered as a clap of thunder sounded close to the house.

"Is somethin' besides the storm troubling you?" Papa asked.

Of course something was troubling her. Something always seemed to be troubling her. She shook her head. "Just the storm. I hope the *wedderleech* doesn't hit anyone's house or barn."

"Lightning strikes are always uninvited. But if it should happen, then we'll simply rebuild." He smiled. "A good barn raising is always a joy."

"A joy? You mean, it's a lot of work, don't you?"

"That, too, but working together with your friends and family can be a happy time."

Miriam couldn't help but admire her father for his optimistic attitude, but try as she might, she couldn't seem to emulate it.

That Sunday, church services were held at Andrew and Sarah's home. Their farm was only three miles away, so the ride by horse and buggy was rather short compared to some.

After Papa helped Mom down from the buggy, he and Lewis joined his two married sons, Jonas and Andrew, behind the barn where the horses had been put in the corral. Miriam and her mother made their way to the front porch to visit with Sarah, Crystal, and some of the other women who had already arrived. The twins were playing on the front lawn with their cousins, Rebekah and Simon, and several other small children.

"I'm going to step inside the kitchen for a drink of water before the service starts," Miriam whispered to Sarah.

Sarah, who was rocking baby Nadine, answered, "Help yourself. There's a pitcher of lemonade in the refrigerator if you'd rather have that."

Miriam shook her head. "Water will be fine, danki."

"Jah. Suit yourself."

When Miriam first entered the kitchen, she thought it was empty, but then she caught sight of someone across the room near the sink. Amos Hilty was bent over Mary Ellen, scrubbing her face with a wet washcloth. The child wiggled and squirmed, and she heard Amos say, "Mary Ellen, please stop *rutschich*."

"Sorry, Papa. I don't mean to do so much squirming." When the child spotted Miriam, she squealed and ran to her side. "Teacher Mim! You look schee today. Doesn't she, Pappy?"

Miriam looked down at her dark blue cotton dress with a white apron worn over the front. She wondered what there was about her that the child thought was pretty, and then she remembered Nick McCormick's comment about her being beautiful. Her gaze met Amos's, and he smiled.

"Your teacher's a fine-looking woman," he said, nodding at Mary Ellen.

Miriam made no reply.

Amos shifted his weight from one foot to the other. "Mary Ellen sampled some raspberries from Sarah's garden when we first arrived. She had sticky red juice all over her face."

Miriam nodded. "I came in for a drink of water. I'll get it and be out of your way."

Amos stepped away from the sink. "Help yourself. I've done about as well as I can with this little scamp's dirty face anyway."

Miriam hurried over to the cupboard and got out a glass; then she went to the sink and filled the glass with enough water to quench her thirst. She wished Amos would leave the room instead of standing there, watching her.

"Mary Ellen, why don't you run outside and play with some of your friends?" he said. "I want to speak with your teacher a few minutes."

The child gave him a questioning look, but obediently, she went out the back door, looking over her shoulder to flash Miriam a dimpled smile.

The last thing Miriam wanted was to be alone with Amos Hilty. She looked around the room, hoping someone would come into the kitchen and rescue her.

Amos pulled out a chair and motioned her to sit down. Reluctantly, she obliged, and Amos took a seat directly across from her.

"Church will be starting soon," Miriam reminded.

Amos glanced at the battery-operated clock hanging on the far wall. "We still have some time yet. I wanted to discuss something with you."

"About Mary Ellen?"

"No, about us."

"Us?" Miriam's voice sounded high-pitched, even to her own ears.

"Jah. It—it's about our relationship."

Miriam looked into Amos's coffee-colored eyes to see if he was serious, while she cleared her throat to stall for time. She wanted to be sure her words were well chosen. "The only relationship we have is the fact that your daughter is one of my students. So, if this isn't about Mary Ellen, then what?"

Amos stood and began pacing the kitchen floor. "Miriam, surely you've been able to tell that I have an interest in you."

Her mouth dropped open. Amos had always seemed rather shy, and she hadn't expected such a bold declaration from him.

"I—I want to spend more time with you—to come calling at your home and court you. Yet every time I ask you to go someplace with Mary Ellen and me, you have an excuse why you can't. Whenever I try to engage you in conversation, you act as though you're trying to avoid me."

"I'm sure you mean well, Amos," Miriam replied, "but I get the feeling that you're only looking for a mother for your little girl."

He looked stunned. "Oh, Miriam, I—"

"You needn't deny it. Everyone knows you're a widower without any family around to help you raise your daughter. It's understandable that you would want to find a wife to help care for her."

The room took on a distinctive chill, as Amos stared at the toes of his boots. "I . . . that is . . . I know Mary Ellen is quite taken with you. In fact, you're all she talked about when she returned from school every day last term. However, I do have some concerns about the type of influence you could have on her young mind."

"What's that supposed to mean?"

"You seem quite melancholy, and I had hoped if we started courting, you might find more joy in life and maybe even—"

"Do you think being courted by you would make me happy enough to have around your daughter? Is that what you're saying?" Miriam felt a trickle of sweat roll down her forehead, and she reached up to swipe it away.

"That . . . that's not what I meant to say at all." A crease formed between Amos's brows, and a pained expression crossed his face. "I—I think we could get along rather well if you'd only give it a chance."

Miriam stood and hurried across the room. When she reached the door, she halted and turned back to face him. "There are several available Amish women in the area, Amos. Some are a bit younger than me, but I'm sure if you use your charms on one of them, you might persuade her to be your wife."

"But I—"

Miriam rushed out the door without waiting to hear the rest of his sentence.

• • •

Amos stood staring at the back door and shaking his head. "She doesn't understand. She doesn't realize how much I care for her or that I would do my best to be a good husband. If only she would give me the opportunity to show her how things could be."

"You talkin' to yourself these days?"

Amos whirled around and was shocked to see one of Miriam's brothers standing in the doorway. "Andrew, I didn't realize you had come into the room."

"I was in the hallway and heard someone gabbin' away in here," Andrew replied with a crooked grin. "Don't tell me you're so desperate for conversation that you've taken up talkin' to yourself as a pastime."

"A few minutes ago, I was talking to your sister—at least, I was trying to—but she didn't stick around long enough to hear all of what I had wanted to say."

"She wouldn't listen, huh?"

"No. To tell you the truth, she doesn't seem to be interested in much of anything I have to say."

Andrew pulled out a chair and sat down. "Is there anything in particular you wanted her to hear? Maybe I could relay the message."

Amos took the seat opposite Miriam's brother. "I asked if I could court her, but she's obviously not interested."

"Did she come right out and say so?"

"Not exactly, but she said I should use my charms on some other Amish woman and try to get her to be my wife." Amos groaned. "If I have any charms, I sure don't know about 'em. Besides, I'm not interested in courting anyone but Miriam."

"How come?" Andrew scratched the side of his head. "I mean, if she's not interested—"

"She's my daughter's teacher, and Mary Ellen's quite taken with her." No way was Amos going to admit to Miriam's brother that he was in love with her and had been for a good many years.

"That's all well and nice, but it doesn't mean Miriam would make you a good wife, Amos."

"But she would make Mary Ellen a good *mudder*, I'm sure of it."

Andrew nodded. "You're probably right. Miriam's done well as a schoolteacher, and she would likely do as well as Mary Ellen's mother."

"Got any ideas how I can make her see that?"

"Guess you need to try harder, and don't give up, 'cause one thing I know for sure is my big sister has no other suitors." Andrew paused and scrubbed a hand down his bearded face. "So do you want me to put in a good word for you or what?"

"You—you would do that for me?"

"Sure thing, because I think you'd be good for my unhappy sister. Truth be told, I wouldn't mind havin' you as a brother-in-law, either."

Amos released a puff of air. "That would be great. I'll appreciate any help I can get on this."

"In case you don't know it, my mamm wants to see you and Miriam together, too."

"Really?"

"Sure. Why do you think she's had you for supper so many times?"

"Maybe I'll have a talk with Anna then, too."

"Might not be a bad idea." Andrew slid his chair back and stood. "A little prayer wouldn't hurt, either."

Heartless . . . heartless . . . heartless . . . The steady rhythm of the buggy wheels echoed in Miriam's ears as they traveled home that evening. The repetitive noise seemed to be calling out a reminder of the heartless way she had behaved toward Amos that morning.

She had probably hurt his feelings by letting him know she wasn't interested in him and thought he was only after her because of Mary Ellen. But he needed to realize there was no chance of them courting, much less of her agreeing to marry him. No matter how hard Miriam tried, she couldn't seem to get over the hurt and pain that lingered in her heart because of William's deception. Now Amos was hurting her even more by using his child to try and gain her favor. How foolish did he believe her to be? She'd been tricked by a man once, only to have her heart torn asunder. She would never allow herself to be hurt like that again.

As Papa pulled their buggy alongside the barn, Miriam pushed her thoughts aside, climbed down, and followed her mother up to the house.

"How about a glass of lemonade or some iced tea?"

Mom asked as they stepped into the kitchen a few minutes later.

Miriam tried to smile but failed. "I'm kind of tired. So if you don't mind, I think I'll head upstairs to my room."

Mom patted Miriam's arm. "Sleep well then, daughter."

"I will. Danki."

Miriam trudged wearily up the stairs, feeling like the weight of the world sat on her shoulders. If only there were some way to remove the heavy burden that made her feel like a prisoner.

CHAPTER 7

The following day after lunch, Anna and Miriam got busy cleaning up the kitchen. The men had gone back to the fields, leaving the women alone with a sink full of dirty dishes.

Anna filled the plastic dishpan with hot water and a touch of liquid detergent. "The men were sure hungry, jah?"

Miriam motioned to the bowl on the cupboard, full of watermelon rinds. "I think Lewis ate three or four pieces of watermelon himself."

"Our men do have some hearty appetites." Anna stepped aside so Miriam could wash the dishes while she dried. "Speaking of men, I was talking with Amos Hilty yesterday after the worship service. He asked me—that is, he was wondering if I would speak to you on his behalf."

Miriam dropped the dishrag into the soapy water so hard that it sent several bubbles drifting toward the ceiling. "Doesn't that man ever give up? I thought I had made myself clear when I spoke to him yesterday. Obviously my words fell on deaf ears."

"Now, Miriam, please don't be upset." Anna spoke in a soothing tone, hoping to calm her daughter. "I've probably made a mistake by bringing this up, but Amos seemed quite upset after he talked with you yesterday."

"I'm sorry about that, but I was upset, too."

"He's afraid you may have the wrong impression of him—of his intentions, that is."

"Oh, his intentions are clear enough. At least, to me they are." Miriam's forehead wrinkled as she turned to face Anna. "Can't you see it, too, Mom? Amos cares nothing for me. He just wants a housekeeper and a mudder for Mary Ellen."

"I'm sure he wants more than that."

"Jah, he probably wants someone to darn his socks, scrub his floors, and cook his meals. Well, I'm sorry, but that someone won't be me."

Anna placed a gentle hand on her daughter's arm. "Miriam, is it so wrong for a man to want those things?"

"Then he ought to get a hired girl to help out. Please tell Amos the next time you see him that I want to be left alone."

"I believe he does have a hired girl who comes in part-time, and you know Amos has no relatives to call on. His parents are both deceased, and his two brothers have farms of their own to run. His in-laws live in another state, so—"

"I'm truly sorry about all that," Miriam interrupted, "but it's certainly not reason enough for me to marry Amos, and I don't appreciate him asking you to speak to me on his behalf."

A ray of hope shone in Anna's soul. "Has he asked you to marry him?"

"Well, no, he just asked if he could come calling."

"I think he only wants to establish a friendship with you for now. In time, you'll both know if there's a chance for love or marriage."

Miriam released a noisy sigh. "I can already tell you that there's no chance for either love or marriage. Not for me."

Anna handed Miriam a few dishes to wash. "Must you always be so negative? Can't you look for some things to be joyous about?"

"What is there to be joyous about?"

Anna nodded toward the open window. "There are so many reasons to smile—the pretty birds chirping and flapping their wings, a clear blue sky on a sunny day, warm apple dumplings with fresh whipping cream for dessert, freshly cut flowers to decorate the table." She smiled. "And of course, knowing one is loved and cherished."

Miriam shrugged and then moved across the room.

She picked up the bulky ceramic bowl and headed for the back door. "I'm going out to the pasture to give these rinds to the cows."

Out in the pasture, the herd of dairy cows grazed contentedly, but they perked up their ears as Miriam approached. She dumped the watermelon rinds over the fence and watched as they ate greedily, nudging each other with their noses.

"You silly old cows. You carry on as though you haven't a thing to eat." She gestured to the field. "See here, you have a whole pasture of green grass to eat, so why all the excitement over a few watermelon rinds?"

Miriam lingered awhile, watching the doting mothers with their young ones. She was in no hurry to get back inside to more of Mom's lectures, so she figured she may as well stay a bit longer. She longed for the day when school started in August, for she looked forward to teaching again. Being at home all summer gave her too much time to think. Even though there were always plenty of chores to do, it wasn't the same as keeping her brain busy. Besides, when she was around home so much, Mom seemed more tempted to meddle in her life.

Miriam leaned on the fence rail and watched with interest as a mother cow washed its baby with a big, rough tongue. For some reason it reminded her of the sight she had witnessed on Sunday when she'd stepped into Sarah's kitchen and found Amos scrubbing his daughter's face. The baby cow squirmed all around, just as Mary Ellen had done.

"I suppose all little ones need a mudder to care for them," she whispered.

Amos had just left his blacksmith shop and was heading to the house to get a jug of iced tea and to check on Mary Ellen, when Andrew Stoltzfus's rig came into the yard.

"Wie geht's?" Andrew called as he stepped down from the buggy.

"I'm doin' all right. How about you?"

"Can't complain." Andrew crossed his arms and leaned against the side of his buggy.

"Were you needing your horse shoed?"

"No. I actually came by to talk to you about my sister."

"Did you put in a good word for me like you said you would?" Amos asked hopefully. If Andrew had achieved any measure of success, then maybe it was time for Amos to invite Miriam on another picnic.

Andrew shook his head. "My mamm spoke to her, but I'm afraid she didn't get very far, so I figured it would be best if I didn't stick my nose in where I'm sure it's not wanted."

"I see." Amos couldn't help but feel disappointed. If Anna hadn't been able to get through to her daughter, it wasn't likely that anyone else in the family could, either. "Maybe it would be best if I gave up on Miriam," he mumbled.

"Or maybe you should try a little harder."

Amos dug the heel of his boot into the ground. "I

invited her to go on a picnic with Mary Ellen and me, but she said no. I sent some wild pansies to school with Mary Ellen, but your sister didn't seem to appreciate them. I even got up the nerve to tell Miriam I wanted to court her, but her response was that I should find someone else."

"My sister's not allergic to flowers, if that makes you feel any better," Andrew said with a slanted grin.

"The only thing that would make me feel better would be if I could see Miriam smile the way she used to do when we were kinner."

Andrew pulled his fingers through the end of his beard as his smile turned upside down. "I don't think I've seen her crack a full-fledged smile since William Graber ran off to Ohio and married some other girl, leaving Miriam with a broken heart and a horrible mistrust of men."

"She doesn't mistrust her daed or any of her *bruders*, does she?"

"I don't believe so. Of course, none of us has ever given her any reason to mistrust us."

Neither have I. If she had given me a chance instead of William when we were teenagers, she would have found out that I wouldn't have let her down the way he did. Amos kicked at a small stone with the toe of his boot. *Course she didn't know the way I felt back then, and she still doesn't know it. Probably wouldn't care even if she did.*

"You okay?" Andrew asked, taking a step toward

Amos. "You're not taking it personally because Miriam's shown no interest in you, I hope."

Amos shrugged. "It's hard not to take it personally."

"I can still put in a good word for you if you think I should."

"It's probably better that you don't. No point in ruffling your sister's feathers any more than they already are. If it's meant for us to be together, then it will happen in God's time. I just need to pray more and leave things in His hands."

Andrew nodded and thumped Amos on the back. "Now that's good thinking."

As Nick sat at his office desk, studying the pictures he'd taken of several covered bridges in the area, he thought about Miriam Stoltzfus. He couldn't believe she had affected him so much that he'd willingly deleted those great shots he'd taken of her drying her hair by the stream. Even though she had explained the reasons for not wanting her picture taken, it made no sense to him. In fact, he didn't understand much about the Amish way of life, and he found Miriam's reference to God and the Bible a bit irritating. Ever since Nick's dad had been killed in a car accident, Nick had made his own decisions about life, and he didn't need any religious crutches in order to deal with life's problems. He believed that a man could be anything he wanted to be, do anything he wanted to do, and deal with whatever came his way.

Sure hope I get the opportunity to see Miriam

again, Nick thought. *I should have asked for her phone number so I could call once in a while.* He slapped the side of his head. *Dummy. Amish don't have phones in their homes, and those who do have phones for business reasons keep them in an outside building. It's not likely that Miriam has a phone, and if someone else in her family does, I'm sure they wouldn't appreciate her receiving calls from a nosy English reporter.*

The phone on Nick's desk rang, rousing him from his musings, and he quickly reached for it. "Nick McCormick here."

"Hi, Nicky. It's Aunt Nora."

"Hey there. How are you doing?" Nick was always glad to hear from his aunt. She was his only relative living in the area, and since he had moved here six months ago, he'd gotten to know her pretty well.

"I'm doing fine. All but one of my rooms is filled with boarders right now," she said. "I'd be happy to give that one to you if you'd like somewhere more peaceful and quiet to live."

"I appreciate the offer, but I like having an apartment in Lancaster because it puts me closer to the newspaper office."

"I understand." There was a short pause. "If you don't have a date for next Friday evening, how would you like to come over for supper?"

"Are you fishing for information about my love life, Auntie?"

"Of course not. I'd never do something like that."

He snickered. “Yeah, right, and frogs walk on their hind legs, too.”

“You would tell me if there was someone special, wouldn’t you, Nicky?”

“Sure I would, but there’s nothing to tell. I’m a contented bachelor and plan to stay one for as long as possible.”

“You’ll change your tune one of these days when the right woman comes along.”

A vision of Miriam Stoltzfus leaped into Nick’s mind, and he blinked several times, trying to dispel it. She wasn’t the right woman for him; he knew that much. She couldn’t be, because they were worlds apart.

CHAPTER 8

It was hard to believe it was August already and that today was the first day of school. Every year, the first day seemed a little hectic and unorganized, and today was certainly no exception. There were several new children in Miriam’s class, and since they were first graders and knew only their Pennsylvania Dutch language, they needed to be taught English. This took extra time on the teacher’s part, and it meant the older students must do more work on their own.

Mary Ellen Hilty was in the second grade and already knew her English fairly well, but she still lacked the discipline and attention span to work on her own for long. From her seat in the second row, the child raised her hand and called out, "Teacher Mim, I need your help."

Miriam tapped her foot impatiently and frowned. She was busy helping Joanna and Nancy with the letters of the alphabet and didn't want to be disturbed.

"Teacher!" Mary Ellen called again.

Miriam put her finger to her lips. "One minute, Mary Ellen. I'll be with you in a minute."

Mary Ellen nodded, folded her hands, and placed them on top of her desk.

When Miriam finished with her explanation to the younger girls, she moved across the room and squatted beside Mary Ellen's desk. "What is it you need?"

"I don't know what this word is." The child pointed to the open primer in front of her.

"That word is *grandfather*," Miriam answered. "You must learn to sound it out. Gr–and–fa–ther."

Mary Ellen looked up at Miriam, her hazel eyes round and large. "My grandpa and grandma Zeeman live far away. Grandpa and Grandma Hilty live in heaven with Jesus. So does Mama."

Miriam saw a look of sadness on the child's face she'd never seen before. Usually there was a light in Mary Ellen's eyes and a sweet smile on her lips. She felt pity for the little girl, knowing she had no one but Amos to look after her. No one but him to love.

The light came back to Mary Ellen's eyes as quickly as it had faded. "Danki—I mean, thank you for helping me, Teacher Mim."

Miriam gently touched the child's arm, pleased that she had remembered to use only English words in her sentence. "You're welcome."

Back at her own desk, Miriam found herself watching Mary Ellen instead of grading the morning spelling papers lying before her. The child never looked terribly unkempt, but her hair always showed telltale signs of not being secured tightly enough in the bun at the back of her head. Her face was always scrubbed squeaky clean, which came as no surprise to Miriam after watching Amos wash the child's face that one Sunday morning in Sarah's kitchen.

Miriam shook her head, bringing her thoughts back to the present. She had no desire to think about that day or to be reminded of the things Amos had said to her. Regardless of everyone's denial, she was convinced that Amos's interest in her was purely selfish. A mother for his little girl was what he wanted most. Though Mary Ellen was a dear child and Miriam did have a soft spot for her, it was certainly not enough reason to marry or even to allow the girl's father to court her. A woman should be in love with the man she planned to marry, and that possibility seemed seriously doubtful for her.

Mary Ellen looked up and offered a warm, heart-melting smile, and Miriam found herself fighting the urge to rush across the room and hold the child in her arms. For one brief moment, she wanted to tell Mary Ellen that she would marry her daed and be her new mamm—that she would love her and take care of her needs. Instead, she turned her attention back to the spelling papers. *What was I thinking? The idea of me marrying Amos is just plain* narrisch—*crazy. I don't love him, and he certainly doesn't love me.*

Miriam knew her students always looked forward to lunchtime, but she dreaded pulling the rope for the noon bell, because she would no doubt be caught up in a stampede as they made a mad dash for their brightly colored lunch buckets. Today was no exception, and she fumed as soon as she pulled the bell and was nearly knocked over by one of the older boys.

"Slow down at once," she scolded. "There's no need for you to rush like that."

Kenneth Freisen grunted an apology, grabbed his lunch box, and walked slowly back to his seat.

It took only five minutes for the children to gobble down their lunches and scamper outside to play for the remaining twenty-five minutes of lunch break. Games of baseball, Drop the Hankie, and hopscotch could be seen being played around the school playground, while some of Miriam's scholars took turns on the swings and teeter-totters.

Miriam stood at the window, watching the children and wondering if the ache she felt between her temples would turn into another one of her pounding migraine headaches. The day was only half over, and already she felt physically and emotionally drained. At moments like this, she wondered if teaching was really her intended calling in life. She often ran out of patience, and when she felt as she did today, she wondered if her mother could be right about her needing to find a husband and get married.

What am I thinking? she chided herself. *Even if I did want to get married, which I don't, I'm not in love with anyone, and I'll never marry without love or trust—both of which I don't feel for Amos.* She shrugged, deciding that her mood was only because it was the first day of school. In a few days when everything became routine again, she would be glad she was teaching school.

When a ruckus broke out in the school yard, Miriam's thoughts came to a halt. She heard laughing and shouting, and when she went to the door, she saw several of the children standing in a circle.

Miriam hurried outside. "What's the trouble?" she asked Kenneth Freisen, who stood nearby.

"The girls were blabbing again."

Miriam pulled two of the girls aside. That was when she noticed Mary Ellen standing in the middle of the circle. Tears streamed down the child's flushed cheeks, and she sniffed between shaky sobs.

"Mary Ellen, what is it?"

"It . . . it's all right, Teacher Mim. They didn't mean it, I'm sure." Mary Ellen managed a weak smile, even through her tears.

"Who didn't mean it? Did someone hurt you?"

"Aw, she's just a little crybaby." Kenneth wrinkled his nose like some foul odor had permeated the air. "She can't even take a bit of teasing."

Miriam eyed him with suspicion. "Who was doing this teasing?"

"It wasn't me, Teacher. It was the girls. Like I said before, they like to blab."

"Which of you girls was involved, and what were you teasing Mary Ellen about?" Miriam's patience was beginning to wane, and the pain in her head had increased. She feared the dizziness and nausea that usually followed would soon be upon her, as well.

The cluster of students remained quiet. Not one child stepped forward to announce his or her part in the teasing.

Miriam frowned and rubbed her forehead. "All right then, the entire class shall stay after school for thirty minutes."

"But, that's not fair! Why should we all be punished for somethin' just a few of the girls said?" Kenneth wailed.

"I didn't do nothin', and I'll be sent to the woodshed for a *bletsching* if I come home late," Karen Lederach whined. "My daed don't like tardiness."

"My mamm has chores waitin' for me," Grace Schrock put in.

Miriam looked at Mary Ellen. "Won't you tell me now who's guilty and what they said?"

Mary Ellen shuffled her feet a few times and motioned for Miriam to come closer. When Miriam bent down, the child whispered in her ear, "I'll tell you in private what they said, but I can't say who said it 'cause that would be tattling, and Pappy don't like a *retschbeddi*. He's warned me against being a tattler many times." She smiled, but the expression never quite reached her tear-filled eyes. "He says the Bible tells us to do to others what we want done to us. I wouldn't want someone to get me in trouble."

Miriam took hold of Mary Ellen's arm and led her inside the school building. Looking at the little girl's sweet face brought a sense of longing to Miriam's soul. She felt an unexplainable need to protect this child, and it went way beyond teacher to student. "All right, Mary Ellen. Please tell me what that was all about."

Mary Ellen looked up at Miriam, and her chin trembled. "Some of the kinner noticed that I don't dress like them."

"What do you mean? You're wearing the same Plain clothes as the rest of the girls in class."

"Today I must have put my dress on backwards, and I never even knew it. That's why some of 'em were laughing." She bit her quivering lip. "But please don't punish anyone on account of me, Teacher Mim."

"I'll worry about that later," Miriam said, as she helped the child out of her dress. *I should have noticed her dress was on backwards. What kind of teacher am I?*

Once the dress was put on correctly, Miriam held Mary Ellen at arm's length and scrutinized her. "You've set a good example for the entire class." She tucked some stray hairs into the bun at the back of the child's head. "I only wish the others would do the same."

"I always try to do what's right. It's what God wants me to do."

Miriam nodded, wondering how a child of Mary Ellen's age could be so full of love and forgiveness, when she, an adult, struggled every day with bitterness and an inability to forgive.

Pushing the thoughts to the back of her mind, Miriam returned to the school yard to speak with her other students while Mary Ellen waited on the porch. "I hope you've all learned something today," she said, shaking her finger. "No one will be required to stay after school this time, but if anything like this ever happens again, I will punish the entire class. I don't care if you all have to go to the woodshed for a spanking when you get home. Is that clear?"

All heads nodded in unison.

"Now get back to your play. Lunchtime will be over soon."

When Miriam stepped onto the porch, Mary Ellen smiled up at her. Miriam couldn't help but offer a smile in return. *She really is a dear little girl. Mary Ellen, the heartsome. Even in the face of difficulty, she still has a forgiving heart.*

"It's good to get out of that blistering sun awhile," Henry said as he washed up at the kitchen sink. "I was sweating buckets out there."

Anna placed a platter of sandwiches on the table, as he turned to reach for a towel hanging on the handle of the refrigerator door. "I'd figured you and Lewis would not only be hungry for lunch but needing some time away from the hot, humid weather."

"And speaking of lunch, I'm hungry enough to eat everything on the table," Lewis said, sneaking up behind his mother and giving her a squeeze.

She chuckled. "The Good Lord may have only blessed me and your daed with four kinner, but ever since you could eat solid food, you've been packing away enough for ten."

"That's a bit of an exaggeration, wouldn't ya say, Anna?" Henry asked, joining them at the table. "It might have been better to say that our youngest son was born with a hole in his leg."

"Puh!" Lewis waved a hand. "You're both exaggerating."

As soon as they were all seated, they bowed their heads for silent prayer. When Henry cleared his throat so the others would know he was done, Anna passed the platter of sandwiches around.

"I wonder how things are goin' for our daughter at the schoolhouse today," Henry said, snatching two bologna sandwiches off the plate, then handing it over to Lewis. "She seemed kind of naerfich today."

"Miriam's always a little nervous on the first day of school because she never knows how things will go with the scholars," Anna said, reaching for the pitcher of goat's milk and pouring some into each of their glasses.

Lewis bit into his sandwich and washed it down with a gulp of milk. "I remember when I was a boy attending the one-room schoolhouse. I always looked forward to the first day of school."

Henry shook his finger at Lewis. "That's because you couldn't wait to tease the girls." He reached for the bowl of cut-up vegetables and plopped two carrots and a handful of radishes onto his plate. "I'm surprised you haven't honed in on one of them girls and gotten married by now."

Lewis's face turned red as a tomato, but he said not a word. Anna had a hunch he'd already found that special girl and was probably secretly courting her. Of course Lewis wasn't likely to volunteer such information, and she wouldn't embarrass him by asking.

"Maybe being back to teaching will make our daughter feel happier," Henry said, bringing the subject back to Miriam again. "I hate seeing her so down-in-the-mouth all the time."

"It is hard to see her that way," Anna agreed. "Guess the best thing we can do is keep praying that God will heal her heart soon."

"And bring her a man to love," Lewis added around a mouthful of food.

Chapter 9

The days rolled quickly by, and Miriam fell back into her role as teacher. She still had moments of frustration and tension, leading to her now-familiar sick headaches, but at least she was keeping busy and doing something she hoped was worthwhile.

One morning, Miriam told her mother that she would pay a call on Crystal after school had been dismissed for the day. It had been awhile since they had taken the time for a good visit, and she was certainly in need of one now.

When Miriam pulled her horse and buggy to a stop in front of Jonas and Crystal's farmhouse, she saw Crystal outside removing her dry laundry from the clothesline. Miriam called to her, and Crystal turned and waved, then motioned for Miriam to follow her to the house.

Crystal deposited the laundry basket on a kitchen chair and pulled out another chair for Miriam. "It's good to see you. You've been on my mind a lot lately, and also in my prayers."

"Oh, really? Why's that?"

Crystal shrugged and began to fold the clothes, placing them in neat stacks on the table. "I've been praying for your happiness."

"Maybe it's not meant for some people to be happy," Miriam said, feeling a deep sense of sadness surround her heart.

"I don't believe that for a single moment, and neither should you." Crystal shook her head. "We've been taught since we were kinner that life offers each of us choices. God gave us the ability to choose what we will think and feel. He expects the believer to make the right choices, and He wants us to be happy and content with our lives."

Miriam shrugged. "That's easy for you to say. You're happily married to a man you love deeply, and you have two beautiful little boys. How could you not be happy?"

Crystal dropped a towel into the basket, pulled out the chair next to Miriam, and sat down. "Please don't be envious of my life. You can have the same happiness, as well."

Miriam stood suddenly, knocking over her chair in the process. "How can you speak to me like that? I thought you were supposed to be my friend."

"I—I am," Crystal stammered.

"Then please don't talk to me as though I'm a child."

"I wasn't. I mean, I don't think of you as a child. I was merely trying to tell you—"

"That I should marry someone? Were you thinking of Amos Hilty?" Miriam bent to pick up the chair, feeling more agitated by the minute. "Marrying Amos would not make me happy."

"How do you know that?"

"For one thing, he doesn't love me." She released a deep sigh as she straightened. "I've said this before, and I'll say it again: All Amos wants is a mother for Mary Ellen and, of course, someone to do his cooking and cleaning. Furthermore, I don't feel any love for him."

"Sometimes one can learn to love."

"Did you have to *learn* to love my brother?"

"Well, no, but—"

"Can't we please change the subject and just enjoy each other's company?" Miriam went to the cupboard and removed a glass. She was beginning to feel another headache coming on and knew she should take some aspirin right away if she was going to stave it off.

"Of course we can change the subject," Crystal was quick to agree. "I'm sorry if I upset or offended you. It's just that I want you to be as happy as I am."

"Please, don't worry and fret over me. I'm doing fine without a husband, and who cares if I'm not truly happy anyway? I've come to accept the fact that life isn't meant to be a bowl of sweet cherries. I . . ." Miriam's voice trailed off when she heard a horse and buggy pull into the yard, and she glanced out the window.

"Who is it?" Crystal asked.

"It looks like Lewis. Mom knew I was coming by here on my way home from school, and she probably sent him over to let me know that she needs my help. It's getting pretty close to suppertime, you know."

Crystal glanced at the clock on the far wall. "You're right. I'm surprised the twins aren't up from their naps yet."

Heavy footsteps could be heard clomping on the porch. The back door flew open, and Lewis burst into the room.

Miriam couldn't remember ever seeing her youngest brother look so upset. "What is it, Lewis? You look as though you've seen something terrible."

Crystal pulled out a chair. "Maybe you'd better sit down."

Lewis shook his head. "There's no time. "We have got to go *schnell*!"

"Go quickly where?" Miriam questioned.

"To the hospital." Lewis's voice quivered, and he seemed close to tears.

"The hospital? Is someone *grank*?"

"No one's sick, Miriam, but I think Papa's in bad trouble."

"What kind of trouble? Did something go wrong in the fields?"

"He seemed fine when we went up to the house at noon, but later on while we were workin' in the fields, he turned really pale, clutched at his chest, and then toppled right over."

Miriam gasped, and Crystal waited silently as Lewis continued. "It took everything I had to get him into the wagon, and as soon as I got him up to the house, I went straight over to Ray Peterson's place so we could call 911 for help." He sucked in a deep breath and wiped the sweat from his forehead with the back of his hand. "The ambulance came soon after that and took Papa to the hospital. Mom rode with Vera Anderson in her van, and I went to let Andrew know and then came over here to tell you."

"Wh—what do you think is wrong with our daed?" Miriam asked with a catch in her voice.

"I thought at first it might be the heat, but the paramedics said they thought it was his heart."

“A heart attack?” Crystal’s mouth hung open.

Lewis nodded. “Where’s Jonas? He needs to know, too.”

“He’s still out in the fields with my daed, but they should be here anytime, I expect,” Crystal said. “If you and Miriam want to get a ride and go ahead to the hospital, I’ll send Jonas there as soon as he comes back to the house.”

“We’d better head out to the field and try to find Jonas now. He can ride with us.”

Miriam shook so hard, she could hardly stay upright. “I’ll leave my buggy here and ride with Lewis, if—if that’s all right,” she stammered, looking over at Crystal.

“Of course. You can get your buggy later on this evening or tomorrow morning.”

Lewis grabbed hold of Miriam’s hand. “Andrew’s on his way to the hospital already, and our other English neighbor, Alan Wiggins, said he’d drive us there, so we need to get Jonas and go now before it’s too late.”

“Too late? What do you mean, too late? Is Papa’s condition that serious?” Miriam felt the blood drain from her face, and tears pricked her eyes.

Lewis nearly pushed her toward the door. “I really don’t know, but Papa wasn’t conscious when the paramedics arrived.”

“Remember Papa in your prayers,” Miriam called to Crystal over her shoulder.

“Jah, I surely will.”

• • •

Nick gripped the steering wheel as he squinted against the glare of the sun streaming through the front window of his sporty new car. He was heading to Lancaster General Hospital to cover a story about an elderly man who had been beaten and robbed at a local mini-mart, and he wasn't looking forward to it one bit.

Ever since Nick's father had been killed after being involved in a five-car pile up on the interstate, Nick had avoided hospitals. He'd only been twelve years old at the time, and for the two days following the accident, Nick and his mother had spent nearly every waking moment at the hospital. It had almost killed Nick to watch Dad slip slowly away, as his body's organs failed from the multiple injuries he'd sustained. Even now, fourteen years later, Nick could visualize his father lying in that hospital bed, hooked up to all sorts of strange-looking machines that had done nothing to save his life. Just driving by a hospital caused Nick to feel nervous, and going inside made his blood run cold.

He had tried to get out of the interview, but his boss wouldn't take no for an answer. In fact, he had told Nick that if he didn't do the interview, he could look for another job. So Nick was on his way to the hospital now, giving himself a pep talk, which he hoped would help conquer his fear.

If you're afraid of something, then reach deep inside and face it head-on. Nick remembered his father reprimanding him for being afraid to ride his bike after he'd crashed and scraped up his knees. *"Grit your teeth and get back on that bicycle,"* Dad had instructed. *"You'll never conquer your fear until you do."*

Nick had spent the better portion of twenty-six years trying to be brave and attempting to do everything in his own strength. He'd pretty much succeeded at it, too, because not much caused him to fear. Except for hospitals, that is, and tonight, he was determined to combat that fear, as well.

He clenched his fingers around the steering wheel tighter and fought the wave of nausea that threatened to overtake him. "I can do this. I can reach inside myself and find the strength I need."

Chapter 10

Soon after Miriam and Lewis arrived at the hospital they learned that their father's condition was quite serious. The doctors confirmed that he had suffered a massive heart attack. Miriam, her mother, and her three brothers stood around Papa's bed as the doctor gave the shocking news that, because his heart was so weak, Papa would probably not survive the night, though they would do all they could for him.

"How can this be?" Mom cried. "My Henry has always been a strong, healthy man."

"Sometimes as we get older—" the doctor began.

"Older? My father is only fifty-seven. He's not old, and he isn't going to die." Miriam shook her head as her face heated up like hot coals.

"Try to calm down. Your outburst isn't helping anyone." Jonas put his arm around Miriam's waist and pulled her off to one side. "If it's the will of God, then Papa shall live. If not—"

"If not, then what? Do we all put on a happy face and go on living as though Papa had never been a part of us?"

"Miriam, don't do this," Mom said tearfully. "We need to remain calm. We need to pray for your daed."

"That's right," Lewis agreed. "*Mir lewe uff hoffning*—we live on hope, so we need to remain hopeful."

Miriam's thoughts drew inward. How many times had she prayed over the last couple of years? How many of her prayers had God answered? Had He kept William from falling in love with someone else? Had He given William back to her? Had God made the pain in her broken heart go away?

Miriam was weary of praying and receiving no answers. Still, she knew that prayer was the only chance Papa had. So she would pray, and she would even plead and bargain with God. Perhaps He would trade her life for Papa's. If she were gone, she wouldn't be so greatly missed, but everyone in the family needed Papa, especially Mom.

"I'll be out in the waiting room," she whispered to Mom, feeling the need to be by herself and untangle the confusion that swirled in her head. "Send Lewis to get me if I'm needed or if Papa wakes up." She glanced once more at her father, lying there so still, hooked up to machines and IVs; then she rushed out of the room.

"What's wrong with Miriam that she can't stay and face this with the rest of her family?" Andrew asked as he turned toward Anna with a pinched expression. "Does she think running away will make anything better?"

Anna shook her head. "I'm not sure what my daughter believes."

"Well, she'll be sorry if she's not here when Papa wakes up," Lewis put in. He moved toward the foot of his father's bed and stood with his head bowed and shoulders shaking.

Jonas stepped up to Anna and put his arm around her shoulders. "Each of us must deal with this in our own way, so it's not our place to judge Miriam."

She nodded, and tears sprang to her eyes. "I don't know what I'm going to do if your daed doesn't make it, but I'm sure God will see me through, just as He will minister to all my children."

" 'God is our refuge and strength, a very present help in trouble,' " Jonas quoted from Psalm 46. "He knows our every need and will help us through this time of trouble."

Lewis turned away from the bed and frowned. "You all talk like Papa has already died. Shouldn't we be praying for our daed's healing instead of talking about how we'll get through it if he dies?"

"Of course we should be praying," Anna was quick to say. She didn't want to see any of her sons at odds with one another, especially not when their father might be dying. *No matter what happens, I'll have to be strong,* she determined in her heart. *With God's help I will set a good example to all my children and keep trusting Him.*

The waiting room was empty when Miriam entered. She was glad for the chance to be alone. For the next half hour, she silently paced, going from the window to the doorway and back again, pleading with God to heal her father.

At one point, Miriam stopped in front of the window and stared at the street below. She saw some cars parked along the curb . . . several more driving past. Some children rode by on bicycles. A bird fluttered past the window and landed in a nearby tree. The world was still going about its business as usual. It was a world that she and her Amish family had chosen to be separate from based on the biblical teachings of nonconformity.

Yet now, due to unwelcome circumstances, they were being forced to accept the modern ways in order to provide her father with the best medical care available. But would modern medicine be enough? Could the doctors save Papa's life and bring him back to them? If by some miracle he did get well enough to come home, would he ever be whole and complete, able to work on the farm again?

The waiting room door suddenly swung open, interrupting Miriam's thoughts and halting her prayers. Jonas and Andrew stood in the doorway, their faces pale and somber. "Papa's gone," Andrew mumbled.

She stared at him numbly. "What?"

"He said, 'Papa is gone,' " Jonas spoke up. *"Er is nimmi am scharfe."*

Papa is gone. He's no longer breathing. The dreaded words resounded in Miriam's head like a woodpecker tapping on a tree. "Is it true?" she asked, looking back at Andrew.

He nodded. "Jah, *sis awwer waricklich so*—yes, it's really so."

Miriam clenched her fingers into tight little balls as she held her arms rigidly at her side. Yet again her prayers had gone unanswered. Once more her heart would ache with pain. It wasn't fair. Life wasn't fair! Without a word to either of her brothers, she dashed from the room.

Tears blinded Miriam's vision as she stumbled down the hospital corridor. Her only thought was to run away—to escape this awful place of death, though she had no idea where she was going. She passed the elevator and ran down two flights of stairs. She flung open the outside door and was about to step into the evening air, when she ran into a strong pair of arms.

"Hey, fair lady! You almost knocked me off my feet."

Miriam looked up into the deep blue eyes of Nick McCormick. They were mesmerizing eyes, and she had to force herself to look away.

"We seem to keep bumping into each other, don't we, Miriam?"

Knowing she needed to put some space between herself and the tall, blond-haired man who stood in front of her, blocking the exit door, she tried to skirt around him. "If—if you'll excuse me, I was on my way out."

"I can see that. You almost ran me over." Nick squinted as he took hold of her arm. "I didn't notice before, but I can see that you're upset. Is there something I can do to help?"

"I—I just need some fresh air."

"No problem." Nick moved to one side and opened the door so that Miriam could walk through.

Once outside, she took several deep breaths, allowing the cool air to fill her lungs and clear her head, then she hurried away.

"Slow down. What's your hurry?" Nick called as he quickened his steps to keep up with Miriam.

She halted and turned to face him. "I—I thought I was alone. I mean, I didn't know you had followed me."

"Do you mind?"

"Don't you have business at the hospital?"

Nick shrugged. "I was there to cover a story about an old man who was beaten and robbed at a minimart."

"Then maybe you should—"

"It can wait." Since Nick was in no hurry to begin his interview, he actually welcomed this little interruption. "I think maybe you need someone to talk to right now."

"Front-page headlines or a back-page article?" she asked in a sarcastic tone.

"You insult my integrity, fair lady. I have no intention of interviewing you, so you can delete that thought right now. I just figured you might need a shoulder to cry on and maybe a little heartfelt sympathy."

Miriam sniffed. "What makes you think I need any sympathy?"

Nick reached out and, using his thumb, wiped away the tears that had dripped onto her cheeks; then he reached into his pocket and retrieved a hankie. "You've obviously been crying," he said, handing it to her.

Miriam blew her nose on the hankie and handed it back to him. "My—my father just died of a heart attack."

"I'm sorry to hear that, but shouldn't you be with your family at a time like this?"

"Probably so, but I—I needed to be alone."

"You want to be alone in your misery, is that it?"

Miriam began walking briskly again, but Nick was not to be put off. Despite her claim of wanting to be alone, he was sure she needed some support, so keeping in step with her, he offered his arm.

She declined with a shake of her head.

"Let's go somewhere for a cup of coffee," he suggested. "It might help if you tell me what happened and talk about the way you're feeling right now."

"I told you already—"

"Yes, I know. You'd rather be alone. Maybe that's how you think you feel, but I'll bet if you searched your heart you would realize that what you really need is someone to talk to." Nick took hold of her arm. "I promise not to include our conversation in my next article on the Amish—and I definitely won't take any pictures."

She released a deep sigh and gave a quick nod.

The small café Nick chose was a few blocks from the hospital, and it was nearly empty when they stepped inside. They took a seat at a booth in the far corner, and Nick ordered them each a cup of coffee and a slice of apple pie.

Miriam declined the pie, saying she wasn't hungry, but Nick insisted that she needed the nourishment and said she would probably feel better if she ate something.

Miriam finally gave in and ate the pie, realizing that she was a bit hungry after all.

"Feeling better?" Nick asked, as he stared at her from across the table.

She nodded. "At least my stomach does. I had no supper tonight. After school let out, I stopped to see my sister-in-law for a few minutes. I planned to be home in plenty of time to help Mom with supper, but then my brother Lewis came by and told us that Papa had collapsed while he was at work in the fields. We rushed to the hospital, and—well, you know the rest."

Miriam blinked back tears and took a deep breath. It turned into a sob. She couldn't believe she was sitting here in a café with a man she barely knew, pouring out her heart to him. Maybe that was why she felt free to do it—because she didn't really know him. He had no expectations of her. He would make no demands on her emotionally.

Nick reached across the table and took her hand, and she made no effort to stop him. The comfort he offered felt good. It was something she hadn't felt in a long time.

"I think I understand how you're feeling right now," he said. "Several years ago, I lost my dad when his car was involved in an accident on the interstate. I was an only child, and Mom and I had it pretty rough for a while."

"How did you manage?"

"It was hard. We lived with my grandparents for a few years. They looked after me while Mom went back to school for some training. She became a nurse, and then she was able to support us by working at a hospital in Chicago. That's where I'm from." Nick stared out the window. "Those were tough times, but I think they helped to strengthen me."

"Where's your mother now?" Miriam asked.

"Still living in Chicago. When I was fifteen, she remarried. I never got along well with her new husband, so after I finished high school, I went off to college, majored in journalism, and worked at several small newspapers after I graduated. When the newspaper in Lancaster offered me a job, I took it." Nick winked at her. "And you know the rest of the story."

Miriam's cheeks warmed. It had been so long since any man had looked at her the way Nick was looking at her now, and she'd forgotten how pleasant it could feel. With her heart aching so, his attention was like a healing balm. Nick had actually made Miriam forget her grief for a few brief moments, and she appreciated it. "Do—do you live in Lancaster alone, or are you—?"

"Married?"

She nodded, wondering what had caused her to be so bold or why she cared whether he was married or not. She felt confused and frightened by the feelings he generated in her, and she quickly pulled her hand out of his, nervously reaching up to straighten her head-covering.

Nick laughed. "No, I'm not married. It's not that I have anything against the state of matrimony. Guess I've just never met a woman who captured my heart enough to make me want to settle down and start a family." He winked again. "Of course, any woman who could put up with me would have to be a real gem."

Miriam smiled in spite of her sadness over losing Papa. "I think I should get back to the hospital now. My family might think I've deserted them."

Nick nodded with a sympathetic expression.

"Thank you for your kindness. I do feel a little better after talking to you, but I know the days ahead will be difficult ones." She gulped as a new realization swept over her. "I—I don't know how we will manage without Papa."

"I suspect you'll get through it, Miriam. I don't know you well, but I get the feeling that you're a strong woman—one with a determined heart."

She nodded. "My three brothers will help out, and Mom won't have to support herself. Of course, I'll be there to help with some money, too."

"I don't imagine an Amish teacher makes much, though."

The magic of the moment was suddenly gone, and Miriam's mind came back into proper focus. This man was a reporter. He didn't care about her as a person. He probably just wanted to satisfy his curiosity. "I make enough," she muttered.

"I meant no harm in asking about your wages," Nick said, lifting one hand as though asking for a truce. "I was only trying to show my concern for your situation, and I was about to say that if there's ever anything I can do to help you or your family, feel free to call my office at the newspaper."

"It's kind of you to offer," Miriam said, her voice softening some, "but—"

"You're not willing to ask favors of a worldly English man?"

"It's not that—I do appreciate your offer," she stammered. "If I should ever need your help, I'll let you know."

Nick smiled as she stood. "Guess I'd better pay for our eats; then I'll walk you back to the hospital."

"Really, there's no need for that. I can find my own way."

"Have you forgotten that I have an interview at the hospital? I was going in as you were going out."

"Okay."

The walk back to the hospital was silent. When they entered the building, Miriam turned to Nick and said, "Thanks again for your kindness."

"It was my pleasure, Miriam." He turned toward the information desk, then looked back again. "Don't forget my offer of help should you ever need a listening ear. Just call the *Daily Express* and ask for Nick McCormick."

CHAPTER 11

The three days following Papa's death were difficult to get through. After the funeral director had done what was necessary to prepare the body for burial and had returned it to the Stoltzfus home, Miriam and her family dressed Papa in his burial clothes. For the next three days, friends and family came to the home for the viewing.

That had been difficult enough, but Miriam wondered how she would ever get through Papa's funeral. She had never lost anyone so close to her before. When Grandma Gehman died, Miriam had only been five years old. Grandpa Gehman, who had moved to Illinois shortly after his wife's death, had passed on nearly ten years ago, when Miriam was still a teenage girl. She had never been close to her maternal grandfather and didn't know him that well. Her paternal grandparents were still living, though their health had failed in the last few years. Miriam figured it wouldn't be long before they were gone, too.

Papa's somber funeral service began early in the morning and was held in the Stoltzfus home. Miriam, dressed all in black, as were the other family members, was relieved that she had managed to get through the ordeal without falling apart. She was determined to be strong for her mother and not give in to the tears pushing against her eyelids, for if Mom saw her daughter crying, she was sure to fall apart.

After the funeral was over, the procession to the cemetery followed, and a short time later, Miriam huddled with her family and friends to watch as Papa's plain pine box was taken from the horse-drawn hearse and set in place at the burial site. She squeezed her eyes shut, trying to block out the memory of her final look at Papa's face before the lid on the coffin had been closed. Though the local undertaker had done a fine job, Miriam's father no longer looked like himself, and the stark reality that Papa was gone was almost more than she could bear.

Why, Lord? Why? she asked, as unbidden tears slipped from under her lashes. *How could You have taken Papa from us?*

Miriam forced her eyes open and glanced to her right, where her mother stood, openly weeping as the bishop said the final words over her husband of thirty-five years. *Is Mom strong enough to make it without Papa? Will I be able to offer her the kind of emotional support she will need in the days to come? Do I have enough strength for the both of us?*

With a heavy heart and a firm resolve, Miriam decided that she must be determined. Through her own sheer will, she would do whatever it took to remain strong for Mom and the rest of the family.

When the graveside service concluded, everyone climbed into their buggies. Then, the buggy Miriam rode in with Mom and Lewis led the way back to their farm, where they would share a meal with those who had come to say good-bye to Miriam's father and offer condolences to the family.

Miriam didn't feel the least bit hungry, but rather than draw attention to the fact that she wasn't eating, she put a sandwich, some dilled cucumbers, and a piece of gingerbread on her plate. Then she picked up a glass of iced tea and made her way to the stream, where she could be alone. Friends and family had been dropping by the house ever since the news of

Papa's death, and today nearly everyone in their community seemed to be present. Miriam needed some quiet time away from all the sympathetic looks and consoling words.

As Miriam approached the stream, she noticed a change in leaves on the trees and realized that they were on the verge of being kissed by crimson colors as fall crept in. Something about the peacefulness of the water gurgling over the rocks and the gentle wind caressing her face caused Miriam to think about Nick McCormick. Perhaps it was only the fact that the two of them had visited in this same spot several months before that brought his name to mind.

Miriam's face flushed. Just thinking about how the obstinate man had sneaked up on her with his camera and how he had taken a picture with her hair uncovered and hanging down her back made her feel almost giddy. Now wouldn't that have made a fine photo for the *Daily Express*?

What was there about Nick that made her feel these unexplained emotions? She had only seen him on three occasions, and each time he had succeeded in making her angry, but he'd also made her smile.

William had been the only man with whom Miriam had ever shared her deepest thoughts and dreams, and when he left her for another woman, she had vowed never to get close to another man again. While she wasn't exactly close to Nick, for some reason she had let her guard down. Was it simply because he seemed easy to talk to, or was it because Nick was an outsider and she knew there was no threat of a possible commitment?

Miriam's thoughts were interrupted when a deep voice called her name. She looked over her shoulder and saw Amos heading toward the stream with a plate of food in his hand.

"I thought you might like something to eat," Amos said when he reached the spot where she sat near the stream.

She held up her half-eaten plate of food. "I haven't finished this."

Feeling more than a little self-conscious, Amos took a seat on the grass beside her. "I already had one helping, but I suppose I could eat another. All this tasty food sure does whet the appetite. I'm not the best cook, so I don't enjoy my own meals so much."

"Where's Mary Ellen?" Miriam asked, making no reference to his cooking. Was he hinting that he needed a wife to cook for him—maybe her, in fact?

"My daughter is playing little mudder to your twin nephews," Amos answered. "Since she's well occupied, I decided to sneak away and check up on you."

"What makes you think I need checking up on?" Miriam's tone was harsh.

"I . . . uh . . . know what it's like to lose someone close to you, and I thought—well, I might have some words of comfort to offer." Hesitantly, he touched Miriam's shoulder, wishing he didn't feel so tongue-tied whenever he was with her. "I—I'm sorry about your daed. He will be missed by everyone in our community, but I'm sure he will be missed by his family even more. Henry was a good man."

Miriam stood, brushing away the pieces of grass that clung to her dress. "I should be getting back to the house. Mom may need me for something." She offered him a quick nod. "Danki for your kindness, but I'm going to be fine. Life is full of hardships and pain, but each of us has the power within to rise above our troubles and take control."

"The power within is God," he reminded.

"It's up to me to help my family get through this time of loss."

"That's fine, but—but what about you? Who will help you in the days ahead?"

"I'll help myself." Miriam pivoted on her heels and darted away.

"When you need me, I will come," Amos whispered.

As Nick left the dentist's office, where he'd gone for a checkup, he spotted a young Amish woman across the street. From this vantage point, she looked a lot like Miriam Stoltzfus.

The woman had just reached the crosswalk when she dropped her sack, tripped over a small red ball that had rolled out, and landed hard on the concrete.

Nick hurried across the street, barely taking the time to look for oncoming cars, and rushed to her side. "Miriam? Are you okay?"

The woman looked up at him, and her cheeks turned pink. "I—I'm not hurt, just skinned my knees a bit. And my name's not Miriam."

Nick was glad the woman hadn't been seriously injured, but he felt a keen sense of disappointment that she wasn't Miriam. He helped her to her feet and then bent down to retrieve the ball and a couple of books that had bounced onto the sidewalk when the sack slipped from her arms.

"I appreciate your help," she said, smoothing her dress and righting the small white cap perched on her head.

Nick handed her the paper sack with the items back inside. "I'm Nick McCormick, and I make it my duty to rescue fair ladies in distress," he said with a smile.

"It's nice to meet you. My name's Katie Yoder."

"Do you live around here?" Since the woman was willing to talk to him, Nick thought she might be agreeable enough to answer a few questions—in case he was ever asked to do another story on the Amish.

She shook her head. "I live in Mifflin County, north of here."

"Guess you must have hired a driver to bring you to Lancaster, huh?"

She nodded. "My brother lives not far from here, and since today's his son's birthday, I wanted to buy something to give the boy before I headed over to their place."

"Say, I've got an idea," Nick said. "Why don't we go have a cup of coffee someplace?"

Katie's dark eyes became huge, and the color in her face darkened. "I—I couldn't do that. I'm betrothed."

"You mean you're engaged to be married?"

She nodded. "Jah, in November."

His forehead wrinkled. "It's not like I'm asking for a date or anything. Just thought we could have a cup of coffee and talk awhile."

"I—I really can't. My driver's supposed to meet me on the next block, and I need to be on my way."

"I could drive you to your brother's house. That would give us time to talk."

"What did you want to talk about?"

"I'm a reporter for the *Daily Express*, and I—"

"You—you want to interview me?" Her voice raised a notch, and she blinked her lashes in rapid succession.

"Interviewing is what reporters do best."

She pursed her lips and stared up at him as though he'd said something horrible. "I have no interest in being interviewed for the English newspaper. Besides, my driver is waiting for me, and I wouldn't feel right about having coffee with you even if you weren't a reporter."

Wow! This little gal was as feisty as Miriam, although now that Nick had seen her up close, he realized she wasn't nearly as beautiful. Maybe Amish women weren't as passive as he'd thought them to be.

"Thanks for helping me, but I really must be going." Clasping the paper sack to her chest, Katie started walking at a brisk pace.

Nick was tempted to tag along but decided against it, figuring she might create a scene if he followed. So he sauntered back across the street where his car was parked as thoughts of Miriam filled his head. Something about her fascinated him. As strange as it might seem, he knew that if he were given the chance to pursue a relationship with her, he might just take it.

"How come we don't go over to Teacher Mim's house for supper no more?" Mary Ellen asked as Amos placed a sandwich on the table in front of her.

Amos didn't know quite how to respond. A few weeks ago Anna had invited him and Mary Ellen to join them for supper again, but he'd declined because he'd decided not to push so hard where Miriam was concerned. That meant not seeing her any more than necessary. Maybe if he gave her some time, she would see that he wasn't trying to force her into a relationship and might even come to him on her own.

"Pappy, did ya hear what I said?" Mary Ellen persisted.

He pulled out a chair and sat down beside her. "I've been real busy in my shop these last few weeks, and it's been easier just to eat at home."

"But I miss Teacher Mim."

"How can you miss her when you see her every day at school?"

"I just do, that's all." Mary Ellen lifted her chin and stared up at him with a peculiar expression on her face. "You think she might wanna be my mamm someday?"

Amos cringed. He wanted that, too. Wanted it more than he cared to admit. But unless God wrought a miracle, he didn't think it was likely that Teacher Mim would ever become his wife.

He patted Mary Ellen's arm. "Let's pray about it, shall we?"

She nodded eagerly. "I have been prayin', Pappy."

CHAPTER 12

The routine of life went on, even for those in mourning. With Papa gone, Lewis had to work twice as hard to keep up with the farm chores. The alfalfa fields needed one final harvesting before winter set in, and even with the help of their Amish family members and neighbors, the work was difficult and time-consuming.

Mom, too, kept busier than ever, working tirelessly from sunrise to sunset. While it was true everyone had more work to do now that Papa was gone, Miriam suspected the main reason her mother stayed so busy was so she wouldn't have to think about Papa so much and about how terribly she missed him. Often in the middle of the night, Miriam would be wakened by the sound of her mother crying. Her parents' marriage had been a good one, and she figured Mom would probably never get over Papa's untimely death.

If only there was some way to erase all the pain in one's life, Miriam found herself thinking as she put the finishing touches on a baby quilt she planned to give Carolyn Zeeman, the mother of one of her students. *God could wipe away all our tears if He wanted to. He has it in His power to keep bad things from happening.*

"What's wrong, Miriam? Did you stick your finger with the needle?" Mom asked, taking a seat in the other chair beside the quilting frame.

"No, I was just thinking."

"Whatever you were thinking about must have been pretty painful, because that frown on your face spoke volumes."

Miriam didn't want to respond. It would be too hurtful to remind Mom that God seemed to have abandoned them and could have saved Papa's life if He had wanted to. "It's nothing," she said, reaching for another spool of thread. "Nothing worth mentioning."

Anna sat beside Miriam for several minutes, watching her slender fingers move in and out of the brightly colored material, as she sewed straight, even stitches. Finally, when Anna could bear the silence no longer, she reached out and touched her daughter's arm. "Did you have a rough day at school? Have some of the kinner been saying unkind things about you again?"

Miriam shook her head, but Anna noticed the tears that had gathered in her eyes. "I—I'm just missing Papa tonight. That's all."

Anna swallowed around the lump in her throat. "I miss him, too. Guess I always will."

"That's understandable. You were married over thirty years."

"Jah, and I have much to be thankful for in that regard."

"What do you mean, Mom?"

"Your daed and I had a good marriage—one that was based on love not only for each other but for our heavenly Father, as well."

Miriam's gaze dropped to the floor, and she released a sigh. "Don't you feel angry that God took Papa away? Don't you want to shout at God for His unfairness?"

Anna gulped back a sob as she wrapped her arms around her daughter's trembling shoulders. "Oh, Miriam, please don't talk like that. Don't you know your daed's in a much better place, where there's no more sickness or dying, no more tears or toiling under a blistering sun?" She closed her eyes as a vision of Henry standing tall and handsome on their wedding day came to mind. "I can only imagine what it's like for him now, up there in heaven with Jesus. As much as I miss him, I take comfort in knowing he's safe and secure in our Father's arms. Why, if I know my Henry, he's running all over those golden streets, happy as a meadowlark in spring."

Miriam sat staring at the floor and breathing quick, shallow breaths like she couldn't get enough air.

"Maybe it would help if you wrote down your feelings," Anna suggested. "In the last article I wrote for *The Budget*, I expressed my deep hurt over the loss of your daed, and just writing it down helped to ease some of the pain."

Miriam looked up and shook her head. "I tried keeping a journal after William left for Ohio, and where did that get me?"

Anna wasn't sure what to say, so she closed her eyes and did the only thing she knew could help. She prayed that the Lord would release Miriam of her pain and help them all in the days ahead.

The fall harvest was finally complete, and everyone's workload had lightened a bit. One afternoon in early November as Miriam dismissed her students at the end of the school day, she noticed that a storm seemed to be brewing. Angry-looking dark clouds hung over the school yard, and the wind whipped fiercely against the trees. Miriam figured a torrential rain was sure to follow, and she hoped everyone would make it home before the earth was drenched from above.

"I'll give you a ride," Miriam told her six-year-old niece.

"Okay." Rebekah smiled and gave Miriam a hug. "Are you ready to go now?"

"In a few minutes. I need to get the blackboard cleaned and gather up a few things before I leave. Then I'll head out to the corral and get my horse hitched to the buggy."

"Is it okay if I wait for you outside?" the child asked.

"Jah, but you'd better wait in the buggy because the clouds look like they're about to burst wide open."

Rebekah darted out the schoolhouse door. "I will," she called over her shoulder.

Miriam hurriedly erased the blackboard and was about to write the next day's assignment, when a clap of thunder rent the air, causing the schoolhouse to vibrate. It was followed by a loud *snap* and then a shrill scream that sent shivers spiraling up Miriam's spine.

She rushed to the door, and a sob caught in her throat when she saw Rebekah lying on the ground next to her buggy, pinned under a tree limb that lay across her back. "Oh, dear God," Miriam cried with a muffled groan. "Please let her be all right."

Rebekah was unconscious when Miriam got to her. A gash on her head was bleeding some, but Miriam couldn't tell the full extent of her niece's injuries. She felt Rebekah's wrist for a pulse and was relieved when she found one, but the tree limb was heavy, and she couldn't lift it off the little girl's back.

She looked around the school yard, feeling helpless and alone. All the other children had already gone home. She knew Rebekah must be taken to the hospital, but she couldn't do that until the limb had been removed. There was a farm down the road, owned by an English couple, but if she went there to phone for help, she would have to leave Rebekah alone.

Miriam seldom found herself wishing for modern conveniences, but at the moment, she would have given anything if there had been a telephone inside the schoolhouse. "Oh, Lord, what should I do?" she prayed, as she wrapped a piece of cloth she'd torn from her apron around Rebekah's head. "I don't ask this for myself but for the dear, sweet child who lies at my feet. Please send someone now, or I must leave her alone and go for help."

Miriam heard the *clip-clop* of a horse's hooves and knew a buggy must be approaching. As soon as it entered the school yard, she realized it was Amos Hilty, who'd probably come to pick up his daughter because of the approaching storm.

"Oh, Amos, Mary Ellen has already gone home, and—and . . . a tree limb fell on my niece." Miriam pointed to the spot where Rebekah lay. "She's alive but unconscious, and I can't lift the limb off her back." Her voice shook with emotion, and her breath came out in short, raspy gasps.

Amos hopped down from his buggy and hurried over to the child. In one quick movement, he lifted the limb and tossed it aside. "Let's put Rebekah in my buggy, and we'll take her to the Andersons' place so we can call for help," he suggested.

"I don't think she should be moved. What if something's broken? What if—" Miriam choked on a sob, and she felt as if there was no strength left in her legs.

"You wait here then, and I'll make the call for help."

Miriam nodded. "Please hurry, Amos. She hasn't opened her eyes, and I think she might be seriously injured."

"I'll go as quickly as I can."

As Amos sped out of the school yard, Miriam feared his horse might trip and fall. *Please let Rebekah be all right, Lord,* she fervently prayed.

For the next twenty minutes, Miriam stood over Rebekah, praying that she would live and that Amos would return with help before it was too late. It seemed like hours until she finally heard the ambulance's siren, and she breathed a sigh of relief. The wind continued to howl, but the rain held off until Rebekah had been strapped to a hard, straight board and placed into the back of the ambulance.

"I need to go to the hospital with her," Miriam told Amos, who had returned to the schoolhouse to offer further assistance. "But someone needs to notify Andrew and Sarah."

"You ride along in the ambulance, and I'll go over to your brother's place and tell them what's happened to their daughter before I head for home."

"My buggy. What about my horse and buggy?"

"I'll see that they get safely home for you." Amos touched her arm. "Try not to worry, Miriam. Just pray."

Miriam nodded and numbly climbed into the ambulance. As the vehicle pulled out of the school yard with its siren blaring, she looked out the back window and saw Amos climbing into his buggy. "I never even told him thank you," she murmured.

• • •

After numerous tests had been run on Rebekah, the doctor's reports were finally given, but the news wasn't good. Rebekah had a concussion and a bad gash on the back of her head where the tree limb had hit. However, the worst news of all was that her spinal cord had been injured, and if the child lived, she would probably never walk again.

Miriam clamped her lips together to keep from screaming, and Sarah sobbed. Andrew wrapped his arms around Sarah as tears coursed down his sunburned cheeks.

Why would God allow this to happen to an innocent young child? Miriam fumed as she clenched her fingers tightly. "I'm so sorry," she said, nodding at Andrew and Sarah. "If I just hadn't allowed Rebekah to wait outside for me. If only—" Her voice broke, and she bolted from the room.

As Miriam made her way down the hospital corridor, she was reminded of that terrible night she had fled the hospital after learning that Papa was dead. When she'd opened the door that led to the street, she half expected to see Nick standing on the other side, but he wasn't there this time to offer words of comfort and a listening ear. Suddenly, she remembered the last words he'd spoken to her. *"If there's ever anything I can do to help you or your family, feel free to call my office at the newspaper."*

Should I call? she wondered. *Should I be turning to an outsider for comfort and support?*

As Miriam turned the corner and headed for the telephone booth at the end of the block, she was relieved that the storm had subsided. She stepped inside and dialed the number of the *Daily Express*, but her fingers trembled so badly she feared she might be hitting the wrong buttons.

"Hello. May I speak to Nick McCormick?" she asked when a woman's voice came on the phone. "He's a reporter at your newspaper."

"One moment, please."

Miriam held her breath and waited anxiously. At least she had reached the newspaper office and hadn't dialed the wrong number.

"This is Nick McCormick. How may I help you?" she heard Nick say a few seconds later.

"It—it's Miriam Stoltzfus. You said I should call if I ever needed anything."

"Sure did, and it's good to hear from you again. What can I do to help?"

Miriam pressed the palm of her hand against the side of her pounding temple. She hoped she wasn't about to be sick. "I . . . uh . . . need to talk. Can we meet somewhere?"

"Where are you now?"

"About a block from Lancaster General Hospital."

"The hospital? Are you all right?"

"It's not me. It's my—" Miriam's voice broke, and she couldn't go on.

"Miriam, whatever's happened, I'm so sorry," Nick

said in a reassuring tone. "Remember the little café where we had coffee a few months ago?"

"I remember."

"Meet me there in fifteen minutes. You can tell me about it then."

CHAPTER 13

Miriam found the café to be full of people when she arrived a short time later. A quick look at the clock on the far wall told her it was the dinner hour. Her eyes sought out an empty booth, but there was none. She stood feeling nervous and self-conscious, as everyone seemed to be looking at her. Was it the fact that she was wearing Plain clothes that made them stare, or was it her red face and swollen eyes?

"May I help you, miss?" the man behind the counter asked.

"I'm . . . uh . . . supposed to meet someone here, and we need a table for two."

"The tables and booths are all filled, but you can take a seat on one of the stools here at the counter, if you'd like."

Not knowing what else to do, Miriam took a seat as the man suggested and studied the menu he'd handed her. Nothing appealed. How could she have an appetite for food when her niece was lying in the hospital, unconscious, with the prospect of being crippled for the rest of her life? Rebekah was such a sweet child, easy to teach and always agreeable; she didn't deserve such a fate.

Miriam gritted her teeth and clenched her fingers around the menu so tightly that her knuckles turned white. *I should never have let Rebekah go outside without me when I knew a storm was brewing.*

A firm hand touched Miriam's shoulder, and she turned her head. "Nick! How did you get here so quickly?"

Nick lifted his arm and pointed to his watch. "It's been over thirty minutes since we talked, and I told you I'd be here in fifteen. So I'm actually late, fair lady, and I'm sorry to have kept you waiting." He looked around. "It's sure crowded in here. Was this the only seat you could find? It won't give us much privacy, you know."

"I've been waiting for one of the booths, but no one seems in much of a hurry to leave."

"Are you hungry?" he asked.

Miriam shook her head, one quick shake, and then another. "I could use something to drink, though, and maybe some aspirin." She rubbed the pulsating spot on her forehead and grimaced.

"Headache?"

She nodded. "I get bad migraines whenever I'm under too much stress, and I don't have any white willow bark herb capsules with me right now. They usually help."

"I'll get you some iced tea to go," Nick offered. "I've got a bottle of aspirin in the glove box of my car. How about if we go for a ride? We can talk better if we have some privacy, and I don't think we'll get any in here."

"I—I suppose it would be all right," Miriam said hesitantly. "But I shouldn't be gone too long. I left my brother and his wife at the hospital, and I didn't tell them where I was going or when I would return. They've got enough on their minds right now, and I don't want them to worry about me."

"I promise not to keep you out past midnight." Nick smiled and gave her a quick wink before turning to the waitress and ordering an iced tea to go.

Heat rushed to Miriam's face, and she tried to hide it by hurrying toward the door. She wasn't used to having a man flirt with her the way Nick did, and whenever he flashed her that grin, she felt as if her insides had turned to mush. Maybe he didn't mean anything by it. It might have been just a friendly gesture or his way of trying to get Miriam to relax.

She walked silently beside him across the parking lot until they came to a small, sporty-looking vehicle. He opened the door on the passenger's side and helped her in.

Miriam could smell the aroma of new leather as she slid into the soft seat. "You have a nice car," she commented after he'd taken his seat on the driver's side.

"Thanks. It'll be even nicer once it's paid for." Nick reached across Miriam and opened the glove box. He pulled out a small bottle of aspirin and handed it to her. "Here, take a couple of these."

"Thank you." As soon as Miriam had swallowed the pills with the iced tea Nick had purchased for her, he turned on the ignition and pulled away from the curb.

"Do you want to tell me what's bothering you now, or would you rather ride around for a while and try to relax and get rid of that headache?"

Miriam clutched the side of her seat with one hand while hanging on to her tea with the other. "Going at this speed, I'm not sure I can think well enough to speak, much less relax."

"How about if I pull over at the park so you can sit and relax while you tell me what's happened?"

"That—that would be fine, I suppose." Miriam pulled nervously on the ties of her *kapp*, where they dangled under her chin. Being alone with Nick made her feel a bit uneasy, since he had such an unsettling way about him. The strange way he kept looking at her stirred something deep within, too, and it made her feel giddy—like she used to feel when she and William had been courting.

Maybe it's just the shock of being told the extent of Rebekah's injuries that has me feeling so quivery, she told herself. *I'm sure I'll calm down once the aspirin takes effect and my headache eases.*

Thinking he might be able to read Miriam's thoughts, Nick glanced over at her and said, "Don't worry. You're safe with me. No harm will come to you, because you're a fair lady, and I'm your knight in shining armor."

Her cheeks flamed, but she silently turned her head toward the window.

Nick figured she probably needed some time to let the aspirin take effect and realize that he wasn't planning to take advantage of her. When they pulled into a parking place at the city park a short time later, he rolled down the window to let in some fresh air.

"Thanks for taking the time to meet me," she said. "I'm sure you're a busy man."

He shrugged. "I was about to call it a day anyhow. So, tell me what's happened. Why were you at the hospital again?"

"It is my niece Rebekah. She's been seriously injured, and I'm afraid it's my fault."

"What happened?" Nick asked as he reached for the notepad he kept tucked inside his window visor.

Miriam seemed to barely notice that he'd taken a pen from his pocket and was prepared to take notes as she continued her story.

"The storm was just beginning when my students headed for home. I told my niece I would give her a ride, and she asked if she could wait outside for me." She drew in a quick breath. "I asked her to get into the buggy and said I would be there soon, but I never thought about the fact that I'd parked my buggy under a tree this morning." She paused for another breath. "Then I heard this terrible snapping sound followed by a scream. I rushed outside and found Rebekah on the ground with a heavy branch lying across her back."

"A branch broke and fell on the child?"

She nodded, as tears pooled in her eyes.

"What happened next?"

Miriam sat up straight and blinked a couple of times as she pointed to his notebook. "You—you're writing this down?"

He nodded. "Please go on. It's a newsworthy item, and I think—"

"I will not go on! I didn't ask you to meet me so you could write a story for your newspaper. When you offered to help before, I thought that included a listening ear."

"I have been listening. The thing is, reporting the news is what I do, so—"

"I think you'd better take me back to the hospital now. I can see what a mistake this has been. I should never have phoned or asked you to meet me."

"Don't get into such a huff." Nick placed the notebook on the seat and returned the pen to his shirt pocket. "I won't write down another thing, Miriam. I didn't think you were going to get so riled up about this. I'm a reporter, so it was only natural for me to take notes on something that seemed like a good story. I'm sorry if I've offended you."

Miriam stared at her hands, clenched tightly in her lap. "I'm not sure I believe you. Maybe you're not the one I should be talking to right now."

"Of course I am." He slipped his arm across Miriam's shoulder, thinking a quick hug might let her know he was sincere. "I'd like to be your friend, Miriam, if you'll let me."

Her lower lip quivered, and when he wrapped both of his arms around her, he felt hot tears against his cheek. "I—I appreciate that," she murmured, "because a friend is exactly what I need right now."

Amos sat at the kitchen table, watching Mary Ellen eat her bowl of vegetable soup while he struggled to eat his own. He had no appetite for food and dreaded having to tell his daughter about her friend's accident. But he knew she would learn about it when she went to school tomorrow, and he didn't want her to find out that way.

He cleared his throat a couple of times, searching for the right words. "There's . . . uh . . . something I need to tell you, Mary Ellen."

She placed her spoon on the table and stared at him with a quizzical expression. "What is it, Pappy? How come you look so *bedauerlich*?"

"I'm feeling a bit sad because one of your friends from school is in the hospital."

Her eyebrows lifted high on her forehead. "Who's in the hospital?"

"Rebekah Stoltzfus."

"How come? Is she sick?"

He shook his head. "After school let out and you and the rest of the kinner had already gone, Rebekah was hit by a tree limb while she waited for Miriam to give her a ride home."

The creases in Mary Ellen's forehead deepened. "Was Rebekah hurt bad? Is—is she gonna be okay?"

Amos groaned inwardly as he pictured Rebekah's still, small frame lying on the ground with a heavy limb pinning her down. He'd seen blood on her head and knew that wasn't good. How he wished he could think of something to tell Mary Ellen that might offer hope that her friend would be all right. But the truth was, it didn't look good for Rebekah Stoltzfus, and he feared she might not make it.

"Pappy?" Mary Ellen's voice quavered. "Rebekah won't die, will she?"

He reached across the table and took hold of her hand, squeezing it gently. "I haven't heard from anyone since they took her to the hospital, so I don't know how badly she was hurt."

Mary Ellen pulled her hand away and jumped up, nearly knocking over her chair. "I want to see her, Pappy. Can we go to the hospital right now so I can talk to Rebekah and find out how she's doin'?"

Amos shook his head. "Rebekah was knocked unconscious when the limb fell from the tree, and I'm sure the doctors are busy running tests on her."

Mary Ellen's eyes filled with tears, and several splashed onto her flushed cheeks. "Is—is Rebekah goin' to heaven, the way Mama did?"

"I don't know," Amos replied honestly. "But I do know that she's in good hands at the hospital, and I'm certain that the doctors and nurses are doing everything they can. We just need to pray."

"I prayed for Mama, and God took her from us anyway," Mary Ellen said tearfully. It was the first time since Ruth's death that the child had shown such emotion, and Amos was at a loss for words.

Mary Ellen's shoulders shook, and convulsing sobs wracked her little body. "If God takes Rebekah away, I don't think I'll ever forgive Him!" She rushed out of the room, and Amos heard her footsteps clomp up the stairs.

Dear Lord, he prayed, *please let Rebekah be all right, and if You choose to take her home, then I'm asking You to help my little girl in dealing with it.*

CHAPTER 14

"I can see that you really do need to talk, and I'm more than willing to listen," Nick assured Miriam. "No more note-taking, I promise."

She nodded slowly. "All right. As I was about to say, the tree branch broke, and it landed across Rebekah's head and back. Amos came along soon after, and he went to call for help."

"Who's Amos?"

"He's the father of one of my students. When the ambulance arrived, I rode to the hospital with Rebekah, and then Amos went to tell my brother Andrew and his wife, who are Rebekah's parents, what had happened."

"What's the child's prognosis—her condition?"

"I know what *prognosis* means," she said in a tone of irritation.

"Sorry. I didn't mean to sound condescending." He squeezed her shoulder. "Now, would you please continue with the story?"

She moistened her lips with the tip of her tongue. "The doctor said Rebekah has a concussion, and that's the reason she's still unconscious."

"Guess that's understandable."

"He also said there's some injury to her spinal cord." Miriam gulped. "Rebekah will probably never walk again."

"Doctors have been known to be wrong," Nick said, thinking his optimism might offer some hope.

"I'm praying for a miracle, but—"

"Oh, that's right, you Amish believe in all that faith stuff, don't you?" Nick wrinkled his nose. "I've never held much stock in any kind of religious conviction."

Miriam frowned. "Faith in God is biblical, Mr. McCormick. It's not just the Amish who believe God is in control of their lives, either."

"Come on now, Miriam. I don't agree with you on something, and now it's back to calling me Mr. McCormick. Is that how it is?"

"I think I was wrong in expecting you to help me sort out my feelings. You're just trying to confuse me."

"Not at all," Nick said with a shake of his head. "I admire you for your faith, but it's just not for me. I'm not one to put others down for their beliefs, but I don't want to rely on anyone but myself. I don't need God or faith."

Miriam stared at her cup of iced tea. "You must think I'm pretty old-fashioned—in appearance as well as in my ideas."

Nick took the iced tea from her and placed it in the cup holder on the dash. "I'm not trying to confuse you, but I'm afraid you have confused me."

"How have I confused you?"

Nick leaned close to her. "I find you to be quite fascinating, Miriam, yet your ways are a bit strange to me and hard to understand. I'd like to find out more about you and your Amish traditions."

"What would you like to know?"

"I know you're expected to remain separate from the rest of the world, but I don't grasp the reasons behind such a lifestyle."

"The Bible tells us that we must present our bodies as a living sacrifice, holy and acceptable to God. It also states that we are not to be conformed to this world, but rather that we be transformed by the renewing of our minds," Miriam said. "In 2 Corinthians it says that we are not to be unequally yoked together with unbelievers. Our entire lifestyle—our dress, language, work, travel, and education are the things we must consider because of this passage in the Bible. We must not be like the rest of the world. We must live as simply and humbly as possible."

"So, things like telephones in your homes, electricity, cars, and gas-powered tractors are worldly and would cause you to be part of the modern world?"

She nodded. "To some, it may seem as if our religion is harsh and uncompromising, but all baptized members are morally committed to the church and its rules."

"It sounds pretty hard to live like that, but I suppose if you're content and feel that your way of life makes you happy, then who am I to say it's wrong?"

Miriam was on the verge of telling Nick she was anything but happy and content, but she decided those words were best left unspoken. Besides, if she had discussed that issue with him, she would have been forced to deal with the nagging doubts that so often swirled in her head.

"I really would like to help you, Miriam," Nick said.

"What kind of help do you have to offer?"

"It sounds to me like your niece is going to be in the hospital for quite a while, and she will no doubt require a lot of physical therapy and medical care."

Miriam nodded. "I suppose so."

"That will cost a lot of money."

"Jah, I suppose it will."

"If I wrote an article for the newspaper about the girl's accident, I'm sure a lot of people would respond to it."

"Respond how?"

"With financial help."

"I'm sure you mean well, Nick, but the cost of Rebekah's medical needs isn't my only concern. Our community has a fund we use when someone has a need, and we will probably have some fundraisers to help, as well."

"I see."

"My mother will no doubt mention Rebekah's accident in her next newspaper article, so my brother's family will probably receive money from some of *The Budget* readers, too."

"Sounds like the Amish take good care of one another."

"We do our best." Miriam grimaced. "I'm just sick about the accident, and I blame myself for it."

"Come now. There was no way you could have known a tree limb would fall on the child when she went outside to wait for you. You can't blame yourself for a freak accident caused by an act of nature." Nick touched his finger against her trembling lips. "If you want my opinion, I think the best thing you can do is face this situation head-on. In matters such as this, no amount of faith in God will get you through. I believe we all have the inner strength to deal with the problems life brings our way."

An unbidden tear slid down Miriam's cheek. Hadn't she decided awhile back that her own determined heart was all she could count on? Perhaps Nick was right. Had faith in God prevented Rebekah's terrible accident, kept Papa from dying, or stopped William from falling in love with another woman? Miriam had dutifully served God all of her twenty-six years, only to end up an old-maid schoolteacher with no father, no husband, and a crippled niece to remind her that God had let her down yet again.

She looked at Nick, so obviously sure of himself, and resolved that she, too, could face life head-on and find her own inner strength.

With a lift of her chin, Miriam said, "I'm ready to go back to the hospital now."

"Sure, okay." Nick smiled. "I've enjoyed being with you, Miriam. Maybe we can get together again."

Miriam returned his smile, feeling as if a special kind of friendship was taking root in her heart.

"Do you have a phone on your property like some Amish folks do?"

She shook her head. "Why do you ask?"

"I'd like to keep in contact—maybe call and check up on you." Nick started up the car. "Since you don't have a phone, I want you to promise to call me if you need more advice or just want to talk."

"All right. I will."

"Or how about this? Since I was on the back side of your property where the stream runs through, I have an idea where your house is, so maybe I can come by for a visit sometime soon."

Miriam shook her head as a sense of panic welled in her chest. "I—I don't think that's such a good idea." The last thing she needed was for Nick to drop by her house. How would she explain the sudden appearance of a good-looking English reporter to her family?

"Why not?"

"You know why, Nick. You're English; I'm Amish. My family might get the wrong idea if—"

"Oh, you mean they might think I was trying to woo you away from the Plain life? Is that what you're afraid of?"

Miriam was at a loss for words. She enjoyed being with Nick, and he made her feel so special, but she was sure no one in the family would believe he was just a friend.

As Amos sat in a chair beside his daughter's bed, he thought about his wife's untimely death and wondered how things would be if she were still alive. Ruth had been a good mother and had always given Mary Ellen the best of care. They'd wanted to have more children, but Ruth hadn't been able to conceive again after Mary Ellen was born. Yet she'd never complained because the Good Lord had only given them just one child. Amos knew that if his wife was still with them, this precious little girl he'd been left to raise wouldn't have to wear dresses that needed mending, put up with unruly hair, or eat slapped-together meals that weren't fit for any growing child.

What Mary Ellen needs is a mother, he thought as he reached out and touched her rosy, damp cheek. The poor little thing had cried herself to sleep after she'd learned about Rebekah's accident.

His thoughts turned to Miriam, as they always did whenever he reminded himself that his daughter should have a mother. If he only felt free to tell

Miriam what was on his heart—that he loved her and wanted her to be his wife. It would be difficult to lay his feelings on the line when he knew the only thing she felt for him was irritation.

Amos pushed the chair aside and stood. Chores in the barn waited to be done. He leaned over and kissed Mary Ellen's forehead. *Bless this child, Lord,* he prayed. *And give her only sweet dreams tonight.*

CHAPTER 15

Get up at five in the morning, light the woodstove, head out to the chicken coop to gather eggs, slop the pigs, and milk the goats. Miriam knew the routine so well she probably could have done it in her sleep. It had been her routine ever since Papa died. This morning was like no other, except that the wind had picked up and it had begun to rain.

As she left the chicken coop and noticed how the wind whipped through the trees, she was reminded of the day Rebekah had been injured. Could it have only been a few weeks ago? It seemed like much longer. Perhaps that was because she kept so busy. Being busy seemed to keep her from thinking too much about the things that caused her heart to feel so heavy.

Rebekah was still in the hospital. She had regained consciousness, but the doctors were fairly certain she would never walk again.

Miriam shuddered. No matter how hard she tried,

she couldn't convince herself that she wasn't partially to blame for the accident. She had made up her mind that the only way to deal with it was to seek her inner strength, as Nick had suggested. She must go on with the business of living, no matter how unhappy she was or how guilty she felt.

Today, after school let out, she planned to hire a driver and go to the hospital. She would take some books to Rebekah and perhaps some of her favorite licorice candy. Maybe she would call Nick and ask him to meet her for coffee again. That thought caused Miriam to quicken her step as she hurried back to the house, carrying a basket of bulky brown eggs. Her day was just beginning, and she still had plenty of inside chores to do before she left for school.

Amos had just left his blacksmith shop after shoeing one of his own buggy horses when he spotted Mary Ellen running across the yard with her lunch pail swinging at her side. "Can I walk to school by myself today?" she called.

"I think it would be best if I take you there," he said when she caught up to him.

Her lower lip jutted out. "Most of the other kinner are allowed to walk. Why can't I?"

Amos grimaced. He knew he was probably being overprotective, but ever since Rebekah's accident, he'd been afraid to let Mary Ellen walk to school by herself for fear that something might happen to her.

There had been a couple of accidents on the road between their place and the schoolhouse in the last month, and some of those had involved Amish walking alongside the road. He'd already lost Mary Ellen's mother, and he couldn't risk losing her, too.

"I feel better taking you to school. It's safer that way, and it gives us more time to be together."

Mary Ellen seemed to be satisfied with that answer, and she smiled up at him. "I packed my own lunch again, and I'm ready to go whenever you are, Pappy."

"I need to run inside and wash my hands first." He held them up and wrinkled his nose. "Old Jake's hooves were pretty dirty."

"I'll wait for you in the buggy then." Mary Ellen headed in that direction but turned back around. "Say, I was wonderin'—"

"What were you wondering?"

"You said I could visit Rebekah soon. Can we go to the hospital to see her after school lets out?"

"Not today, daughter."

"But I made her a card last night, and I want to take it to her."

Amos didn't think going to the hospital and seeing Rebekah unable to stand or move her legs would be good for Mary Ellen. It might upset the child. "Why don't you give the card to your teacher? I heard that Miriam goes to the hospital often, so maybe she can give Rebekah your card."

Mary Ellen frowned. "But that's not the same as me seeing Rebekah. She might think I've forgotten her."

He shook his head. "I'm sure she won't think that. I believe it would be best if you wait 'til Rebekah comes home from the hospital to pay her a call."

"How come?"

"She'll be stronger and feeling better by then. Probably be more up to company comin' by."

"Jah," Mary Ellen said with a nod. "When she goes home, I'll make another card and maybe give her one of the horseshoes I've painted."

Not another headache, thought Miriam as she stood at the door, watching the last of her pupils leave the school yard. *Why must I always get a migraine when I have something important to do? Well, I won't let this one stop me from going to the hospital.*

Miriam crossed the room and opened the top drawer of her desk. Inside was a bottle of white willow bark capsules. She took two and washed them down with some cold water from her Thermos. She could only hope that today the herbals would work quickly. Was it the stress of knowing she was going to the hospital later, or was it the fact that John Lapp had given her a hard time in class today that had brought on the headache? *Probably a bit of both,* she decided. She was determined not to give in to the pain or stressful feelings. John had been punished for his shenanigans by losing his playtime during lunch, and she would force herself to go to the hospital no matter how much it distressed her to see Rebekah lying helplessly in her hospital bed.

• • •

When Miriam arrived at the hospital later that day, she discovered that Rebekah wasn't in her room. She was informed by one of the nurses that the child had been taken upstairs for another CT scan and would be back in half an hour or so. Miriam could either wait in Rebekah's room or in the waiting room down the hall.

She left the candy and books on Rebekah's nightstand and made her way down the hall toward the waiting room.

Except for an elderly gentleman, the room was empty. Miriam took a seat and thumbed through a stack of magazines. Nothing looked interesting, and she was about to leave in search of a phone so she could call Nick when she noticed a copy of the *Daily Express* lying on the table in front of her. She picked up the paper and read the front page, then turned to page two. She stifled a gasp. Halfway down the page was a picture of a young girl lying in a hospital bed. It was Rebekah, and a four-column story accompanied the photo.

Miriam fumed as she read the reporter's name—Nick McCormick. "How dare he do such a thing! I had hoped I could trust him."

She read the entire story, pausing only to mumble or gasp as she read how Rebekah had been struck down by a tree limb during a storm that had swept through Lancaster County. The article went on to say that the little Amish girl would probably never walk again and that the hospital and doctor bills would be nearly impossible for her parents to pay. The story closed by asking for charitable contributions to the hospital on the child's behalf.

Miriam slammed the paper onto the table with such force that the elderly man seated across from her jumped. She mumbled an apology and stormed out of the room.

Miriam had nearly reached a phone booth at the end of the hall when she saw Andrew and Sarah heading her way.

"Miriam, we didn't know you were here," Andrew said. "We dropped Simon and Nadine off at Mom's, but she didn't tell us you were at the hospital."

"Mom doesn't know," Miriam answered. "Gladys Andrews drove me here after school let out."

"You look really upset. Is something wrong? Is it Rebekah? Is she worse?" Sarah's eyes widened, and deep wrinkles formed in her forehead.

"It's not Rebekah. She's having another CT scan, and I was waiting until she came out. It's what I found in the waiting room that upset me so." She lifted a shaky hand to touch her forehead. Her headache, which had previously eased, was back again with a vengeance.

"Miriam, you're trembling," Andrew said. "What did you see in that room?"

"A newspaper article with a picture."

"The news can be unsettling at times," Sarah interjected. "There are so many murders, robberies, and—"

"No, no, it's nothing like that. It's a story about Rebekah."

"Rebekah?" Andrew and Sarah said in unison.

Miriam nodded. "The article tells about her accident and how you won't have enough money to pay all the bills. There's even a picture of Rebekah lying in her hospital bed."

"What?" Andrew asked a bit too loudly. A nurse walking by gave him a warning look, but he didn't seem to notice.

"Who would do such a thing, and how'd they know about Rebekah's accident?" Sarah questioned.

"Let's go to the waiting room, and I'll show you the article." Miriam led the way down the hall.

The newspaper still lay on the table where she had angrily tossed it, and she bent down to pick it up, then handed it to Andrew.

"Who's responsible for this?" he asked, his dark eyes flashing angrily.

"I'm afraid I am." Miriam stared at the floor as a feeling of shame washed over her. She should never have gotten friendly with Nick or shared anything about her family with him. He'd pretended to be her friend, but he had only been using her as a means to get information for one of his newspaper articles.

Andrew raised his eyebrows. "You?"

She nodded. "I told the reporter about Rebekah's accident."

"You called the newspaper and asked them to write an article about our daughter?" Sarah's wounded expression revealed obvious hurt and betrayal.

Miriam placed a hand on her sister-in-law's arm. "Please don't think for one minute that I called the *Daily Express* or wanted anything like this to be printed."

"Then how did the reporter know about it?" Andrew asked.

Miriam suggested that they all sit down; then she told her brother and his wife everything except for the fact that she had nearly been taken in by Nick McCormick—even allowing herself to feel tingly and excited when she'd been with him. She would never have admitted that to anyone.

Nick had just entered his office when his boss stormed in. "I wanted to talk to you about this," Pete said, tossing a folded newspaper onto Nick's desk.

Nick glanced at the article, recognizing it as the one he'd written on Rebekah Stoltzfus, the child who had been hit by a tree limb that had left her legs paralyzed. "What about it? You did put your stamp of approval on it before it was released, remember?"

Pete nodded. "I just didn't realize you were going to include a close-up shot of the little Amish girl."

"I thought it would add more appeal to the story if the readers could see how pathetic she looked lying in her hospital bed, unable to walk."

"Maybe you should have thought more about how the girl's family would feel about the whole county seeing their daughter's face in the newspaper."

Nick could tell by the tone of Pete's voice that he was irritated, and the deep furrows in his forehead drove the point home.

"Have you had a complaint about this?" he asked. "Or did you simply become concerned that I might have offended someone?"

Pete pulled out the chair across from Nick and sat down. "The child's aunt phoned yesterday evening after you'd left to do that story about the drug bust on the other side of town."

"Miriam called? Did she ask for me?"

Pete nodded. "Fran took the call, but since you weren't in your office and the woman on the phone mentioned the article you had written, Fran forwarded the call to me."

"So what did Miriam say?"

Pete thumped the article with the tip of his pen and frowned. "She was upset and said you knew how the Amish feel about having their pictures taken, yet you sneaked into her niece's hospital room and snapped a picture of her anyway, without asking the family's permission." He gave the newspaper another quick tap. "I thought the article was well-written, but I'd like you to do a follow-up story and include an apology for that picture you used."

CHAPTER 16

As Miriam sat at the kitchen table, reading the newspaper one evening, she thought about Nick and how he'd let her down by writing that article on Rebekah and including a picture with it. Had she really been so naive as to believe he was different than other men? To think that she'd nearly phoned him to ask if they might meet again for coffee. She promised never again to allow her emotions to get in the way of good judgment.

Rebekah had been in the hospital for nearly three weeks already, and Miriam knew the medical bills were adding up. She had a little money put aside from her teaching position, which she would give to Andrew to use toward the mounting bills. She also planned to sell the beautiful quilts she had made for her hope chest at one of the firemen's benefit auctions, which were known as "mud sales" because they were held in the early spring when the ground was still muddy. Since Miriam never planned to marry, the quilts were useless to her, anyway. Tourists were always on the lookout for items made by the Amish, so she was sure she would have no trouble selling the quilts to the general store in town if they didn't sell during one of the mud sales.

Miriam was aware that several other Amish families had given money to help with Rebekah's hospital bills, and it made her thankful she belonged to a group of people who helped one another in times of need.

"I think I'll hire Gladys to drive me to the hospital tomorrow so I can see Rebekah again," Miriam said, glancing at her mother, who sat across the table, reading her Bible. "Would you like to go along?"

Mom looked up and smiled. "I appreciate the offer, but I went this morning with Sarah. Barbara Nyce, the Mennonite woman she usually hires, took us there."

Miriam frowned. "How come you didn't mention it earlier? I would think you would have wanted to give us a report."

"I did say something to Lewis about it when he came to the house at noon, but when you came home from school today, you said you had a headache and needed to lie down, so I didn't mention it."

"I see. How was Rebekah doing?"

"As well as can be expected. Her spirits are up, and that's a good thing."

Miriam released a heavy sigh. "How I wish the doctors had been wrong about her not being able to use her legs. It won't be easy for that sweet little girl to spend the rest of her life confined to a wheelchair, relying on others to do everything for her."

Mom clucked her tongue. "That's not true. There are many things Rebekah can do while she's sitting down."

Miriam opened her mouth to comment, but her mother rushed on.

"The child has a determined spirit, and I don't think

she will let her handicap keep her from living life to the fullest."

Miriam folded her arms and leaned on the table. "Thanks to me being foolish enough to let her go outside, she'll only be living half a life."

Mom shook her head and looked hard at Miriam. "I wish you would stop being so negative."

"I'm not being negative; I'm just facing the truth."

"The truth is you have a lot to learn about how God wants us to live, and unless you allow Him to fill your heart with joy and love, I'm afraid you'll be living less of a life than my crippled granddaughter."

Mom's harsh words pricked Miriam's heart, but she would not allow them to penetrate the wall of defense she had built around her wounded soul. She pushed the newspaper aside and stood. "I'm going upstairs to bed. It's been a long day, and I'm awfully tired."

Long after Miriam left the room, Anna stayed at the table, reading her Bible and praying. She knew only one answer for her daughter's troubled spirit, and that was to open her heart to God's unconditional love and allow Him to fill her life with His joy and peace.

"Is there any of that good-tasting gingerbread cake left?" Lewis asked as he stepped into the kitchen, rousing Anna from her time of prayer and meditation. "I wouldn't mind a piece if there is."

"I think that can be arranged." Anna slid her chair back and stood. "Would you like a glass of milk or some tea to go with it?"

He smacked his lips. "Ice cold milk sounds good to me."

"If you want ice cold, maybe you'd better take it outside," she said with a chuckle. "The weather's turned frigid this week, and I'm thinking that soon we'll be having some snow."

He took a seat at the table. "I believe you're right about that."

Anna placed a hunk of gingerbread and a tall glass of milk in front of Lewis; then she returned to her seat across from him.

"Aren't you having any?" he asked around a mouthful of cake. "This is sure tasty."

She shook her head. "I'm still full from supper, and I had a big lunch today after Sarah and I went to see Rebekah."

"You think she'll be goin' home soon?"

"I don't know. Her therapy sessions are going well, so maybe it won't be too long before the doctor says she's ready to leave the hospital."

"It's a good thing Miriam's been giving her a few lessons while she's there." Lewis took a swallow of milk. "Otherwise Rebekah would be way behind when she returned to school."

Anna drummed her fingers along the edge of the table. "It might be some time before Rebekah's up to going back to school. Even with Miriam giving her lessons to do at home, she's likely to have a lot of makeup to do."

"You think she may be held back and have to do this year over again?"

"Might could be."

Lewis reached for a napkin and wiped a spot on his chin where some crumbs had accumulated. "I remember when I entered eighth grade and knew I'd be graduating that year. I wanted to be held back a year and even tried to fail just so Katherine Yoder wouldn't graduate me."

Anna's forehead wrinkled. "This is the first I've heard of that. Why would you have wanted to fail?"

His ears turned pink, and he stared at his empty plate. "You want the truth?"

"Of course."

"As you know, Grace Zepp is a year younger than me, and since I'd be leaving school after eighth grade and she still had another year, I didn't want to graduate yet."

"Ah, I see. You cared for Grace even back then?"

He nodded. "Of course, she made me see reason when I told her my plan to flunk all my tests that year so I wouldn't have to graduate."

"What did Grace say?"

"She reminded me that the sooner I learned a trade, the sooner I'd be ready to marry and begin a family." The color that permeated Lewis's ears spread quickly to the rest of his face. "I think I'm almost ready for that, Mom."

She smiled and reached across the table to touch his hand. "I think so, too."

Whenever Miriam went to the hospital to visit Rebekah, she always took a book to read, as well as some of the child's favorite licorice candy. Today was one of those days, but Miriam found herself dreading the visit. Would she ever stop feeling guilty whenever she looked at the sweet young child lying so helpless in her bed? Maybe Rebekah would be asleep when she arrived, and then she could leave the treat and book on the table by her bed and retreat to the protection and solitude of home.

As Gladys pulled her van into the hospital parking lot, Miriam thanked her. "I'll be ready to head for home in about an hour."

"That's fine," Gladys replied. "I'll run a few errands and meet you here at five o'clock."

"All right." As Miriam stepped out of the car, it started to rain, so she hurried toward the hospital's main entrance. Just as she was about to step inside, she collided with a man. When she looked up, she found herself staring into the familiar blue eyes of Nick McCormick. She trembled, fighting the urge to pound her fists against his chest.

Nick smiled, apparently unaware of her irritation. "Miriam, it's good to see you again. As usual, you look a bit flustered, but beautiful, nonetheless. Is there something I can do to help?"

Miriam clasped her hands tightly behind her back,

trying to maintain control of herself. She had never been so close to striking anyone. Strangely, Nick seemed to bring out the worst in her, yet he also brought out the best.

"I have no patience with a liar," she mumbled.

"Excuse me?"

She lifted her chin and met his piercing gaze. "I'm referring to the fact that you promised not to do a story about my niece but then went ahead and did it anyway. Your word meant absolutely nothing, did it?"

Nick reached up to scratch the back of his head while giving her a sheepish-looking grin. "Guess you caught me red-handed. When I wrote the article, I didn't think about how some Amish probably read the *Daily Express*."

"We're not ignorant, you know."

"I'm sure you're not."

"My people aren't perfect and don't claim to be, but we do strive for honesty, which is more than I can say for some."

"My, my, aren't you a feisty little thing today?" He chuckled. "I like spunky women—but I also like women who get their facts straight."

"What's that supposed to mean?"

"Fact number one: I never actually promised that I wouldn't do a story about your niece."

"But you said—"

"That I wouldn't do any more note-taking while you were talking to me. I kept true to my word and put away my paper and pen."

"But when you mentioned that you wanted to do an article about Rebekah's accident and include something about the cost of her medical bills, I asked you not to, and I assumed you would abide by my wishes."

He gave no reply, just staring at her in a most disconcerting way.

"And I certainly never thought you would sneak into her hospital room and take her picture," Miriam added, putting emphasis on the word *picture*.

"I did what I thought best—as a reporter and as your friend."

"What kind of friend goes behind someone's back and does something so sneaky?"

"The kind who believes he's doing the right thing." Nick pulled Miriam into the little waiting area across the hall. "Fact number two: I really do care about you, and I believed I was doing something helpful for your family. I apologize if it upset you or if you thought I had betrayed you." He sank into a chair. "If it makes you feel any better, I got a good chewing-out from my boss for including the picture I took of your niece, and that's why I wrote the apology letter that went into the paper a few days later. Did you happen to read it?"

She shook her head.

"Well, it's true. I didn't want anyone to think I had done anything to intentionally step on the Plain People's toes—especially not your pretty toes."

Miriam's anger receded some. It was hard to remain

in control when she was in Nick's presence. And when he looked at her with such a tender expression, she could barely think or breathe. Did she really need acceptance so badly that she would go outside her Amish faith to get it? Despite her desires, she couldn't allow this man to deceive her into believing he actually cared for her.

"I need to go see my niece now," she said, starting for the door. "I appreciate your apology, but I would ask that you not see Rebekah again."

Nick stood and moved toward her, but before he could give a reply, she dashed from the room.

"That sure went well," Nick muttered under his breath. "I wait all this time to see Miriam again, and then I can't think of anything to say that might redeem myself and make her willing to spend time with me again."

He groaned. *If she knew why I'd come to the hospital today, she would really be mad. Maybe it's good that she left the room before I ended up telling her where I just came from and how I bribed her niece into letting me take her picture again.* He grabbed his camera bag, which he'd placed on a chair when they'd come into the room, and started for the door. *I didn't take any face-on shots of Rebekah this time, so at least I shouldn't catch any flak from Pete for doing it.*

As Nick left the waiting room, he glanced down the long corridor, hoping to catch a glimpse of Miriam.

She was nowhere in sight. *It's probably just as well. After my next article comes out, she'll probably never speak to me again.*

When Miriam entered Rebekah's room, she found the child propped up on pillows. *So innocent, sweet, and helpless,* she thought.

"Aunt Miriam!" Rebekah smiled and reached her small hand out to Miriam.

"How's my best pupil and favorite niece today?" Miriam asked as she took the child's hand in her own.

"Better. My head don't hurt no more. Doctor said I can go home soon."

Miriam cringed at the thought of Rebekah returning to her family as a cripple. Rebekah had never made mention of it, though. Was it possible that she wasn't yet aware of the fact that she could no longer walk? How would the once-active child handle the probability of spending the rest of her days confined to a wheelchair?

"I'm glad you're feeling better," Miriam said, trying to make her voice sound light and cheerful.

"Did you bring me some licorice?" Rebekah asked with an expectant look.

"Jah, and another book to read for your English lessons, as well as a get-well card from your friend Mary Ellen." Miriam handed the card and candy to Rebekah; then she seated herself in the chair next to the bed. "Would you like to look at Mary Ellen's card before we start the lesson?"

Rebekah nodded and tore open the envelope. Her smile stretched ear to ear as she read the card:

Dear Rebekah,

I miss not seeing you at school. Pappy says I can come visit when you get home. I pray for you every night—that God will make you well.

Your friend,
Mary Ellen

Tears welled in Miriam's eyes, and she blinked to keep them from spilling over. Rebekah was paralyzed and would never be whole again, so Mary Ellen's prayers were wasted. But she wouldn't tell Rebekah that; it would be too cruel.

"A man took my picture," Rebekah surprised her by saying.

"I know, but that man will never bother you again." It was then that Miriam noticed the teddy bear sitting on the table near Rebekah's bed. She picked it up. "Where did you get this, Rebekah?"

"The man gave it to me."

"When was that?"

"Awhile ago."

"What man?"

"The picture man."

Miriam's head started to throb, and she pressed her hands against her temples, trying to halt the pain. So Nick must have just come from Rebekah's room when she'd bumped into him at the hospital entrance.

Had he come out of concern for the child? Was his gift one of genuine compassion, or had he used it to bribe Rebekah in order to take additional pictures? Now that Miriam thought about it, Nick had been carrying his camera bag when she'd first seen him, and he'd set it on a chair in the waiting room while they talked.

"Rebekah, did the man take more pictures of you today?"

The child nodded. "He gave me the bear, and then he asked me to turn my head to the wall, so's he could use his camera without makin' everyone mad."

CHAPTER 17

One month after Rebekah's accident, the doctors released her from the hospital. She would still need to return for physical therapy twice a week, but at least her days and nights could be spent with family.

On Rebekah's first day home, Mom suggested that she and Miriam ride over to see if they could help out. "Sarah's certainly going to have her hands full now," she said. "Just taking care of a *boppli* and two small kinner is a job in itself, but now this?"

"Since today's Saturday and there's no school, I have all day to help out." Miriam pulled her jacket from the wall peg. "I'll go out and feed the animals while you start breakfast. Then we can go."

"Jah," Mom agreed with a nod.

A blast of cold air greeted Miriam as she stepped onto the porch. It was early December, and a definite feeling of winter hung in the air. She shivered and pulled her collar up around her neck. "I hate winter!" The truth was, she was beginning to dislike all seasons. Perhaps it was life in general that she hated. *Is it all right for a believer to feel hate toward anything—even the weather?*

Another thought entered her mind. Maybe she wasn't a believer anymore. Her faith in God had diminished so much over the last several months. She got very little from the biweekly preaching services she attended with her friends and family. She no longer did her daily devotions, and her prayers were few and far between. When she did pray, she offered more of a complaint to God rather than heartfelt prayers and petitions. Where was God anyway, and what had happened to her longing to seek His face?

Miriam trudged wearily toward the barn and forced her thoughts onto the tasks that lay before her.

On her way back to the house half an hour later, she noticed a clump of wild pansies growing near the fence that ran parallel to the pasture. Pansies were hardy flowers, blooming almost continuously from early spring until late fall. The delicate yellow and lavender blossoms made her think of Mary Ellen and the day she'd given her the bouquet of heartsease. *Children like Rebekah and Mary Ellen are a lot like wild pansies,* she thought. *They're small and delicate, yet able to withstand so much.*

Thoughts of Mary Ellen made Miriam think about Amos. She'd seen him only a few times since the day of Rebekah's accident. Those times had been at preaching services. It seemed strange that he wasn't coming around anymore. He hadn't even come over for supper at Mom's most recent invitation. Perhaps he'd been too busy with his blacksmith duties or taking care of Mary Ellen. Or maybe he'd finally come to realize that Miriam had no interest in him, so he'd given up on his pursuit of her. Regardless of the reason, Miriam was glad he wasn't coming around anymore. The last thing she needed was an unwanted suitor. Her life was complicated enough.

She bent down and picked several of the colorful pansies. They would make a lovely bouquet to give Rebekah.

When they arrived at Sarah and Andrew's place, Anna noticed Sarah sitting on the front porch, with her head bent and shoulders shaking. She quickly got down from the buggy and rushed to Sarah's side, leaving Miriam to unhitch the horse. "What is it, Sarah? Why are you sitting out here in the cold?"

Sarah lifted her head. Tears coursed down her cheeks. "Oh, Anna, please remember me in your prayers."

"Jah, I surely will," Anna answered, taking a seat beside her daughter-in-law and reaching for her hand. "What has you so upset?"

"I'm happy to have Rebekah home again, but there isn't enough of me to go around." Sarah sniffed and dabbed at her eyes with the corner of her apron. "Simon's into everything, the baby always seems to need me for something, and taking care of Rebekah will be a full-time job. She's only been home half a day, and already I can't seem to manage."

"There, there," Anna comforted. She slipped her arm around Sarah's shoulders. "We'll work something out."

"Is there anything I can do to help?" Miriam asked as she joined the women on the porch.

Anna spoke before Sarah could reply. "Miriam, would you please go inside and check on the kinner while I speak to Sarah?"

"Jah. I want to give Rebekah the flowers I picked for her this morning," she said, holding the bouquet in front of her.

As soon as Miriam had gone into the house, Anna turned back to Sarah. "When I learned that Rebekah was coming home, I became concerned that her care would be too much for you to handle alone."

Sarah nodded and released a shuddering sigh. "I want to do right by all my kinner, but caring for Rebekah is going to take up so much of my time, and we really can't afford to hire a *maad* right now."

"There's no need for you to hire a maid," Anna said with a shake of her head. "I think I may have the answer to your problem."

When Miriam entered the kitchen, she spotted Rebekah sitting in her wheelchair next to the table, coloring a picture. The child looked up and smiled. "Hi, Aunt Miriam. Do you like my picture?"

"Jah, it's nice." Miriam placed the flowers on the table. "These are for you."

"Danki. They're very pretty."

"Where are Simon and baby Nadine?"

Rebekah pointed across the room.

Miriam gasped when she spotted three-year-old Simon sitting on the floor with a jar of petroleum jelly he had obviously rubbed all over his face and hair. The baby, who sat on the braided rug next to Simon, had some in her hair, as well.

"*Was in der welt*—what in the world? How did you get this, you little *schtinker*?" Miriam rushed across the room and grabbed the slippery jar out of his hands. "That is a no-no!"

Simon's lower lip trembled, and tears gathered in his big, blue eyes.

"Come over to the sink with me, and let's get you cleaned up. Then I'll tend to the boppli."

Just as Miriam finished cleaning both children, Mom and Sarah entered the kitchen. Sarah's eyes were red and swollen, but at least she was no longer crying.

"Our help is definitely needed here today, and there's much to be done," Mom said with a nod in Miriam's direction. "So now, let's get ourselves busy."

By the time they reached home that evening, Miriam felt exhausted. The last thing she wanted to do was chores, but farm duties didn't wait, so she climbed down from the buggy with a sigh, prepared to head for the barn.

"If you don't mind, I'd like to talk before we have our supper," Mom said as she stepped down from the buggy. "When you go out to the barn, if Lewis is there, would you ask him to come up to the house with you if he's not busy? The matter I have to discuss pertains to both of you."

Miriam tipped her head in question, but when Mom gave no explanation, she nodded and started for the barn, wondering what her mother could have to talk about that would affect both her and Lewis.

She found her brother grooming one of their horses when she entered the barn leading Harvey, her buggy horse. "Here's another one for you," she called. "When you're done, Mom wants to see you up at the house."

Lewis looked up from his job. "What's up?"

"She said she has something to discuss and that it pertains to both of us."

"Tell her I'll be there in a while," Lewis answered with a nod.

As Miriam left the barn a few minutes later, a chill ran through her body. She shivered and hurried toward the house. Was the cool evening air the cause of her chilliness—or was it the fear she felt in her heart? Fear that whatever Mom had to tell them was bad news.

By the time Miriam entered the house, Anna had steaming cups of hot chocolate waiting and a kettle o soup simmering on the stove. “Is Lewis coming?” she asked, after Miriam had removed her heavy black shawl and hung it over a peg near the back door.

“He said he’d be in when he’s done with the horses.” Miriam moved away from the door and took a seat at the table. When Anna offered her a cup of hot chocolate, she smiled and said, “Danki.”

“You’re welcome.” Anna settled herself into the rocking chair near the stove and reached into a basket on the floor. She pulled one of Lewis’s holey socks out and began to mend it as she made small talk with Miriam. “I figured I may as well keep my hands busy while the soup heats. After Lewis comes in and we’ve had our talk, we can make some sandwiches.”

“Okay.”

“Winter’s in the air. Can you feel it?”

Miriam lifted the cup of hot chocolate to her lips. “Jah, I nearly froze to death this morning when I went out to do my chores. I suppose I’ll have to get out my heavier jacket soon. A shawl sure isn’t enough for these crisp, cold mornings and evenings.”

“The hens aren’t laying as many eggs, either,” Anna said. “It’s a sure sign that winter’s here.”

The back door creaked open, and Lewis entered the kitchen. “Yum . . . I smell hot chocolate. I’d recognize that delicious odor even if I was blindfolded and still out on the porch.” He smiled at Anna. “Miriam said you wanted to talk to us?”

She nodded, laid the sock aside, and cleared her throat a couple of times. “I . . . uh . . . was wondering

. . . that is, how would you two feel about me moving in with Andrew and Sarah? Could you manage on your own?"

Neither Lewis nor Miriam spoke for several minutes; then Miriam broke the silence. "For how long, Mom?"

"Indefinitely."

"Indefinitely?" Lewis echoed.

"Jah. Now that Rebekah's confined to a wheelchair and what with all the work the other two kinner will take, Sarah's going to need all the help she can get for a good long while."

"But Mom, how do you expect Lewis and me to manage here by ourselves?" Miriam asked in a shrill tone.

"You're both capable adults. I'm sure you can manage fine without me."

"I think we could do all right," Lewis said with a nod.

"I know that my moving out will cause some discomfort for you," Anna continued. "However, I'm sorely needed over at Andrew and Sarah's right now."

"What about Sarah's folks? Can't they help out?" Lewis questioned.

"Their place is several miles away. Besides, they still have young kinner living at home to care for."

"It's just like you to make such a sacrifice, Mom," Lewis said. "You have a heart of compassion."

Miriam left her seat at the table and knelt next to Anna's chair. "It should be me that goes. I'll quit my job teaching and care for Rebekah. After all, it was my fault she was injured."

Anna placed her hand on top of Miriam's head. "It was not your fault, and I wish you would quit blaming yourself. It was an accident, plain and simple. It was something bad that God allowed to happen. You are in no way responsible. You're a fine teacher, and you're needed at the school. Sarah and I talked things over today, and I've made my decision. I'll be moving to their place this weekend, and I hope I have your blessing on this."

Miriam rose to her feet. "If you're determined to go, then I'll abide by your decision."

"And we'll do our best to keep this place runnin'," Lewis added with a grin.

Anna smiled despite the tears running down her cheeks. How grateful she was to have such a supportive family during times of need.

Chapter 18

The winter months seemed to drag unmercifully. With all the work to be done, the days should have passed quickly, but Miriam's tired body and saddened soul made her feel as if each day were endless. The snow lay deep on the ground, which made the outside chores even more difficult. And the cold—Miriam couldn't remember a winter that had been as cold as this one. She wondered if it was because the temperatures often dipped below zero, or was it simply because her heart had turned so cold?

Valentine's Day was only a few weeks away, and she knew her pupils would expect to have a party, with refreshments and the exchange of valentine hearts with one another. The last thing she felt like was a party, but she would force herself to get through it somehow.

As Miriam returned home from school one afternoon and entered the quiet, lonely kitchen, she admitted to herself that she missed her mother terribly. She knew Mom was doing a good thing and that her help was needed at Andrew and Sarah's, but they hardly got to see Mom anymore, for she was too busy caring for Rebekah and her siblings. Miriam had many chores to do, as well, and the foul weather made it difficult to travel. Only for those things that were necessary, such as school and church, did Miriam go out.

Lewis had begun to officially court Grace Zepp. He'd taken her to a couple of singings and more recently had begun to call on Grace at her home. Miriam worried about him because, ever since Papa's death, Lewis had been forced to do the work of two men. Of course, she was doing the work of two women, but she wasn't taking the time for courting. Maybe it was good that Lewis was young and obviously in love. How else could he have managed the extra activity of courting?

The scholars were full of excitement on the day of the Valentine's Day party. Nearly everyone brought goodies. There were cookies sprinkled with red sugar crystals; cupcakes frosted in pink icing; candy hearts; glazed, sugared, and powdered donuts; and a pink and white decorated cake. Miriam furnished a beverage of cold apple cider.

The party was held after lunch, and the children began by eating refreshments and followed their snack by playing some games. Finally, they exchanged valentine cards. Some of the cards were store-bought, but most of them had been made by hand, using construction paper and white paper doilies.

Every child had taken a cardboard shoebox and decorated it, then cut a hole in the top and placed it on their school desk. As Miriam sat at her desk, watching the proceedings, the scholars took turns walking around the room, placing their valentines into one another's special boxes. Miriam had instructed the class earlier in the week that each child was expected to give a card to everyone. That way nobody would be left out or go home with only a handful of valentines. She even thought to make a box for Rebekah, which she had placed on her own desk, reminding the class that Rebekah was unable to come to school right now because of her accident and would probably be studying at home for some time.

Miriam hoped some valentines, a cupcake, and a few cookies might cheer Rebekah, and she planned to deliver them after school today. It had been several weeks since she'd been over to Sarah and Andrew's, and she looked forward to a much-needed visit with

Rebekah, Mom, and Sarah. The chores at home would have to wait.

Miriam forced her thoughts aside as Mary Ellen approached her desk. The child had a large valentine heart, and she handed it to Miriam. "This is for you, Teacher Mim. It's from me and Pappy."

Miriam nodded and tried to smile. "Danki, Mary Ellen. That was nice of you."

"And Pappy, too. He helped me make it and even wrote some words on it. I think Pappy likes you, Teacher."

Miriam placed the valentine on her desk. "Tell your daed I said danki for his thoughts, as well."

"Aren't you gonna read it, Teacher Mim?"

"I'll look at it later. Right now it's time for the class to begin cleaning up the room."

Mary Ellen's eyes were downcast, but she obediently returned to her seat.

Just when I thought Amos had forgotten about me, Miriam fumed inwardly. She placed the valentine on her desk along with a stack of papers she would be taking home to correct; then she turned her attention back to the class.

As Amos forked hay into his horses' stalls, he thought about Miriam and wondered what her reaction would be to the valentine card he and Mary Ellen had made for her last night. It was the first effort he'd made in a while to reach Miriam, and he hoped she wouldn't take it wrong or think he was being too pushy. He hoped that, by giving her some time and space, she might have reconsidered his offer to court her. Maybe receiving the valentine would soften her heart and make her willing to speak with him the next time he decided to broach the subject of them courting.

"And when will that be, Lord?" he asked, setting his pitchfork aside and looking up at the rafters. "Will You let me know when the time is right to speak with Miriam again? Will You make her heart open to the idea of my courting her?"

No answer. Only the gentle nicker of the buggy horses could be heard.

Amos thought about a recent message their bishop had given on the subject of friendship. It had been based on Proverbs 18, verse 24: "A man that hath friends must shew himself friendly: and there is a friend that sticketh closer than a brother."

"Maybe that's all I need to do where Miriam's concerned," he murmured. "I just need to show myself friendly, so she will know I'm her friend."

Nick headed across the parking lot to his car, his feet slipping on the ice with every step he took. "Stupid weather!" he fumed. "I hate getting out in this slick stuff in order to conduct an interview." That afternoon, he was on his way back from a fire station across town, where he'd met with the fire chief about a benefit auction, called a "mud sale," that would be held later in the month.

Nick had learned that local people, both English

and Amish, would turn out to support the volunteer firefighters by buying crafts, food, horses, farm equipment, buggies, washing machines, plants, furniture, livestock, and various handmade items like quilts and wall hangings. Part of the sale would be held inside the building, but much of the proceedings would take place outside, where the ground was churned into mud by the feet of hundreds of people. Thus the name "mud sale."

"I'll bet anything Pete will find the story I'm doing today so interesting that he'll want me to be there on the day of the sale so I can learn more and write up another article for the newspaper."

Nick blew out his breath and watched it curl into the air like steam pouring from a teakettle. *If Amish are going to be at this shindig, maybe there's a chance I'll see Miriam Stoltzfus there.* That thought brought a smile to his lips, and as he climbed into his car, he began to whistle.

CHAPTER 19

Snow was beginning to fall again as Miriam climbed into her buggy and headed for Andrew and Sarah's place. But today she didn't care. She wasn't going to let a little bad weather stop her from an overdue visit with her family. This was a special day—a day when folks showed others how much they cared.

She placed the stack of school papers on the seat next to her and was about to pick up the reins when she noticed the red and white valentine heart sticking out between two pieces of paper. "I suppose I may as well read it now," she murmured.

On the inside, something had been written on both sides of the card. She read the left side first. It was printed and obviously done in a child's handwriting:

Dear Teacher Mim,

I wanted to bake you some cookies, but I don't know how to bake yet. I think you're smart and pretty, too.

Love,
Mary Ellen

Miriam sighed. "What a sweet little girl." She turned her attention to the other side of the card. It was written in cursive writing:

Dear Miriam,

I think of you often and wonder how you're doing. Let me know if I can be of any help to you or your family. I say a prayer for you every day.

Sincerely,
Amos Hilty

Miriam felt moisture on her cheeks and reached up to wipe it away. Had the snowflakes drifted inside the buggy? She thought all the windows had been closed, but then she felt a familiar burning in the back of her throat and realized she was crying. *But why?* she wondered. *Surely Amos has no real concern for my well-being. He's only worried about himself and his daughter.*

She drew in a deep breath and blew it out quickly. Maybe she had been too quick to judge Amos. Was it possible that he did care for her in some small way? He had experienced the pain of losing someone close to him when Ruth died. He might have been sincere in expressing his desire to help. Maybe it was time to let go of the terrible ache in her heart and move on with life.

Miriam sniffed. Even though her head told her to let go of her bitterness, it would mean she must risk being hurt again, and she couldn't take that chance.

"I don't care if Amos Hilty is sincere," she mumbled as she picked up the reins and got the buggy moving down the snow-covered road that would take her to Andrew's place. "I can't allow him to court me."

Anna was sitting at the kitchen table, writing her next article for *The Budget*, when Miriam showed up carrying a paper sack in her hand and wearing a disgruntled look on her face. Rather than make an issue of Miriam's obvious bad mood, Anna smiled and said, "It's good to see you, daughter. What brings you by on this snowy, cold afternoon?"

"I brought some valentine cards for Rebekah that

her classmates made." Miriam placed the sack on the table, slipped out of her heavy coat, draped it over the back of a chair, and sat down with an audible sigh.

"What's wrong?" Anna asked. "Do you have another one of your headaches this afternoon, or are you feeling stressed because the roads are so icy?"

Miriam glanced around the room. "Where is everyone? I'd rather that no one else knows what is irritating me so."

Anna nodded toward the door leading to the hallway. "Sarah's upstairs with the younger ones, and Rebekah's on the sofa in the living room, reading a book."

"Where's Andrew?"

"He went out to the barn some time ago to check on the batch of pups his chocolate Lab had last week."

"I'll bet the kinner are excited about having new puppies around."

Anna nodded and poured Miriam a cup of tea from the pot that sat in the center of the table. She had a feeling her daughter was trying to avoid talking about what was bothering her.

"Danki. I can use a cup of warm tea about now."

"You're welcome." Anna waited until Miriam had taken a sip of tea and seemed a bit more relaxed before she asked, "Now what's got you looking so down in the mouth today?"

"I got a valentine card—from Amos Hilty."

"Oh?"

"Actually, it was from both him and Mary Ellen, but

I have a hunch he had more to do with it than she did." She groaned. "The way he's pushing like this makes me kind of angry."

Anna clicked her tongue. "Miriam, Miriam, will you never learn?"

Miriam's forehead wrinkled as she set her cup down. "What do you mean, Mom?"

"I mean that you should not kick a gift horse in the mouth."

"You think Amos is a horse?"

"That's just an old expression, and you know it." Anna leaned forward, resting her elbows on the table. "I'm trying to tell you that you should stop questioning Amos's motives and enjoy the attention he's giving you."

"I might be able to do that if I didn't know that he has an ulterior motive."

Anna opened her mouth to reply, but Andrew stepped into the kitchen just then, interrupting their conversation.

"Brr," he said, briskly rubbing his hands together. "It's getting colder by the minute out there." He started across the room but halted when he saw Miriam. "I didn't realize you were here, sister."

"I came to bring Rebekah some valentine cards the scholars made for her."

"That's nice, but do you really think you should be out on your own this close to dark—especially with the roads being so icy?"

"I did fine on the way over here," she said, wrinkling her nose at him. "I'm sure I'll do fine going home."

"Maybe so, but being out alone after dark is not good. Too much could happen between our place and yours."

"Like what?"

"The horse could lose its footing on the icy pavement, or the buggy might slide off the road." He made a swooping gesture with his hand as though he thought she needed a picture drawn.

"Just because I'm a woman doesn't mean I'm helpless, and for your information, I think I'm doing rather well on my own."

Andrew removed his jacket and hung it on a wall peg. "I'm thinkin' what you need is a man in your life."

Miriam's face flamed, but before she could open her mouth to reply, Anna spoke up. "I'm sure Miriam wouldn't have driven over here if she didn't believe she could handle the horse and buggy in the dark or on the icy road," she said, coming to her daughter's defense.

"It's nice to know that somebody's on my side," Miriam said with a smug smile.

Anna held up her hand. "Only on that one issue." She nodded at Andrew as he took a seat at the table. "I must agree with your bruder on the other issue. When I was your age, I was happily married, and your daed and I had already begun our family."

Miriam's lips compressed into a thin line as her

eyes narrowed. "Isn't there anyone in this family who doesn't think I need a man in order to be happy?"

Andrew stared at his sister. "Can you honestly say that you're happy now?"

She shrugged.

"Miriam, why don't you take the valentines into the living room and give them to Rebekah? After you've visited awhile, you can join us for supper," Anna suggested.

"I'd be happy to follow you home in my buggy," Andrew put in.

Miriam shook her head. "I'll visit with Rebekah a few minutes, but then I'll be heading for home. Lewis will no doubt expect *his* supper to be waiting."

CHAPTER 20

The first sign of spring came on Saturday morning when Miriam, preparing to leave for the mud sale in Strasburg, discovered some yellow crocuses poking their heads between clumps of grass that were surrounded by patches of snow not far from the barn. How she wished the new life spring brought could give her a new life, too. She wanted to wake up every morning with a feeling of joy and peace. She wanted to find a reason to begin each new day with anticipation, knowing it truly was a day the Lord had created, and she wanted to enjoy every day to the fullest.

The sound of a horse and buggy plodding up the

graveled driveway caused Miriam to turn away from the flowers. She shielded her eyes against the sun, wondering who would be coming by so early in the morning. As the buggy approached, she took a few steps toward it to get a better look.

When the buggy was a few feet away, it stopped, and Amos Hilty stepped down. He smiled at Miriam and said, "Guder mariye. It's a beautiful day, wouldn't you say?"

Her only reply was a quick nod.

"I know there's still snow on the ground in places, but the sun's shining bright as a new penny, and there's a definite promise of spring in the air."

Miriam mumbled something about the crocuses she had just seen, then quickly added, "What brings you out here so early in the day, Amos? There's nothing wrong with Mary Ellen, is there?" She really did feel concern for the young girl who always seemed so determined to make "Teacher Mim" like her.

"Mary Ellen's fine. Since this is Saturday, and there's no school, I allowed her to spend last night with her friend Becky Weaver."

"I see. Then if it's not about Mary Ellen—"

"I came by to see if Lewis has any horses he might like to sell."

"If you're looking for a new horse, then why not ask Henry Yoder? He raises horses for the purpose of selling, you know."

"That's true, but I thought maybe Lewis could use the money."

"We are not destitute, Amos Hilty!"

"I—I'm sorry if I've offended you. I don't think you need charity. It's just that . . . well, with Lewis planning to get married in the fall, I thought he could probably use some extra money to put away. I'm in need of a couple of horses anyway, and—"

"Married? Who told you Lewis is planning to be married?"

"He did. I thought you knew." Amos looked flustered, and he shifted from one foot to the other.

"I know Lewis has been courting Grace Zepp, but he hasn't said anything to me about marriage in the fall," Miriam said, trying to gain control of her quivering voice.

"I—I'm sorry. I guess I shouldn't have said anything. I think maybe I've put my big boot in my mouth."

"No, you were only telling me something you thought I already knew."

"I can't believe Lewis hasn't told you," he said with a shake of his head.

"Since the wedding is several months off, he probably figured it could wait awhile." Miriam frowned. "Or maybe he didn't want to upset me."

"Why would it upset you if Lewis married a nice girl like Grace?"

"I have nothing against Grace. It's just that our life has been full of so many changes in the last year or so. If Lewis marries Grace, it will mean more changes—especially for me."

"You mean because she'll be moving into your house?"

"I suppose she will. The farm is Lewis's now that Papa's gone, and Mom isn't likely to move back since she's needed at Andrew's to help with Rebekah." Miriam shrugged. "The only logical thing for me to do is move out before they get married."

"But where would you go?"

"I'm not sure. I just know I don't want to stay here once they're married."

"Two hens in the same henhouse? Is that it?" Amos asked with a crooked grin.

Miriam had to bite her lower lip to keep from smiling. She could almost picture Grace and her running around the kitchen, cackling and chasing each other the way the hens in the coop often did. "Grace and I would probably get on fine together," she said. "But it wouldn't be fair to the newlyweds to have Lewis's big sister hanging around all the time."

"That's considerate, Miriam. You're a good woman."

Miriam's face grew warm and she looked away, hoping Amos wouldn't notice. The truth was, the idea of living in the same house with Lewis and his new wife was too painful for her. It would be a constant reminder of what she would never have—a loving husband and the hope of children to raise someday. It would also mean giving up the control she had gained in the house since Mom had moved out, and that wouldn't be easy.

• • •

Amos could see that he had embarrassed Miriam, and impulsively he reached out and touched her arm. "I—I think I might have an answer to your problem."

"Oh?"

He nodded. "You could marry me and move to my place. Mary Ellen loves you, and—"

"Are you joking?"

"About Mary Ellen's feelings toward you?"

She shook her head. "Are you joking about me marrying you?"

"No, I . . . that is . . . I've been thinking on this for some time." Amos paused a moment to calm his nerves. "I'll admit that I do have some concerns because you don't seem to be as interested in spiritual things as you should, but from what I know of you in the past—"

"My spiritual life is none of your business." She squinted. "Besides, how would you know what I think or feel about God?"

Amos cleared his throat. "I—I've been watching you for some time, and I've noted during our preaching services that you often stare out the window rather than concentrate on the sermons being preached. You don't even participate much during the time of singing. Are you bitter because of your daed's untimely death, or does the problem go back further, to when William Graber jilted you?"

"Why must you bring that up?" Miriam stared at the ground. "Are you trying to pour salt in my wounds?"

"Of course not. It's just that William and I used to be friends, until he—"

"My personal life is none of your business, and I think this discussion had better end now."

Gathering up a bit more courage, Amos took a step toward her, but she backed away, almost bumping into her buggy, which was parked next to the barn. "I—I'm sorry if I've taken you by surprise or said things that hurt you," he mumbled. "But I hope you'll at least give the matter of marrying me some deep thought. I believe we can work through your bitterness together."

She opened her mouth as if to say something, but he rushed on before he lost his nerve. "My main concern is for Mary Ellen. If we were to marry, I would hope you wouldn't let your attitude affect her. I don't want my child to have feelings of distrust toward God."

Miriam shook her head. "I would never do anything to hurt Mary Ellen's belief in God. She must draw her own conclusions as she matures and is dealt more of life's harsh blows. Now, regarding your proposal of marriage—you haven't said anything about love."

"I told you that Mary Ellen loves you, and—"

Miriam held up her hand. "You needn't say anything more, Amos, because I'm not in love with you, either."

Amos gave his beard a quick tug. Miriam's truthful words had stopped him from making a fool of himself, yet her announcement had hurt his pride more than he cared to admit. Even so, he was still willing to marry her in the hope that someday she might come to care for him the way he did her. For now, he would bide his time and keep praying for a miracle. He moistened his lips with the tip of his tongue and forced a smile. “There’s . . . uh . . . still plenty of time before Lewis and Grace’s wedding, so you don’t have to give me your answer right now. But I hope you will at least pray about it.”

Miriam looked dumbfounded, but she didn’t say a word. He figured her silence probably meant she had no plans to change her mind about marrying him.

With a quick nod in her direction, Amos headed into the barn to find Lewis.

“Men,” he heard Miriam mutter. “They would trade their heart in exchange for a live-in housekeeper.”

Nick had never been to a mud sale before, and if he’d had his way he wouldn’t be at this one, either. It was only ten in the morning, and already the ground outside the firehouse had been churned into mud by the hundreds of people milling around.

Despite the fact that he knew the Amish didn’t like to have their pictures taken, Nick couldn’t resist this chance to get some good shots of the Plain People buying and selling their wares while they interacted with others not of their faith. He spotted one teenage Amish boy pedaling furiously on an exercise bike. Two Amish girls stood in front of an English vendor’s table, playing with the brightly colored plastic toys that were for sale, while a couple of young English boys pretended to shoot each other with plastic squirt guns. Adults stood around, conversing with one another and bidding on the merchandise being sold in the auction rings. Everything from plain, old-fashioned wringer washing machines to fancy, modern speedboats was available to buy or bid on. Nick noticed a tent had been set up to shelter the horses that would soon be auctioned off. He started toward that area but stopped when he spotted an Amish woman plodding through the mud, carrying a box in her arms. It was Miriam Stoltzfus.

"Miriam, wait up!" he called, slipping his camera back into the bag and trudging after her.

She halted and turned to look at him. "What are you doing here, Nick?"

"Came to cover the mud sale for an article I've been asked to do for the newspaper."

"I'm not surprised," she said with a sniff. "You seem to be good at doing stories that involve my people."

"You're still mad at me for writing that article about your niece, aren't you?"

"It wasn't what you said in the article; it was the picture you took of Rebekah that upset me so."

"I said I was sorry."

"Yes, but then you went back to her room again and bribed her with a stuffed animal so you could take more pictures."

Nick knew he was caught, so he decided to change the subject. "Are you here to buy or sell?"

Miriam nodded at the box in her arms. “I’ve brought a couple of quilts for the auction that will be held later on. The money will go to help with Rebekah’s hospital bills.” She started walking in the direction of the building again, and he followed.

“How’s your niece doing? Is she getting along okay?”

She halted before they reached the door. “Rebekah’s legs are paralyzed, and she’s in a wheelchair. My mother has moved to my brother Andrew’s house to help care for her.”

“Does that mean you’re living alone?”

She shook her head. “My brother Lewis is still at home, and he will continue to live there even after he’s married in the fall.”

Miriam’s serious expression made Nick wonder if she might disapprove of her brother’s choice for a wife. “Are you opposed to the idea of your brother getting married?” he asked.

Her lips compressed into a thin, straight line. “Of course not. It’s just that things won’t be the same for me after Grace moves into the house, and if I can find someplace else to live before the wedding, I may move.”

“My aunt runs a boarding home not far from here,” Nick said. “Want me to see if she has any spare rooms?”

“No, thank you. I’ll find somewhere to go, and when I do, it will be within the Amish community.” Someone opened the door to exit the building just then, and Miriam stepped quickly inside. “I need to get this quilt in for the auction before it's too late. I hope you get all you need for your mud-sale story," she called over her shoulder.

Nick chuckled as he watched her retreating form. "I think that woman likes me. She just doesn't know it."

CHAPTER 21

Miriam made her way to the house as though she were moving in slow motion. Her mind was filled with thoughts of the conversation she'd had with Nick at the mud sale, and she wondered what kind of hold he had on her that she always managed to tell him more than she wanted him to know about her personal life. What had she been thinking, blurting out that information about Lewis's marriage plans? She hadn't even told Lewis she knew, and since his plans to marry Grace hadn't officially been published during church yet, she had no right to tell anyone.

By the time Miriam reached the back porch, her thoughts took her in another direction as she remembered the marriage proposal she'd had from Amos that morning. She wondered if the man actually thought he'd be doing her a favor by marrying her, solving the problem of where she would live after Lewis's marriage to Grace and all. If she were to marry Amos, it would be her doing him the favor, not the other way around.

She entered the kitchen and tried to focus her thoughts on what she should be doing. Baking some muffins and making a pot of baked beans for tonight's supper—wasn't that what she'd planned to do after returning home from the mud sale? Maybe if she got busy, it would take her mind off Amos Hilty and Nick McCormick.

"How could Lewis keep something as important as his decision to marry Grace from me and yet tell Amos?" Miriam fumed as she pulled a tin of flour down from the cupboard. "Men are all alike. None of them can be trusted! I wonder who else Lewis has told, and how many other people have been hiding the truth from me. If people would talk behind my back about how William jilted me, then who knows what else they're saying?"

Miriam soon had her pot of beans cooking on top of the stove and had just put a pan of muffins in the oven when she heard the sound of heavy footsteps clomping up the porch steps. A few seconds later, Lewis entered the kitchen with a broken harness hanging over one arm. "Umm . . . something smells good," he said, sniffing the air.

"It's muffins and baked beans for supper," Miriam said.

Lewis dropped the harness to the floor, then pulled out a chair and sat down. "How'd the mud sale go today?"

"Fine. I sold both of my quilts, and that gives me a little more money toward Rebekah's hospital bills."

"That's good to hear."

Miriam stirred the pot of beans but said nothing more. She was afraid if she voiced the thoughts in her head, she and Lewis might end up in an argument.

He cleared his throat a couple of times. "Uh, Miriam, I think the two of us need to have a little heart-to-heart talk."

She turned down the burner on the stove and took a seat at the table across from him. "If it's about you and Grace, I already know."

"Jah, Amos told me he'd let the cat out of the bag. I'm sorry you had to hear it secondhand. I was planning to tell you, but I was just waiting for the right time."

"Didn't you think I could handle the news? Don't you know by now that I can handle most anything that comes my way—even disappointments?" Miriam's voice sounded harsh even to her own ears.

"You're disappointed because Grace and I plan to be married?" Lewis shook his head. "I never expected you to be jealous."

It was true. Miriam was jealous, but she never would have admitted that to her brother. "This has nothing to do with jealousy. It has to do with the fact that you told Amos, who isn't even a family member, before you told me, your only sister." She paused for a breath. "With so many other changes having gone on in our lives lately, this news is a bit too much to take."

"What do you mean by that?"

"First, Papa dies, and then Rebekah gets injured. Next, Mom moves out of the house, and now I have to move out, as well."

"I don't expect you to move out. This is your home, too, and I want you to stay here as long as you like."

"I'm sure you're only saying that to be kind, Lewis. I would never dream of staying on here once you and Grace are married. It wouldn't be fair to either of you. And quite frankly, I'm not sure I would enjoy it much, either."

Lewis's forehead wrinkled. "Why not?"

"I've had complete control of the household for several months now, and another woman in the house would be a difficult adjustment. I have my own ways of doing things, and I'm certain Grace has hers, as well."

"But I'm sure Grace would be most understanding," Lewis argued. "Besides, she'll probably need your help with a lot of things."

Miriam shook her head. "For a time she might, but soon she would come to think of the house as hers and want to run it her own way. It's only normal that she would, and I won't stand in her way. Besides, you newlyweds will need your privacy. When is the wedding to take place? Have you set a date yet?"

"We're planning to be married on the third Thursday of November."

Miriam nodded stiffly. "Maybe I'll see if Mom's willing to move back home, and then I could move in with Andrew and Sarah when the time gets closer to the wedding."

"I suppose there's nothing I can say to change your mind?"

"No, nothing."

"I can't believe I was dumb enough to propose to Miriam this morning," Amos mumbled as he traveled down the road in his buggy toward the Weavers' place, where his daughter had spent the previous night and would be waiting for him to pick her up. "Now Miriam's really convinced that I only want to marry her for the sake of convenience."

He gave his horse the signal to trot, hoping a brisker ride might smooth the edges of his frayed nerves a bit. All day he had berated himself for everything he'd said to Miriam—first telling her about Lewis's plans to marry Grace; then asking her to marry him; and finally, allowing her to believe he didn't love her, but only wanted a mother for Mary Ellen. What a *dummkopp* he had been!

I do love Miriam and have for a long time, he thought ruefully. *But what good is that if she doesn't return my feelings?* Miriam had made it clear by her actions that she felt no love for Amos, and today, when she'd actually spoken the words, he had been crushed. At that point he would have made a bigger fool of himself if he had opened his heart to her, and he was sure her response would have only pierced him further by a firm rejection.

"Well, I won't ask again," he shouted into the wind. "If Miriam changes her mind, then she'll have to come to me."

On Monday after school let out for the day, Miriam went to Strasburg to do some shopping. As she passed a boardinghouse situated on a quiet street on the south side of town, she remembered Nick mentioning that his aunt ran a boardinghouse. Miriam thought this particular home, tall and stately, shaded by leafy elm trees, and surrounded by a white picket fence, looked like the perfect place to live. It would offer solitude, seclusion, and no more farm duties or household chores to take up her time. Living in a boardinghouse would probably mean that all of her meals would be provided, and her only real responsibilities would be to keep her room clean and, of course, continue to teach at the Amish schoolhouse.

Just think of all the free time I would have for reading, quilting, and visiting friends and family, she told herself. But of course, that idea was about as ridiculous as the thought of her marrying Amos Hilty. The boardinghouse wasn't run by anyone Amish, which was obvious by the electrical wires running to it. And Miriam was too committed to her family to do anything that would hurt them or get her shunned.

She moved on down the street but had only taken a few steps when she bumped into a man. Her mouth dropped open. "Nick!"

• • •

Nick couldn't believe his good fortune. He had run into Miriam twice in one week, and that pleased him more than he cared to admit. He smiled and winked at her. "It's good to see you again, Miriam. I've been thinking about you and wondering how you're doing."

"I'm managing."

"You're looking well—as beautiful as ever in fact."

Miriam wrinkled her nose. "Are you trying to flatter me?"

"Not at all." He took a step toward her. "So, what are you doing in this neck of the woods?"

"I was about to ask you the same question."

"My aunt lives here." He turned and pointed to the stately home Miriam had been admiring. "That's the boardinghouse she runs. Too bad you don't live in Strasburg. I come here frequently to see my aunt, and if you lived in Strasburg, we'd be able to see each other more often, too."

Miriam's cheeks turned pink, and she stared at the ground.

"If we saw each other more, we'd be able to find out if we could ever see eye-to-eye on anything."

"I—I would like to move," Miriam said as she lifted her gaze to meet his. "But it won't be here."

"How come?"

"I'm sure you know why, Nick. An Amish woman's place is with her family."

"What if your family lived here? Then would you consider moving?"

"Of course, but I have no family living in Strasburg."

"What if I was your family?"

"Wh—what are you saying?" she croaked, her voice all but gone.

"I'm saying that you could marry me. I'm not getting any younger, and maybe it's time I settled down with a good woman—and a beautiful one at that."

Miriam's face turned even redder, and he noticed that perspiration had beaded up on her forehead.

"You're making fun of me, aren't you?" she asked in a near whisper.

"No, I'm not. Listen, I've surprised myself as much as I have you by popping the question, but now that I have, I kind of like the idea." Nick scrubbed his hand across his chin, realizing that he'd forgotten to shave that morning. "You know, I never thought I'd hear myself say this, but the thought of coming home at night to a good, home-cooked meal and a beautiful wife waiting for me is kind of appealing."

He took another step toward her and was glad when she didn't back away. "I know we're about as different as your buggy horse and my sports car, but maybe we could make it work. After all, we do seem to find one another easy to talk to, and there's a certain kind of chemistry between us. In fact, this could turn out to be the adventure of our lives."

"But . . . but—I would have to leave the Amish faith if I were to marry an outsider," she stammered. "I'd be excommunicated and shunned by my family and friends."

Nick reached for her hand and pulled her toward his car. "Let's go for a ride and talk this over."

At first, Miriam looked as if she might go with him, but then she halted and slowly shook her head. "You've not said anything about love, Nick."

He shrugged and pulled his fingers through the back of his hair. "Who says there has to be love in a marriage? There's chemistry between us; you can't deny it."

"I could never marry without love, and leaving my faith to marry you is impossible." She turned on her heel and started to walk away, but he reached out and took hold of her arm so she was facing him again.

"If two people are as attracted to each other as I believe we are, then nothing else should matter."

Tears pooled in Miriam's eyes, and she pulled away. "I—I'm sure you meant well, asking me to leave my faith and marry you, but I can't. We hardly know each other, and even if we did, I think we both know that things could never work out between us. My faith has weakened in the last several months, but I won't let my family down by leaving our church for a relationship that's built on nothing more than a physical attraction."

"Is that your final word?"

"It has to be." She turned toward her buggy, parked across the street. "I need to go. I have chores to do at home."

Nick felt a strange mixture of relief and disappointment as he watched Miriam climb into her buggy. He didn't know what had come over him to pop the question like that, and now he felt kind of stupid. It wasn't his style to let his guard down like that or make himself so vulnerable. Asking Miriam to marry him, when they were so different, bordered on ridiculous. Maybe that was why he'd proposed—because he knew it would never work and that she would say no.

As Miriam was about to pull away from the curb, Nick gathered his wits and called, "I wish you the best, Miriam. If you ever need a shoulder to cry on or just want to talk, you know where to reach me."

Miriam sat up in bed and wiped the perspiration from her forehead. She'd been dreaming about three men. First there had been William Graber, smiling and waving at her as he drove away in his buggy with his new bride. Then Nick McCormick had come onto the scene, traipsing after her with his camera and calling her "fair lady." Miriam had pulled her dark bonnet down over her face, and when she removed it again, Nick was gone. Amos Hilty stood before her, holding a bouquet of pansies. *What did that strange dream mean?* she wondered. *Was there any significance to it?*

She glanced at the clock on the table by her bed and frowned. It was only four in the morning. She didn't have to get up for another hour, yet she was afraid to go back to sleep. What if her dream continued? She didn't want to think about William, Nick, or Amos. For that matter, it would suit her fine if she never thought of any man ever again!

CHAPTER

22

As the months flew by and Lewis's wedding drew closer, Miriam began to feel a sense of panic. Mom wasn't willing to move back home and allow Miriam to take her place at Andrew and Sarah's, so Miriam had about decided that she would have to stay at the house with Lewis and Grace after they were married. She hoped the newlyweds would understand and that she would be able to handle not being in charge of the house once Grace took over.

One morning on the way to school, Miriam passed Amos's rig. He and Mary Ellen were obviously headed for the schoolhouse. Mary Ellen leaned out the window and waved. "Hello, Teacher Mim!"

Miriam waved in response and urged her horse into a trot. She didn't think it would be right for any of her students to arrive at school before their teacher did.

As she pulled into the school yard a short time later, she was relieved to see that none of the other children were there yet. She halted her horse, climbed down from the buggy, and had just started to unhitch the mare when the Hiltys showed up.

Miriam watched as Amos got out and went around to help his daughter down. In spite of her mistrust of the man, she had to admit that he was a good father, and Mary Ellen obviously loved him very much.

Just as the child stepped down from the buggy, her

foot snagged in the hem of her dress. She looked down and gasped. "It's torn! Pappy, please don't make me go to school today. The others will laugh at me; I just know they will."

The sympathetic look Amos first gave his daughter turned to obvious frustration. "I can't do anything about your dress right now, Mary Ellen. We'll take it over to Maudie Miller's after school lets out. She can mend it for you then."

Mary Ellen shot him an imploring look. "No, Pappy, please. I don't want to wait that long."

Feeling the child's embarrassment as if it were her own, Miriam stepped forward. "Let me get my horse put in the corral, and then we'll go inside the schoolhouse. I'll mend your dress before the others get here."

When Amos turned to face Miriam, he wore a look of astonishment. "Would you really do that for her? Do you have the necessary tools?"

Miriam gave a small laugh. "You needn't be so surprised, Amos. In spite of what some may say about me, I've actually been known to do a few acts of kindness."

"I—I didn't mean to say—"

"Never mind. Just go on your way, and Mary Ellen will be fine."

"Well, let me take care of your horse then."

"Danki." Miriam put her hand across Mary Ellen's back and guided her toward the schoolhouse; then she turned back and called to Amos, "Oh, and by the way—you don't use tools to sew, but I do keep a small kit full of sewing supplies in my desk for such an emergency as this."

Amos mumbled something under his breath and headed over to Miriam's buggy to unhitch the horse.

When Miriam entered the schoolhouse with Mary Ellen, she saw right away that the child's face was streaked with tears. The first thing she did was to dip a clean cloth into the bucket of water she kept nearby and gently wipe the little girl's face. "Now stand on this chair while I hem up your dress," she instructed.

"How come?"

"It would be quicker and easier if your dress was off, but some of the other kinner may arrive soon, and you wouldn't want to be caught without your dress on, would you?"

Mary Ellen shook her head. "No, Teacher Mim."

"Now, hold real still, and no rutsching."

"I'll try not to squirm, I promise."

Miriam threaded a needle and began the task of putting Mary Ellen's hem back into place. When the job was completed, Mary Ellen smiled happily and jumped down from the chair. "Danki, Teacher. You did a good job, and it looks real nice now."

"Gern gschehne—you are welcome," Miriam replied as the door opened and three of the Hoelwarth boys burst into the room.

She was glad the sewing job had been completed, because the Hoelwarths were all teases, and they would probably have taunted Mary Ellen if they'd seen her standing on a chair getting her dress mended.

• • •

All the way home, Amos thought about Miriam and how she had seemed so concerned about Mary Ellen's torn dress.

"Miriam has a lot of good in her, Lord," he said out loud. "Trouble is she doesn't seem to know it. So maybe what we need here is some way to bring out all that goodness."

Keeping his focus straight ahead, Amos guided his horse and buggy down the road, allowing his thoughts to wander back to the day when he and Miriam were still kinner in school. . . .

"Let's get a game of baseball going," Noah Troyer shouted when the school children were dismissed for morning recess.

Amos always enjoyed a good game of ball, so he eagerly grabbed the baseball glove from under his desk and headed outside to the playground. It was a hot, humid day, and before he joined the game, he made a quick trip to the pump around back for a drink of water. He came across Miriam and her youngest brother, Lewis, whose face was wet with tears. "I wanna play ball," the boy wailed, "but Noah says I'm too young, and he told me to go play on the swings with the girls."

Miriam dropped to her knees and wrapped her arms around her brother. "It's okay. You and I can have our own game of ball."

Lewis looked up at her, and a slight smile tugged at the corners of his lips. "Really?"

She nodded. "I was going to read for a while, but I'll go inside and get a ball from Teacher Leah."

Amos was tempted to ask if he might join in their game, but the shyness he felt whenever he was around girls prevented him from saying anything. So he gave the pump handle a couple of thrusts and took a big drink of water.

Miriam's got such a kind heart, he thought, as he headed over to the ball field a few minutes later. *Someday, if I ever get up the nerve, I'm gonna ask that girl to marry me.*

"Well, I've finally asked her to marry me," Amos mumbled, as his thoughts returned to the present. "But unless God changes Miriam's heart, I'll never have the chance to show how much I love her."

A truck sped by Amos's buggy just then, causing the horse to spook and veer off to the left. Amos gripped the reins and shouted, "Whoa, there. Steady, boy!"

He struggled to gain control of the skittish animal, but it was too late. The buggy flipped onto its side as the horse broke free and took off down the road. Except for a couple of bumps and bruises, Amos was relieved that he had escaped serious injury. The last thing Mary Ellen needed was to lose another parent or to have him end up in the hospital.

He reached over and pushed the opposite door of the buggy open, then crawled out. "That's what I get for letting my mind wander and not paying better attention to my driving," he muttered. "Now I've got a buggy to repair, not to mention a runaway horse that needs to be found."

The morning went by quickly, and soon it was lunchtime. Miriam watched as Mary Ellen opened her metal lunch box. The child ate hungrily, but Miriam was appalled to see what Amos had given his daughter to eat. The contents of the lunch box revealed a biscuit, some dried beef jerky, a green apple, and a bottle of water.

Miriam wondered if Mary Ellen's father had been in a hurry that morning or was completely ignorant as to a child's nutritional needs. She had seen some of the pitiful lunches he'd made Mary Ellen in the past, but none of them had looked this bad.

Miriam shook her head and sighed, wishing she hadn't already eaten her own lunch, for she would have shared some of her sandwich with Mary Ellen. *That man really does need a wife, and Mary Ellen surely needs a mother.*

She looked away from the little girl and directed her gaze out the window. She had to get her mind on something else. She could feel one of her sick headaches coming on and knew she had to ward it off, so she reached into her desk drawer and retrieved a bottle of white willow bark capsules. The Thermos of water that normally sat on her desk was half full, so she popped two capsules into her mouth and swallowed them down.

Miriam was relieved when all the children had finished their lunches and filed outside to play. Now maybe she would have a few minutes of peace. But that was not to be. After only a brief time, a commotion outside ended her solitude.

When Miriam went out to investigate, she found a group of children gathered around Mary Ellen. This was not the first time she'd witnessed some of them picking on the child, and she wondered what the problem could be.

Mary Ellen lay crumpled on the ground, whimpering pathetically, while several of the older boys, including two of the Hoelwarths, pointed at her and jeered. John Hoelwarth held a long stick in his hand and was poking Mary Ellen with it. "Get up, baby Hilty. Quit your cryin'. You're such a little boppli!"

Angrily, Miriam grabbed the stick from John and whirled him around to face her. "What is going on here, and why are you poking at a defenseless little girl and calling her a baby?"

John hung his head as he made little circles in the dirt with the toe of his boot. "I was only tryin' to make her quit bawling. She sounds like one of my daed's heifers."

The children's laughter rang out, vibrating through Miriam's tensed body. "Quiet!" she shouted. "I want to know why Mary Ellen was crying, and why you've been teasing her again."

"Look at her hair, Teacher," Sara King said. "She

hasn't got a mamm, and her daed can't fix it so it stays up the way it should. She looks pretty silly, don't ya think?"

Miriam bent down and gently pulled Mary Ellen to her feet. "Come inside now. I'll fix your hair and clean you up." To the other children, she said, "You may all stay outside until I call you. Then we'll discuss what's happened here." She turned and led Mary Ellen to the schoolhouse.

It took nearly half an hour for Miriam to get the child calmed down, cleaned up, and her hair put back in place.

"Try not to let the kinner's teasing bother you," Miriam said. "Some of the older ones like to make trouble. Everyone but you will be made to stay after school."

"It don't matter," Mary Ellen said with a shake of her head. "They'll always tease me, 'cause I have no mamm. If Mama were alive still, she'd sew my dresses so the hems stayed up. She would fix me good lunches like the others have, and she'd do better with my hair than Pappy does. He tries real hard, but he can't do some things the way a mudder can." Mary Ellen sniffed deeply, although she did manage a weak smile. "Teacher Mim, I sure wish you was my mamm."

Miriam swallowed hard. There was no doubt about it. Mary Ellen needed her. For that matter, Amos probably did, too. And as much as she hated to admit it, she needed them—or at least their home to live in.

She knew she could never give up her faith to marry Nick, and perhaps a marriage without love wouldn't be such a bad thing. If she married Amos, all concerned would have mutual needs met.

Heartrending though the decision was, Miriam knew what she wanted to do. She would tell Amos that she had changed her mind and decided to accept his proposal, and she must do it soon before she lost her nerve.

CHAPTER 23

"I will not tease" had been written on the blackboard one hundred times by each of the boys who had tormented Mary Ellen, and Miriam had kept the entire class after school and given them a lecture on kindness.

It had been a long, emotionally exhausting day at school, and Miriam was glad it was finally over. Now she must ride over to the Hiltys' and speak to Amos before she lost her nerve. The decision to marry him had not been an easy one, and her mind was full of questions. Would he still want to marry her? Would Mary Ellen be happy about it? What would her own family think? Most of all, she wondered if she could really make herself go through with it.

Miriam poured herself a glass of water and swallowed the two white willow bark capsules she had put in her mouth. If she was going to face Amos, it had better not be with a pounding headache. With a sigh of resignation, she gathered up her things and headed out the door.

"I love you, Grandma," Rebekah said as she smiled up at Anna, her pale blue eyes gleaming in the sunlight that streamed through Anna's bedroom window.

Anna smiled in return and pushed Rebekah's wheelchair closer to the African violets sitting on her window ledge. "I love you, too, child."

"I like the purple ones best," Rebekah said, reaching out to touch the tip of one leafy bloom.

"Jah, I agree."

Anna knew there weren't many things Rebekah could do without the use of her legs, but helping water and prune the plants was one thing she could do to make herself feel useful. Besides, Rebekah seemed taken with the pretty flowers and was always eager to help out whenever Anna said it was time for watering, pruning, or repotting some of the plants that had grown too big for their containers.

"I'm glad you came to live with us, Grandma. Otherwise, I would have had to come all the way over to your house to see your pretty houseplants." Rebekah sighed. "Of course, someone would have to drive me there, since I can't walk to your place the way I used to do."

A stab of regret pierced Anna's heart. She hated to see any of her family suffer.

"I'm glad I live here, too," she said, patting Rebekah on top of her head.

"Mama says you write stories about me sometimes for the newspaper," Rebekah said, changing the subject.

"Jah, that's true. I write about many things that go on in our community."

"Do you think I could write some stories for the paper?"

Anna smiled. "I don't see why not. In fact, someday after I'm gone, maybe you can take over my column."

"I'd like that, but I don't want you to leave—not ever."

"If God allows it, I hope to be around for a long time yet." Anna motioned to another one of her plants. "After all, who would keep these pretty violets watered if I wasn't here?"

Rebekah giggled. "I guess I could water 'em, but it's a lot more fun when we do it together, don't ya think?"

"Jah, everything is always more fun when you have someone to do it with." Anna's thoughts turned to Miriam, who seemed to prefer being alone these days. *Or maybe she just doesn't like me butting into her business.*

Anna closed her eyes and lifted a silent prayer. *Heavenly Father, I've asked this before, I know, but I'm beseeching You to fill my daughter's heart with peace, joy, and love. Oh, and would You remind me if necessary that it's You who can work on Miriam's heart, not me? Amen.*

• • •

Mary Ellen was sitting on the front porch, playing with a fluffy white kitten, when Miriam pulled into the yard. The child waved and ran toward Miriam as soon as she climbed down from her buggy. "Teacher Mim, you came to visit! Look, my hem's still in place," she said, lifting the corner of her dress.

Miriam nodded. "I see that, and I also see that your hair is in place yet."

Mary Ellen's grin stretched ear to ear. "You did a good job with it. Don't tell Pappy I said so, but you're much better at fixin' hair than he is."

Miriam smiled. She couldn't help but like the sweet little girl. Mary Ellen obviously needed a woman to train her to do all the feminine things her father was unable to do. "Speaking of your daed," Miriam said, "where is he? I need to talk to him."

"He's out in his shop. I can take you there, if you want."

"Danki for offering, but I think it would be best if you stayed on the porch and played with your kitten. Your daed and I have some grown-up things we need to say to each other. We'll join you on the porch when we're done. How's that sound?"

Mary Ellen's eyes widened. "You're not gonna tell Pappy about those boys teasin' me today, are you?"

Miriam shook her head. "What I have to say to him has nothing to do with the Hoelwarth boys."

The child released a sigh of obvious relief. "I'll play

'til you're done talking. Then maybe we can all have cookies and milk."

"Jah, maybe so," she said, turning toward Amos's blacksmith shop.

Miriam had never been inside his shop before, and when she entered the building a few minutes later, she saw no sign of Amos but was surprised at how neat and orderly everything looked. She noticed a large wooden table with several small compartments, each filled neatly with tools of all shapes and sizes. A stack of firewood stood along one wall next to a tall brick fireplace and an anvil. A large rack also rested nearby, with horseshoes of all sizes hanging from it. A metal desk, a few chairs, and a filing cabinet took up the corner area near the door, and a stack of magazines lay on a small table nearby. *Probably for customers to browse as they wait for their horses to be shod,* she thought. *Amos may not do such a good job of putting his daughter's hair in place, but he sure runs a neat, organized place of business.*

"Amos, are you about?" Miriam called, cupping her hands around her mouth.

A few seconds later, he stepped through the doorway of the smaller room that was attached to the main part of his shop. "Oh, it's you, Miriam. I—I was just cleanin' things up in the other room and didn't realize anyone had come in," he said, looking kind of red-faced and flustered.

"I just came in." Miriam made a sweeping gesture

of the room. "This is quite impressive. There must be a lot of work involved in what you do."

He nodded. "Jah, always seems to be a lot of horses that need shoeing."

Feeling the need to stall for time, as her resolve began to weaken, Miriam decided to question him about his business. "How often do horses need to be shod?"

"You don't know?"

She shook her head. "Papa used to take care of that kind of thing, and now that he's gone, it's become Lewis's job to see that our horses are looked after."

"Well, most need shoeing every six to eight weeks on the average. In the summertime the pavement is softer because of the heat, so that can loosen the shoes." Amos leaned against his workbench and folded his arms. "Plus, the horses are stamping at flies all the time, and that action can wear down the shoes pretty good."

"Do they need to be shod that often during the winter?"

"Not usually. Most horses can go eight or even ten weeks between visits to my shop during the colder months."

"I see." Miriam shuffled her feet a few times, wondering how best to broach the subject of his earlier marriage proposal.

"I want to thank you for mending Mary Ellen's dress this morning," Amos said, taking their conversation in a different direction.

"No problem. I was glad to do it."

"So what brings you out our way? Does your horse need new shoes or did you need to speak with me about Mary Ellen?"

"Neither one. Actually, I . . . uh . . . came to talk about your offer of marriage."

"Really?"

She nodded.

"Have you been thinking it over then?"

"I have, and if the offer's still open, then I've decided that I will marry you."

Amos dropped his arms to his sides and took a step toward Miriam. "I don't know what caused you to change your mind, but I'm glad you did. I think Mary Ellen will be real pleased about this, too."

"Mary Ellen is the reason I did change my mind," Miriam stated truthfully. No point in letting him think otherwise. "I've come to the conclusion that the child needs a woman's care." She paused for a quick breath, hoping she hadn't offended him. "It's not that you aren't doing a fine job with her, but—"

"I understand what you're trying to say. My daughter needs a mudder. She needs someone who can do all the feminine things I can't do for her. As you know, I do have some concerns about how your attitude might affect Mary Ellen, and if there's to be a marriage, I need your word that you won't let Mary Ellen see your bitterness. It's important that you help me train her in God's ways, and we both must set a good example for her." He reached out and touched her arm.

Miriam pulled away, feeling as if she'd been stung by a bee and wondering if she had done the right thing after all. Could she really keep from letting her bitter heart be noticeable to Mary Ellen? Could she set the child a good example?

"I—I promise to do my best by Mary Ellen," she finally murmured.

"Danki." Amos smiled. "I need you as well, Miriam. I need a wife."

She gulped. "Do—do you mean just for cooking and cleaning, or in every way?"

He shuffled his feet and stared at the concrete floor. "I . . . that is . . . of course I would like a physical relationship with my wife, but if you don't feel ready—"

"I'm not ready. I may never be ready for that, and if this will be a problem for you, then it might be best if we forget about getting married."

He shook his head. "No, please. I'll wait until you feel ready for my physical touch. Until then, we'll live together as friends and learn more about one another. Maybe as our friendship grows, things will change between us."

"I don't want to give you any false hope, Amos. I don't think I can ever love you," Miriam said as gently as she knew how.

"We'll see how it goes." Amos turned toward the door with his shoulders slumped. "Shall we go up to the house and tell Mary Ellen our news? I'm sure she will be glad."

"I—I hope so." Miriam could hardly believe Amos

had accepted her conditions so easily. She figured he must be desperate for a housekeeper and a mother for his child. Of course, she'd had to agree to set a good example for Mary Ellen and teach her about spiritual things. She just hoped she wouldn't fall short of that promise.

Mary Ellen was still on the porch playing with her kitten when Amos and Miriam joined her a few minutes later. She looked up at them expectantly. "Can we have some cookies and milk, Pappy?"

He smiled down at her. "Jah. That sounds like a fine idea. Let's go inside, and we'll sit at the table, eat our cookies, and have a little talk. Miriam and I have something important we want to tell you."

When they entered the house, Miriam realized it was the first time she'd been inside the Hilty home since Ruth's funeral. The place wasn't dirty, just cluttered and unkempt. If there had ever been any doubt in her mind about whether Amos needed a wife or not, it was erased. The touch of a woman in the house was greatly needed.

Amos poured tall glasses of milk, while Mary Ellen went to the cookie jar and got out some cookies that were obviously store-bought. When they'd all taken seats at the table, Amos cleared his throat a couple of times and said, "Mary Ellen, how would you like it if Pappy got married again?"

The child tipped her head and looked at him with a quizzical expression. "A new mamm for me?"

Amos nodded. "And a *fraa* for me."

Mary Ellen turned to face Miriam. "Is it you, Teacher Mim? Are you gonna be Pappy's wife?"

"How would you feel about that?" Miriam asked.

"I'd like it very much." Mary Ellen gave Miriam a wide grin. "When can ya come to live with us?"

Amos chuckled. "Not 'til we're married, little one."

"When will that be?"

Amos looked at Miriam, and she shrugged. "As soon as possible, I suppose."

He nodded in agreement. "I'll speak to Bishop Benner right away."

CHAPTER 24

Miriam's family seemed pleased when she told them she was going to marry Amos—Mom most of all. Miriam was certain that everyone thought she was marrying Amos because she had changed her mind about him and perhaps had even come to love him. She had no intention of telling them otherwise.

However, Miriam had a hunch that Crystal hadn't been so easily deceived. She had acted a bit strange when Miriam gave her and Jonas the news, although she hadn't said anything more than a pleasant "congratulations."

I suppose I'll have to tell her the truth if she asks, Miriam thought as she cleaned up the kitchen after breakfast one morning. Crystal had always been able to see right through her, even when they were children and Miriam had tried to hide her feelings when she was upset about something.

Forcing her thoughts aside, Miriam finished her cleaning and had just decided to take a walk, when Crystal showed up.

"I came by to see if you'd like to go to town with me to do some shopping," she said, stepping into the kitchen.

"Right now?"

"Jah."

"I don't feel much like shopping today," Miriam said as the two of them took seats at the table. "But I appreciate you asking."

"Do you have other plans for the day?"

"Not really. Just the usual work around here." Miriam chose not to mention that she had planned to take a walk.

"Then let's get out for a while. It'll do us both some good. Ever since school let out for the summer, you've been staying around here too much."

"I like being at home. It feels safe, and I don't have to answer to anyone." Miriam's chin quivered as she sat on the edge of her kitchen chair, blinking back the tears that had gathered in her eyes. She felt Crystal's arm encircle her shoulders.

"What is it, Miriam? Why are you crying?"

"It—it's just that . . ." Miriam's voice faltered. "I'm not sure how things will go once Amos and I are married."

"You're already having second thoughts?"

Miriam's only reply was a quick nod.

"I was afraid of that, and your tight muscles are proof of it." Crystal massaged the knots in Miriam's neck and shoulders. "When you gave Jonas and me the news about you and Amos, I suspected that your heart wasn't in the decision. Why are you marrying him, Miriam? What changed your mind?"

"I only agreed to marry Amos because of Mary Ellen." Miriam sniffed deeply. "That sweet little girl needs a mother so badly." She wiped the tears from her face with the back of her hand. "I know I've said many times that I would never marry without love, but there will be love—Mary Ellen's love for me, and my love for her."

"I understand, but what about love for Amos?"

"He's a nice enough man, but I must admit that I don't love him."

"Then how can you marry him when there's no love between you?"

Miriam shrugged. "I can live without a man's love; I've done it for some time. My biggest concern has to do with trust."

"What do you mean?"

"I don't know if I can trust Amos."

"Trust him how?"

"He's agreed not to force a physical relationship on me, but men are selfish, and—"

"Miriam, all men are not like William Graber. Amos appears to be an honest and upright man. I don't believe he will hurt you the way William did.

However, since you obviously feel no love for him and you say he doesn't love you, then—"

"He doesn't love me."

"Then maybe it would be best if you don't make a lifelong commitment to him. As you know, divorce isn't an acceptable option among the Old Order Amish, and it isn't fair of you to expect Amos to enter into a relationship that won't be a real marriage."

"You think I should tell Amos I've changed my mind and call off the wedding?"

"I'm only saying that I feel you need to give the matter more prayer and thought. I want to see you happy, and if you marry someone you don't love, how can you ever be truly happy?"

Miriam shrugged. "I've come to realize that life's not always so joyous."

"Until you get rid of your feelings of mistrust and allow God to fill your heart with peace, you'll never find love or happiness."

"I've learned to manage without those things." Miriam swallowed against the bitter taste of bile rising to her throat. "Besides, if I marry Amos, it will benefit others, as well."

"Like who?"

"First of all, I won't be living here with Lewis and Grace, so they'll be happier. Then there's Mom. I'm sure she will be pleased to see me married off. Mary Ellen will have a mother to care for her needs properly. And of course, Amos will have someone to cook and clean for him."

"What about your needs, Miriam? How will they be met?"

"My needs will be provided—I'll have a roof over my head and a child to help Amos raise." Miriam drew in a deep breath. "I hope that as my best friend, you will support me in this decision."

"Of course I support you," Crystal said with a nod. "I'll help with your wedding plans in any way I can. If you're doing what you feel your heart is telling you to do, then I'll support you with my love and prayers, too."

Miriam stared at a dark spot on the tablecloth. It was probably a coffee stain that would never come clean—just like the stain of William's deception that would never leave her heart. "I—I feel that this is the right thing to do."

"All right then; enough has been said." Crystal patted Miriam gently on the back. "Now, are you sure you won't go shopping with me?"

Miriam pushed her chair aside and stood. "I guess there are a few things I might need before the wedding. So, jah, I'll go along."

"How come you're staring at the newspaper and smiling, Grandma?" Rebekah asked, as she rolled her wheelchair up to the table where Anna sat. "Is there somethin' funny in that paper?"

Anna smiled. "I was reading an article written in our Amish newspaper by a woman who lives in Kentucky. She found a nest of baby mice in her box of wedding china."

Rebekah giggled. "I bet Aunt Miriam would scream if she found a baby *maus* in with her wedding dishes."

"You're probably right about that."

"I'm glad Aunt Miriam is gonna marry Mary Ellen's daed. That will make my best friend my cousin, jah?"

"I expect it will." *I just hope things turn out well between my daughter and Amos,* Anna thought. *I've got a feeling things aren't quite right between those two.*

The Country Store was Miriam's favorite place to shop, and today she found it unusually busy. Not only were there several Amish customers milling about, but a lot of tourists had crowded into the small building. Miriam disliked crowds, especially when she knew they were watching her and all the other Amish who often shopped here. Crystal had gone across the street to the quilt shop, and Miriam wondered if it was crowded there, too.

When she moved to the back of the store where the household items were kept, she spotted an oil lamp she wanted to look at, but it was too high to reach. She glanced around, hoping to find a store clerk to help, but none were in sight. She turned away, deciding to look at some other items instead.

"Are you in need of some help?"

Thinking one of the clerks had seen her and had come to help, Miriam replied, "Jah, I would like to see—" Her mouth fell open as she turned her head. "Nick! What are you doing here?"

He smiled his usual heart-melting smile. "I like to come here on weekends. I get lots of story ideas from watching the people."

"You mean *my* people, don't you?"

Nick gave her a playful wink. "The Amish are quite interesting. Especially you, fair lady."

Every nerve in Miriam's body tingled, and her cheeks grew warm. She'd always considered herself quite plain, but in Nick's presence, she almost believed she was pretty.

"You know, I wonder if this could be fate, us always running into each other." Nick brought his head close to hers. "Maybe we really are meant to be together, Miriam."

She leaned away. What if someone she knew saw her engaged in such a personal conversation with this man? "We're not meant to be together, Nick. I'm sure you know that."

"Yeah, you're probably right," he whispered. "But if you weren't Amish, I might not have given up so easily on pursuing a relationship with you."

Miriam's hands felt clammy, and her heart beat fast against her chest. She had to get away from Nick as quickly as possible. Yet she didn't want to leave the store until she had completed her shopping. "If you'll excuse me, I must find a clerk for some assistance."

"What kind of help do you need?"

She pointed to the shelf above. "I'd like to see that kerosene lamp."

"No problem." Nick easily reached for the lamp and handed it down to her. "Here you go."

"Thank you."

"So, how are things with you these days?"

"Fine. I'm . . . uh . . . getting married in a few weeks."

Nick's eyebrows lifted in obvious surprise. "What was that?"

"I said, 'I'm getting married in a few weeks.' "

"Kind of sudden, isn't it?"

She stared at the floor for a few seconds, then finally lifted her gaze.

"Not really. I've been thinking about it for some time."

He grunted. "And who's the lucky fellow?"

"He—he's a nice Amish man."

"I didn't think he'd be anything but Amish. You made it pretty clear the day I proposed that you could never be happy with someone who didn't share your beliefs and traditions. So as much as I hate to admit it, you were right to turn down my offer of marriage. We both know it probably wouldn't have worked for us."

Nick lifted his shoulders in a shrug. "Besides, I'll be moving next week, and I doubt you'd have wanted to move to Ohio, much less become English."

Her mouth dropped open. "You're leaving Lancaster and going to Ohio?"

He nodded. "Got a job offer at the newspaper in Columbus, and I couldn't say no to the paycheck they're offering."

"I see."

"I won't be but a few hours from Holmes County, which I understand is where a large settlement of Amish is, so maybe I'll get the privilege of writing some more stories about your people."

"*The Budget* office is located in Sugarcreek, Ohio," Miriam said. "Maybe you can stop in there sometime and see how they put it together."

"That's not a bad idea. And if the job at the newspaper in Columbus doesn't work out, I could put in my résumé at *The Budget*." Nick chuckled and leaned close to her again. "I don't suppose I dare ask for a kiss from the bride-to-be before we part ways?"

Miriam's face heated up as she shook her head and took a step back.

"Well, you can't blame a guy for trying." He winked. "Guess a word of congratulations would be more appropriate under the circumstances, huh?"

"Jah."

"Well, congratulations then."

Before Miriam could comment, he smiled and said, "Say, I'd like to do something for you, if you'll let me."

"Wh—what is it?"

"Let me buy that oil lamp. It will be my wedding present to you. Whenever you look at it, maybe you'll remember me and know that I'm happy you've found true love."

Miriam swallowed against the lump rising in her throat. How could Nick possibly know she hadn't found love at all but was only marrying Amos so she would have another place to live and Mary Ellen could have a mother? If she tried to explain things, would he understand? Probably not, since his way of life was so different than hers.

"Please, don't deny me the pleasure of giving you the lamp," he said in a pleading tone. "It would make me happy to do something special for you."

Miriam shrugged as she released a sigh. "I suppose it will be all right." After all, who was she to stand in the way of anyone's happiness?

CHAPTER 25

As Miriam's wedding day approached, she found herself feeling increasingly anxious. She wondered at times if she could make herself go through with the marriage or if she should cancel it and go back to teaching. But then she would think about how she really did want to find another place to live before Lewis married Grace. Besides, Mary Ellen desperately needed her. With those thoughts firmly in mind, Miriam determined in her heart to follow through with the commitment she'd made to marry Amos.

On the day of the wedding, Miriam awoke with a headache. "Oh, no," she groaned as she climbed out of bed. "Not today of all days!" She forced herself to get dressed and headed downstairs to the kitchen with a firm resolve that she could make it through the day without any regrets.

As she sat at the table, drinking a cup of peppermint tea, she reflected on her past. So many memories swirled around in her head. She'd been born here in this old farmhouse—upstairs in what used to be Mom and Papa's room. She'd grown up here and had never known any other home, but that was about to change. In just a few hours, Miriam would become Amos's live-in housekeeper and Mary Ellen's new mamm. Nothing would ever be the same.

She swallowed hard, trying to force that ever-familiar lump out of her throat. Oh, how she would miss this house filled with so many memories of her happy childhood, when things hadn't been nearly so complicated or painful as they were now that she was an adult.

"Guder mariye, bride-to-be."

Miriam turned and saw Lewis standing in the doorway, stretching both arms over his head as he yawned.

"Good morning," she mumbled.

"This is your big day. Are you feeling a bit naerfich?"

"Jah, I am a little nervous," she admitted.

Lewis smiled. "I'm sure I'll be naerfich when Grace and I get married, too."

"Grace is a special girl. The two of you should be quite happy living here together."

"I hope we can be as happy as Mom and Papa were for so many years." His smile widened. "I'm happy for you and Amos. You've both been through a lot and deserve some joy in your lives."

Miriam groaned inwardly, but outwardly, she managed a weak smile. She was glad her brother was happy about his upcoming wedding. She only wished she didn't feel so anxious on her own wedding day.

Amos paced from his dresser to the bed and back again. He couldn't remember when he had been so nervous. Even on his and Ruth's wedding day, he hadn't felt this keyed up or suffered with such sweaty palms and shaky hands. Of course, he'd known that Ruth loved him and was marrying him for the right reasons. Not so with Miriam.

He moved over to the window and stared into the yard below. The morning had dawned with a clear, blue sky, and he spotted a cardinal sitting on a branch of the maple tree near the house, looking eager to begin its day.

I should be eager, too, he thought, as he opened the window and drew in a couple of deep breaths. *I hope I didn't make a mistake in asking Miriam to marry me, and I hope her agreeing to do so isn't a mistake. I know she doesn't love me, and even though I love her, I haven't been able to tell her, because I'm afraid it might drive her further away.*

He pressed his palms against the window ledge and inhaled again. *Dear Lord, please let me know when it's the right time to tell her how I feel, and I pray that You will bless our union, even though it's a marriage of convenience and will be in name only.*

• • •

Miriam, wearing a navy blue dress draped with a white cape and apron, grew more anxious by the moment as she sat rigidly in her seat, waiting to become Mrs. Amos Hilty. She glanced across the room where Amos sat straight and tall, wearing a white shirt, black trousers, and a matching vest and jacket. Did he feel as nervous as she did about this marriage? Was he having second thoughts, too? His stoic expression gave no indication as to what he might be thinking.

Should I have accepted Nick's proposal? Maybe I would have been happier being married to him. Miriam mentally shook herself. She wasn't marrying Amos so she could be happy. She was doing it for Mary Ellen, so the child would have a mother and so that Miriam would have a home. Things wouldn't have worked out between her and Nick. Besides, she didn't love him, nor did he love her. The feelings she'd had for him had only been a silly attraction, and she would never have risked hurting her family or being shunned just to satisfy a need for affection or even a home. By marrying Amos, she would be gaining a daughter, and she wouldn't have to give up her family or the only way of life she had ever known.

The wedding ceremony, which was similar to a regular Sunday preaching service, began at 8:30 a.m. Miriam did all right during the first part of the service, but as the time drew closer for her and Amos to stand before the bishop and say their vows, she became increasingly apprehensive. Miriam knew that both men and women of the Amish faith took their wedding vows seriously. Divorce would not be an acceptable option if things didn't go well between her and Amos. Married couples were expected to work out their problems and, above all else, remain true to the vows they had spoken before God and man.

Though Miriam's intent was to remain married to Amos until death parted them, it would not be easy for her to promise to love him. She was sure she would never feel anything more than mutual respect for Amos, but for Mary Ellen's sake, she would go through with the wedding. No one but Miriam and Amos, and perhaps Crystal, would know this was not a marriage based on love. No one need know the reasons behind her decision to marry him.

When it was time for Miriam and Amos to stand before the bishop, she pushed her nagging doubts to the back of her mind and took her place beside her groom.

If Bishop Benner knew about my lack of faith in God and the circumstances of my marriage to Amos, I'm sure he would never have agreed to perform the ceremony, she thought as a lump formed in her throat.

"Brother," the bishop said, looking at Amos, "can you confess that you accept this our sister as your wife, and that you will not leave her until death separates you? And do you believe that this is from the Lord and that you have come thus far by your faith and prayers?"

With only a slight hesitation, Amos answered, "Jah."

Bishop Benner then directed his words to Miriam. "Can you confess, sister, that you accept this our brother as your husband, and that you will not leave him until death separates you? And do you believe that this is from the Lord and that you have come thus far by your faith and prayers?"

Miriam cringed inside because of her deception, but in a clear voice, she answered, "Jah."

The bishop spoke to Amos again. "Because you have confessed that you want to take this our sister for your wife, do you promise to be loyal to her and care for her if she may have adversity, affliction, sickness, or weakness, as is appropriate for a Christian, God-fearing husband?"

"Jah."

Bishop Benner addressed the same question to Miriam, and she, too, replied affirmatively. He then took Miriam's right hand and placed it in Amos's right hand, putting his own hands above and beneath their hands. Offering a blessing, he said, "The God of Abraham, the God of Isaac, and the God of Jacob be with you together and give His rich blessing upon you and be merciful to you. To this I wish you the blessings of God for a good beginning, and may you hold out until a blessed end. Through Jesus Christ our Lord, amen."

At the end of the blessing, Miriam, Amos, and Bishop Benner bowed their knees in prayer. When they stood, he said, "Go forth in the name of the Lord. You are now man and wife."

Amos and Miriam returned to their respective seats, and one of the ordained ministers gave a testimony, followed by two other ministers expressing agreement with the sermon and wishing Amos and Miriam God's blessings.

When that was done, the bishop made a few closing comments and asked the congregation to kneel, at which time he read a prayer from the prayer book. Then the congregation rose to their feet, and the meeting was closed with a final hymn.

Miriam clenched her fingers as she blinked against stinging tears. It was done. There was no going back. She was now Amos's Miriam and would remain so until the day they were separated by death.

As several men began to set up tables for the wedding meal, Amos stole a glance at Miriam's three brothers, who stood off to one side, talking and laughing like this was a most joyous occasion.

And it should be, Amos thought painfully as he reflected on the somber expression he'd seen on his bride's face as they had each responded to the bishop's questions during their wedding vows. For many years before Amos had married Ruth, he had wished that Miriam could be his wife. Now that it had finally happened, it seemed bittersweet, for he knew she had only married him because of Mary Ellen's need for a mother, not because she felt any love for him.

Amos clenched his fingers until his nails bit into the palms of his hands. *Dear Lord, what have I done? I've married a woman who will never fully be my wife. I've given my word that I won't put any physical demands on her, and since we won't have an intimate relationship, we'll never have any kinner of our own. Miriam doesn't love me, and short of a miracle, she probably never will.*

Chapter 26

Miriam had only been living in Amos's house a few days, and already he wondered if he had made the biggest mistake of his life. Since today was an off-Sunday and there would be no preaching services, he hoped they could use this time together to discuss a few things concerning their marriage.

Mary Ellen, who was playing on the kitchen floor with her kitten, looked up at Miriam and smiled. "I'm glad you've come to live with Pappy and me. Can I call you Mama Mim from now on?"

Miriam smiled at the child. "If you like."

Amos's chair scraped against the linoleum as he pushed it away from the table and stood. He went over to the stove and removed the coffeepot, deciding that now might be a good time to say what was on his mind. "Mary Ellen, would you please go upstairs and play for a while?"

"Can I play outside on the porch instead?"

"Jah."

Mary Ellen looked at him with questioning eyes. "You and Mama Mim want to be alone, don't you, Pappy?"

If only that were true. I'm sure the last thing Miriam wants is to be alone with me.

"Miriam and I need to talk," he said, nodding at the child. "If the rain stops, maybe we'll go for a picnic at the lake later on."

"Really, Pappy? I love picnics!" Mary Ellen scooped the fluffy kitten into her arms and headed for the back door.

"Don't forget your jacket," Miriam called to her. "Since it's still raining, be sure you stay on the porch."

Mary Ellen grabbed her jacket from a low-hanging wall peg and bounded out the door.

"Do you think it was a good idea to get her excited about a picnic when it may not stop raining?" Miriam asked, turning to look at Amos with a frown.

"We'll see how it goes," he mumbled as he placed the coffeepot on the table.

She stood. "Well, I have dishes to do."

"Please, stay seated awhile. We need to discuss a few things."

She gave him a brief nod and sat down.

Amos poured coffee for them both and took the chair across from her. "I—I'm not sure what you believe about our marriage, but I want you to know that I . . . well, I think God brought us together." He wanted desperately to reach out and caress Miriam's cheek. Instead, he grabbed hold of the coffee mug and took a sip.

She opened her mouth as if to respond, but he held up one hand to silence her, knowing he needed to get this said while he had the chance and before he lost his nerve.

"I also think God will bless our marriage if we're faithful to Him and to one another."

"I'll be faithful to our vows, Amos. Divorce will never be an option for me."

"Nor for me." He took another sip from his cup as he searched for the right words. "I know we have many adjustments to make, and some of them might take some getting used to on both our parts."

Miriam blew on her coffee. "You're right about that."

"As I'm sure you know, the Bible teaches us in Ephesians 5:23 that the man is to be the head of the house, just as Christ is the head of the church." Amos paused to gauge her reaction, but she just stared at the table. "So, while I may want to consult with you on certain matters," he continued, "I believe that the final decisions should always be made by me."

Miriam looked up and stared at him with her forehead wrinkled and her lips compressed. After a moment, she asked, "Are you saying that I must do whatever you tell me to do?"

"No, it's just that I need to know that you respect my opinion, and I—I have a need to—to be able to touch you, Miriam." Amos tentatively reached for her hand, but she quickly pulled it away as soon as his fingers made contact with her skin, as though repulsed by his touch.

"You—you promised our marriage wouldn't have to be a physical one. Are you going back on your word now, Amos?"

"No. No, I'm not." He pushed away from the table and began pacing the floor, wishing he could somehow ask or even insist that she be his wife in every respect, knowing that he couldn't. "I will keep true to my word, Miriam. We'll continue to sleep in separate rooms just as we've done since our wedding night."

"I—I appreciate that," she murmured, staring down at the table again.

Amos cringed as he reflected on their wedding night. It certainly hadn't gone the way he would have liked, but a promise was a promise, and he wouldn't go back on it no matter how much he wanted to make Miriam his wife in every sense of the word. He knew that if he was ever to win her heart, he would have to remain honest and trustworthy. And he must remember never to try to touch her again unless she let him know first that it was what she wanted.

Miriam sat silently as Amos paced back and forth across the kitchen floor, his face red and his breathing heavy. "Was there anything else you wanted to talk to me about?"

He gave a quick nod and returned to the table. "Jah. I have some things to say about Mary Ellen."

"What about her?"

"I would appreciate it if you didn't mother my daughter so much."

"What? I thought that's why you agreed to marry me—so she would have a mudder."

Amos pulled his fingers through the end of his beard. "I'm not saying you shouldn't be like a mother to her. I just don't think she needs smothering."

"Smothering? How am I smothering the child?"

"Making her put on a jacket when it's warm outside and reminding her to stay on the porch."

"But it's raining, Amos. Surely you don't want your daughter to be outside playing in the rain."

He took a long drink from his cup. "I played in the rain a lot when I was boy, and it never did me any harm."

Miriam clasped her fingers tightly around her mug to keep them from shaking. She could hardly believe they were having this conversation. "I'm only concerned for her well-being. It may still be summer, but it's kind of nippy outside this morning."

"If I thought my daughter needed to put on her jacket or stay on the porch, don't you think I would have said something?"

She pursed her lips. "Maybe so. Maybe not."

He gave his beard a quick pull. "I—I'm sorry if I upset you. It's just that I've been Mary Ellen's only parent for a year now, and—"

"If you didn't think Mary Ellen needed a woman's care, then why did you marry me?"

"Because I—" Amos broke off in mid-sentence, pushed his chair aside, and stood. He tromped across the room, snatched his straw hat from the wall peg, and went out the back door, letting it slam shut.

Miriam's throat constricted, and a tight sob threatened to escape her lips. In an effort to regain control of her emotions, she dropped her head into her hands and squeezed her eyes shut. *Being married is nothing like I imagined it would be when I thought William was going to marry me.*

So far nothing had gone right—from the wedding ceremony, where she had made promises she wasn't sure she could keep, to their wedding night, when she had slept alone in the room next to Amos's.

After tucking Mary Ellen into her own bed that evening, Miriam had slipped quietly into the bedroom across the hall. For some time after she'd crawled into bed, she had heard Amos moving about in his own room next door. She had lain awake for most of the night, worrying that he might change his mind and come to her room, and wondering if she'd made the biggest mistake of her life by agreeing to marry him.

She was grateful Amos had been true to his word on their wedding night, but when he had reached for her hand a few minutes ago and said he wanted her touch, she'd become full of new doubts about whether he could be trusted.

She lifted her head and blinked a couple of times to

chase away the tears in her eyes. "I will get through this. I'll reach deep inside myself and find the courage to face each new day. And despite what Amos says or thinks, I do know what's best for Mary Ellen."

A routine was quickly established at the Hilty home, and even though Miriam found herself adapting to it, she didn't think she would ever adjust to being Amos's wife. Her heart longed for something more than wifely chores to do, but without love, a real husband-and-wife relationship was out of the question. Being a stepmother to Mary Ellen helped to fill a part of Miriam that seemed to be missing, but she knew it would never completely fill the void in her heart.

She didn't want to admit it, not even to herself, but she found Amos's presence to be unnerving. It made her keenly aware of the emptiness in her life. In the past, she had managed to keep her life fairly uncomplicated because she'd forgotten what love felt like. But now she had the strange desire—a need really—to love and to be loved.

Longing for love doesn't bring love into one's life, she told herself one evening as she washed the supper dishes. *The best thing I can do is keep busy, and I've certainly been doing a good job of that since I came to live here.* Her jaw clenched as she forced herself to concentrate on the task at hand.

Soon after Miriam had put the last dish away, Amos picked up his Bible to read as he had done every night since they had married. At first, she'd been irritated by the practice, since she had long ago given up reading her Bible every day. But now she was able to tolerate the ritual he'd established. It was a time when the three of them sat around the kitchen table, reading God's Word as a family. Mary Ellen usually had questions, and Amos seemed to take pleasure in being able to interpret the scriptures for her.

"Tonight I'll be reading in Proverbs," Amos said as he opened the Bible. " 'Whoso findeth a wife findeth a good thing, and obtaineth favour of the Lord.' " He looked up and smiled. "That was chapter 18, verse 22."

Does he think I'm stupid? Miriam fumed. *I may not have the kind of faith Amos has, but I'm well acquainted with the Bible.*

Mary Ellen gave her father's shirtsleeve a little tug. "Mama Mim's a good wife, isn't she, Pappy?"

"Jah, she is." Amos glanced over at Miriam and smiled.

His piercing gaze made her feel uncomfortable, and she looked away, hoping he hadn't seen the blush she was sure had come to her cheeks.

"Is there more in the Bible about Mama Mim?" Mary Ellen questioned.

"Let's see," Amos thumbed through the pages. "Here in Proverbs 31, verse 27, it says, 'She looketh well to the ways of her household, and eateth not the bread of idleness.' "

The child gasped. "Pappy, do you mean that Mama Mim isn't supposed to eat any bread? Won't she get awfully hungry?"

Amos laughed, and Miriam did, too. It felt good to laugh. It was something she did so seldom.

Mary Ellen stared up at her father, her hazel eyes wide and expectant. Amos patted the top of her head. "The verse isn't talking about real bread, Mary Ellen. The bread of idleness refers to someone who's lazy and doesn't want to work."

Mary Ellen's forehead wrinkled as she frowned. "But Mama Mim's busy all the time. She ain't one bit lazy."

"Isn't, Mary Ellen," Miriam corrected. She glanced at Amos, hoping she hadn't overstepped her bounds.

To her surprise, Amos nodded and smiled. "You're right, daughter. Your new mamm is a hard worker." He pointed to the Bible. "The verse is saying that a good wife isn't idle or lazy, and it's speakin' about someone like Mama Mim. She looks well to our house and takes good care of us. She doesn't eat the bread of idleness, because she's not lazy."

Mary Ellen grinned, revealing cute little dimples in both cheeks. "I'm so glad we have Mama Mim livin' with us now."

Amos looked over at Miriam and smiled. "I'm glad, too."

Miriam's face grew warm again, and she wasn't sure how to respond. So she merely nodded and said, "I made some pumpkin pie today. Would anyone like a piece?"

"I do! I do!" Mary Ellen shouted.

Amos nodded. "Jah, that sounds real good."

CHAPTER 27

Miriam looked at the kitchen clock on the wall above her head. It was one thirty in the afternoon, and Mary Ellen wouldn't be home from school for a few hours yet. Amos was out in his blacksmith shop, and since he'd taken his lunch with him today, Miriam had been alone all morning. She found that no matter how busy she kept, the loneliness and sense of longing that had crept into her heart never went away. The longer she lived under Amos's roof, the more those emotions intensified.

A knock at the back door brought her thoughts to a halt. Surely it couldn't be Amos. He wouldn't knock on his own door.

The door creaked as Miriam opened it, and a ray of sun bathed the room with its pale light. She was surprised to see her mother on the porch, holding a basket draped with a cloth. "What a surprise! I didn't hear your buggy drive in, Mom."

"I left it parked in front of Amos's shop while he shoes my horse."

"Ah, I see." Miriam motioned to the table. "Have a seat, and let's visit awhile."

Mom set the basket on the table, then removed her dark shawl and hung it over the back of a chair. "I brought you a loaf of oatmeal bread," she said, lifting the cloth from the basket.

"It looks good. Should I slice a few pieces? We can have some with a cup of tea."

"Jah, that'd be nice."

Miriam took the bread over to the cutting board. "How are things at Andrew and Sarah's, and how did you manage to get away by yourself?" she asked as she sliced the bread and placed a few pieces on a plate.

"Things are going along okay, and I was given the day off because baby Nadine had a checkup at the doctor's today."

"Oh?"

"Jah, and Andrew and Sarah decided to take all the kinner along and make some time for shopping and a meal out after Nadine's appointment."

Miriam set the plate of bread on the table. "Didn't they invite you to go with them?"

"They did, but I turned them down because I thought they should have some time alone as a family without me tagging along. Besides, I needed to get my horse shoed, and I saw it as a good chance to come visit with you for a while."

Miriam smiled. It was nice to see her mother in the middle of the week. To be able to spend some time together over a cup of tea and some oatmeal bread made Miriam's day seem less gloomy. She poured them each a cup of tea from the pot she'd placed on the table a few minutes before Mom had arrived and took a seat. "I'm glad you're here. We don't get to see each other much anymore now that I'm married."

"That's true, but we didn't see each other much before you were married, either."

"There was a good reason for that," Miriam said. "Between my job teaching school and all the work you were doing at Andrew's place, we were both too busy to spend much time visiting."

Mom took a sip of tea. "I know how much you enjoyed teaching. Do you miss it now that you're a *hausfraa*?"

"I do miss it some," Miriam admitted as tears stung the back of her eyes. "But I'm learning to adjust to the role of being a housewife and a mother."

"Speaking of being a mother," Mom said, "I just found out yesterday that my sister Clara's daughter Ada is going to have her first boppli later this fall. Ada's due around the time of Lewis and Grace's wedding in November."

"That's nice," Miriam said, trying to make her voice sound as excited as possible. "I'm happy for Cousin Ada and her husband, Sam."

"What about you, daughter? When do you think you and Amos will be starting your own family?"

Miriam reached for a piece of bread and took a bite, wondering how to let her mother know that she would never have any children of her own. It was a touchy topic, to be sure. One Miriam would rather not talk about.

"Miriam, did you hear what I said?"

She nodded. "I—I already have a family. Mary Ellen's a good child, and—"

"I'm sure she is, but wouldn't you like some kinner of your own?"

Miriam's eyes flooded with tears, and she quickly looked away so Mom wouldn't notice. How could she explain that her heart longed for a baby but that having a child with Amos wasn't possible because they didn't share the same bed? And that no matter how badly she might want a boppli, it simply wasn't meant to be.

"You and Amos haven't been married long, so there's still plenty of time for you to conceive. You just need to be patient, because kinner will come in God's time, not yours."

Miriam swallowed hard. "When you go out to Amos's shop to get your horse, please don't say anything to him about my not being pregnant yet. It might upset him."

"Of course not. I won't mention it to anyone, but I will be praying." Mom patted Miriam's arm. "My heart longs to be a *grossmudder* many times over, just as I'm sure your heart longs to be a mudder."

Miriam picked up her cup and took a drink. *If you only knew the truth about my so-called marriage to Amos.*

Amos had just returned to his shop after shoeing Anna's horse and hitching him to her buggy, when she stepped into the room. "Done visiting already?" he asked.

She nodded. "I figured you'd probably be finished

with Harvey by now, and I really do need to go back home and get supper started before the rest of the family returns from their day in town."

Amos smiled as he looked up from the metal desk where he sat. "I hope Andrew knows how fortunate he is to have such a caring mudder."

Anna's face turned a light shade of pink, and she waved her hand like she was fanning herself. "Ah, I don't do anything so special. And if I thought I did, then I would be *hochmut*."

"There's nothing prideful about admitting that you work hard." He smiled. "And you do work hard, since you help care for Andrew and Sarah's kinner, do a multitude of chores around their place, and offer support and encouragement to Sarah whenever she feels down."

"You know about her bouts with depression?"

He nodded. "Andrew's shared a few things with me."

"It's not been easy for Andrew or Sarah to see Rebekah confined to a wheelchair, struggling to deal with her handicap, but Sarah has taken it the hardest." Anna sighed. "I try to spend as much time with the child as I can, and since I discovered that she's taken with the plants I have in my room, it gives us something we can do together—something Rebekah doesn't need much help with at all."

Amos leaned against his chair and folded his arms. "You've been as good for Andrew's Rebekah as Miriam's been for my Mary Ellen."

Anna smiled, and her blue eyes fairly twinkled. "From what I can tell, Miriam loves your little girl as if she were her own flesh-and-blood daughter. She seems devoted to caring for that child."

Amos couldn't argue with that. Many times he'd seen or heard Miriam do or say something that had let him know how much she cared for Mary Ellen. *If only she cared that much for me,* he thought, as a feeling of regret coursed through his body.

"Have I said something wrong?" Anna asked in a tone of concern. "You look so solemn all of a sudden."

He was about to reply, when Bishop Benner entered the shop, saying he had a couple of horses he wanted shoed.

"I'd better be on my way home," Anna said. "It was good talking with you, Amos, and danki for hitching the horse up to my buggy again."

"You're welcome." Amos saw Anna out; then he turned to face the bishop. "Did you bring your horses with you, or do you need me to head out to your place to get the job done?"

The bishop motioned toward the door. "I brought 'em along."

"All right then. Guess I'd best get to it." Amos was glad he kept so busy these days. It helped take his mind off Miriam, who seemed to consume his thoughts more than ever. He knew that only the good Lord could change things between them, and he would continue to pray for such a miracle.

CHAPTER

28

Miriam could hardly believe fall was behind them already and winter was well on the way. The month of November had been a busy one, with Lewis and Grace's wedding, and then Thanksgiving a week after that. Soon Christmas would be here, and that would mean the opportunity for her to spend more time with family and friends.

Not that Mary Ellen and Amos aren't family, she thought as she sat at the treadle sewing machine, preparing to make Mary Ellen a new dress for school. The child had grown so much in the last month, and everything she wore seemed much too short for her gangly body.

When Miriam had agreed to marry Amos, she hadn't realized how demanding the role of motherhood would be, but she found herself enjoying the responsibility of being Mary Ellen's mother, although it caused her heart to ache for a child of her own.

At times like now, she found herself thinking about William Graber and the love they'd once shared, knowing that if they had married, she might have one or two children by now.

Miriam shook her head to clear the troubling thoughts and reminded herself that it did no good to dwell on such things. The past was in the past, and now she had a new life to think about. Mary Ellen would be the only child she would ever be able to help raise, and being around the little girl had given Miriam a reason to laugh and smile again.

Miriam found that she was even becoming more relaxed around Amos. He was a soft-spoken man with an easy, pleasant way about him. Though he wasn't what she would consider handsome, he certainly wasn't ugly. Being near him didn't make her heart pound wildly the way it had when she'd been with William or Nick, but she did feel respect for Amos, which was something William certainly hadn't earned.

One evening as Amos opened the Bible, he announced to Miriam and Mary Ellen that he would be reading from Psalm 127:3–5. " 'Lo, children are an heritage of the Lord: and the fruit of the womb is his reward. As arrows are in the hand of a mighty man; so are children of the youth. Happy is the man that hath his quiver full of them.' "

"What's a quiver, Pappy?" Mary Ellen asked.

Amos stroked his beard and looked thoughtful. "A quiver is a case for carrying arrows."

"Do you have a quiver?"

He grinned. "I have no case full of arrows, but I do have a home, and God's Word is saying that men are happy when they have a home full of children."

Mary Ellen's forehead wrinkled. "You only have one child, Pappy, so you must be awful sad."

Miriam cringed. Mary Ellen had hit a nerve, for Miriam knew she wasn't as happy as she could be, and one of the reasons was her deep desire for a baby.

Amos pulled Mary Ellen from her chair and into his lap. "I must admit, having more kinner would be nice, but I'm happy with just one."

Mary Ellen cuddled against his chest. "I hope God sends us a boppli sometime. I want a little bruder or *schweschder* to play with."

The tears that had formed behind Miriam's eyes threatened to spill over, and it took all her willpower to hold them at bay.

"If God wishes you to have a brother or sister someday, then it will happen, but it will be in His time," Amos told the child.

"Then I'll pray and ask God to hurry up," she said eagerly.

Amos looked as though he was about to say something more, but he closed the Bible instead, and then in a surprising gesture, he lifted his hand to brush away the tears that lay on Miriam's cheeks.

A deep-seated longing coursed through her body, and she quickly pulled back.

"Sorry. I—I didn't mean to offend you or go back on my word." Amos pushed away from the table. "There are a few things outside I must tend to."

As Miriam watched his retreating form, she felt relieved that he'd left the room, yet that sensation was mixed with disappointment. She didn't bother to analyze her feelings, but she knew one thing for certain—Amos Hilty, her husband in name only, was as miserable as she was right now.

• • •

Feeling the need to work off his frustrations, Amos grabbed an axe and a kerosene lantern from the woodshed and headed around back to the pile of logs he'd been planning to split for firewood.

"Miriam hates it whenever I touch her," he mumbled, placing the first hunk of wood on the chopping block. "I had promised her I wouldn't, yet I touched her anyway."

Crack! The axe came down hard, splitting the wood in two and sending both chunks into the air. They landed a few feet away, and Amos grunted as he bent to pick up another hunk of wood. He positioned it on the chopping block, raised his arms, and let the axe fall once more.

It seems like she always has to be moving—jumping up and down to check something on the stove, racing back and forth from the table to the refrigerator. She tries to keep busy so she doesn't have to talk to me, and when we do talk, there's either an invisible wall between us, or I say or do the wrong thing.

For the next half hour, Amos chopped wood with a frenzy as he thought about Miriam and how much he loved her. "I was a fool to marry that woman!" he shouted into the night sky. *Crack!* "Why can't she look at me with tenderness and love, the way she does Mary Ellen?" *Crack!* "How can I go on living with her when I can't touch her or let her know how much I love her?"

He swiped at the rivulets of sweat rolling down his

forehead with the back of his hand and grabbed another piece of wood. Placing it on the chopping block, he gritted his teeth. "I don't think I can do this much longer. I can't stand not being able to touch Miriam when I love her so much. Oh, Lord, give me the strength to endure this test."

Crack! The axe came down hard, shattering the wood into several pieces and sending them flying. Amos ducked as one came his way, but it was too late. The wood smacked him in the head quicker than he could blink. At first, all he felt was a dull ache, but soon his head began to throb. He lifted his hand to touch the spot, and thick, coppery blood oozed out between his fingers.

"Dummkopp!" he mumbled. "I'm a dunce for thinking too much and not watching what I was doing."

Amos knew the cut needed to be looked after, and he hoped it wasn't so deep that it would require stitches. The last thing he needed tonight was a trip to the hospital. He leaned the axe against the chopping block.

Feeling very foolish and a bit woozy, he turned for the house. A few minutes later, he found Miriam and Mary Ellen sitting at the kitchen table, putting a puzzle together and eating popcorn.

"Pappy, your head's bleeding!" Mary Ellen shouted.

Miriam was immediately on her feet and rushing to his side. "Oh, Amos, what happened?"

"I was choppin' wood out behind the shed, and one of the pieces flew up and hit me in the head."

"Come, sit at the table and let me look at that."

Miriam took hold of Amos's arm and led him across the room. As soon as he was seated, she leaned over and examined the wound, shaking her head and clicking her tongue.

Mary Ellen peered up at them with a worried expression. "Is Pappy gonna be okay?"

"The cut doesn't look too deep. I think it just needs to be cleaned and bandaged." Miriam hurried across the room and pulled a small towel from one of the cupboards. Then she went to the sink and wet it. She returned to the table and placed the towel against Amos's forehead. "Hold this here while I run upstairs and get some bandages."

When Miriam left the room, he smiled at Mary Ellen and said, "Now wipe that frown from your face, little one. I'm not hurt so much, and Mama Mim will be back soon to put a bandage on for me."

Mary Ellen's chin quivered, but she managed a weak smile. "I'm sure glad you married her, Pappy, 'cause I wouldn't know what to do if you came in here bleedin' like that."

Amos patted the top of his daughter's head. "Jah, I'm glad I married Mim, too."

Miriam's hands shook as she dabbed some antiseptic on Amos's wound and covered it with a bandage. What if the cut had been deeper? What if the wood had hit him in a vital spot?

She straightened and stepped away from him. "There. I think you'll be good as new."

"Pappy ain't old, Mama Mim." Mary Ellen stared at Miriam with a wide-eyed expression.

"I don't think that's what Miriam meant when she said I'd be good as new," Amos said before Miriam could reply.

Miriam touched the little girl's shoulder. "I guess I should have said that your daed will be fine and dandy now. The bleeding has stopped, and in a few days, the cut will be all healed up."

"I'm glad to hear it." Mary Ellen pivoted toward the table and pointed to the bowl of popcorn. "Now can we finish eatin' our snack?"

Amos chuckled, and Miriam felt herself relax. For the first time since she had become Mrs. Amos Hilty, she felt as if they were a real family. If only that feeling could last.

CHAPTER 29

The days moved on, bringing frosty cold mornings with plenty of snow on the ground. One afternoon in the middle of February, Miriam decided to leave a little early when she went to pick up Mary Ellen after school so she could pay a call on Crystal.

"Be careful today," Amos called to her from the door of his blacksmith shop. "The roads could be icy what with that snow we had last night."

"I'll watch out for it," she said as she climbed into her buggy. It was nice to know Amos was concerned, but she wondered if his apprehension over her driving on icy roads was because he cared about her welfare, or if he was merely worried that if something happened to her, he would have to find another mother for Mary Ellen.

She shook the thought aside and reached for the reins. At least Amos had kept true to his word and not tried to touch her again.

Half an hour later, Miriam guided her horse and buggy up her brother and sister-in-law's long driveway. She spotted Crystal right away, standing on the front porch, sweeping snow that had probably been blown in from the wind they'd had last night. When Crystal saw Miriam, she waved and set the broom aside. "It's good to see you," she called.

Miriam stepped down from her buggy and started toward the house, being careful not to slip on the icy path. "It has been awhile, hasn't it?"

Crystal nodded. "I've been wondering how you're doing on these cold, snowy days."

Miriam stepped onto the porch. "It's still kind of hard for me to take Mary Ellen to school each day, then turn around and go back home to an empty house. Teaching the scholars was a part of my life for several years, and I still miss it some."

Crystal opened the door and led the way into her warm, cozy kitchen. "But you have Mary Ellen to train and teach at home. The role of motherhood can be very rewarding. You'll see that even more once other kinner come along." She took Miriam's coat and hung it on a wall peg, then motioned to the table where a teapot sat. "Why, you'll be so busy changing *windle* and doing extra laundry, you won't have time to think about anything else."

"Other children? Changing diapers?" Miriam sank into a chair with a moan. "Have you been talking to Mom by any chance?"

"About what?"

"Me having a boppli."

"You're in a family way?" Crystal's face broke into a wide smile, and she leaned over to grab Miriam in a hug.

"I'm not going to have a baby," Miriam said. "Not now. Not ever."

Crystal clicked her tongue. "Miriam, it's only been six months since you and Amos were married. You need to give it more time. It's God's time anyway, and it will happen when He's ready for it to."

Shortly before Miriam's wedding, she had told Crystal why she was marrying Amos, and she'd thought she had made it clear that there was no love between them. However, she hadn't spoken of the matter since that day, so she was sure Crystal didn't understand the extent of how distant things really were between her and Amos. Miriam felt ashamed to admit that she slept in her own room and Amos in his. There had been no physical union between them, so there would be no babies.

She drew in a deep breath and decided that, despite her embarrassment, maybe it would help if she confided in someone who might give her a little understanding and sympathy. "I'll never get pregnant," she whispered with a catch in her voice.

"Now, Miriam, good things come to those who wait."

Tears slipped out from under Miriam's lashes and splashed onto the front of her dress. "Amos and I—we haven't consummated our marriage."

Crystal's mouth fell open. "You mean—"

"We sleep in separate rooms. We're man and wife in name only." Miriam grabbed a napkin from the basket in the center of the table and wiped her eyes. She hated to cry and saw tears as a sign of weakness, yet she'd been giving in to weepiness a lot these days.

"Has Amos agreed to such an arrangement?" Crystal asked, staring at Miriam in obvious disbelief. "I know you only married him because of Mary Ellen, but I thought that by now you—"

"He knows I don't love him, and he feels no love for me. Our marriage is still one of convenience. He provides a home and food for me, and I cook, clean, and take care of his daughter."

Crystal placed a gentle hand on Miriam's arm. "Miriam, he could have simply hired a maad for those tasks. Surely Amos needs a wife and not just a housekeeper."

"Then he should have married someone else. Someone he could love and cherish. Someone who would love him in return." More tears dribbled down Miriam's cheeks, and she sniffed deeply. "I'm afraid I have ruined Amos's life—and mine, as well."

"How can you say that? You obviously care deeply about his daughter."

"I do," Miriam admitted. "Mary Ellen's a wonderful child, and I feel almost as if she's my own little girl." She sniffed again, nearly choking on the tears clogging her throat. "I've come to love her so much."

"You see," Crystal said with a nod. "You just said that you have *come* to love Mary Ellen. It didn't happen overnight. It happened gradually, so maybe you can learn to love Amos in the same way."

"But I—I'm afraid of being in love."

"I think you fear falling in love because you're afraid of losing control."

Miriam's throat burned, and she swallowed hard. She wanted to argue with Crystal, but she couldn't, because she knew her friend's words were true. She did like to be in control, and since she'd married Amos, she felt as if she'd lost control of everything.

Crystal took hold of Miriam's hand and gave it a gentle squeeze. "Please think about what I've said. Why don't you ask God to fill your heart with love toward the man you've chosen to be your husband? I feel certain that, with God's help, things can work out between you and Amos."

When Miriam left Crystal's house a short time later and headed for the schoolhouse, her heart was full of questions. She knew her friend cared for her and wanted her to be happy, and she wondered if Crystal might possibly be right. Could she learn to love

Amos? Was love a feeling that was simply there? Or was it a matter of choosing to love someone, as Crystal had said?

Miriam shook her confusing thoughts aside, knowing she needed to concentrate on the road ahead. The once-cloudless sky had darkened, and soon the heavens opened, dropping thick snowflakes that nearly blinded her vision.

She turned on the battery-operated windshield wipers and gripped the reins to hold the horse steady. She'd left Crystal's later than she had planned, and she was worried that she might be late picking Mary Ellen up from school.

As the snow came down harder and stuck to the road, the wheels of the buggy started to spin. Miriam strained to see the road ahead and fought to keep her rig on the road. The battery-operated lights on the front of the buggy did little to light the way.

Miriam found herself wishing she hadn't taken the time to stop and see Crystal. She would have been at the schoolhouse by now, and she wouldn't have ended up telling her friend the truth about her and Amos. She was sure she could trust Crystal to keep the information she had shared to herself, but she didn't want Crystal's pity—and she wasn't sure she wanted her advice, either.

The buggy lurched as it hit a patch of ice, jolting Miriam's thoughts back to the task at hand. She shivered from the cold as well as from her fear of the near-blizzard-like conditions. Suddenly, the horse's hooves slipped, and the buggy lunged to the right. Miriam pulled back on the reins, calling, "Whoa, now! Steady, boy!"

The gelding whinnied and reared its head, jerking against the reins and causing the buggy to sway back and forth. It was dangerously close to the centerline, and when Miriam saw the headlights of an oncoming car, she gave a sharp tug on the reins.

The horse reared up, and before Miriam could think what to do, the buggy flipped onto its side, skidded along the edge of the road, and finally came to a halt.

She strained to see out the front window. The horse must have broken free, for it was nowhere to be seen. She pushed unsuccessfully against the door on the driver's side and winced in pain. Her side and shoulder hurt terribly, and she knew she must have a gash on her head. It not only stung, but she felt warm blood dripping down her face. She managed to rip a piece of her apron off and place it against her head to stop the bleeding.

In spite of Miriam's predicament, her first concern was for Mary Ellen. She knew the child would be waiting for her at the schoolhouse and might be frightened. *There must be some way to get out of here. Surely someone will see the buggy and stop to help. Oh, what about the horse? Is Amos's gelding all right?*

As Miriam's head continued to throb, making her feel helpless and dizzy, she was overtaken by a sense of panic, and she swallowed several times to keep from vomiting. She, who had always been so determined to solve her own problems, was now trapped inside the buggy, unable to find an answer to her dilemma. "Oh, dear God!" she cried. "Please help me!"

She squeezed her eyes shut and tried to think of scripture verses she had committed to memory. "Second Timothy 1, verse 7," she recited. " 'For God hath not given us the spirit of fear; but of power, and of love, and of a sound mind.' Psalm 23, verse 4, 'Yea, though I walk through the valley of the shadow of death, I will fear no evil: for thou art with me; thy rod and thy staff they comfort me.' Mark 4, verse 40, 'And he said unto them, Why are ye so fearful? how is it that ye have no faith?' "

She drew in a deep breath and tried to calm down. Then a sudden sense of peace came over her like a gentle spring rain. She had been so far from God for such a long time, yet now she was keenly aware that she was not alone. She was confident that the Lord was with her now, and she had nothing to fear.

Amos glanced at the battery-operated clock sitting in the middle of his desk. It was four o'clock. Miriam and Mary Ellen should have been home by now.

He left the desk and moved to the window. It was snowing—large, heavy flakes swirling in the howling wind. Had she gotten stuck in the snow somewhere along the way? Had the buggy slipped on a patch of ice? Could she have been involved in an accident?

"If Miriam's carriage doesn't come into the yard in the next ten minutes, I'm going out to look for them."

For the next ten minutes, Amos paced to the window, keeping an eye on the worsening weather, and then back to his desk, where the clock reminded him with every tick that his wife and daughter were still not at home. Finally, he grabbed his jacket and hat from the wall peg near the door and left the blacksmith shop, his heart pounding with dread. It was time to go looking.

"Miriam, can you hear me? Are you hurt?"

Miriam's eyes snapped open, and she winced when she tried to sit up. Then she remembered that the buggy was tipped on its side. Had she been asleep? If so, for how long? Had someone called out to her?

The voice came again. "Miriam, please answer me!"

It was Amos, and he'd come to rescue her. Tears burned Miriam's eyes as she turned her head to the left. "I'm here. I'm hurting, but I don't think my injuries are serious."

"The door is jammed shut, and I can't get it open," Amos hollered. "I'll have to go for help. Can you hang on awhile longer?"

"I'll be fine."

"What was that?"

"I'll be fine, Amos," Miriam said, her voice all but gone. "I'm not alone any longer; God is with me." Her eyes closed, and she drifted off.

• • •

"I love you, Miriam. I love you, Miriam. . . ." The resounding words ran through Miriam's mind as she struggled to become fully awake and focus on her surroundings. Where was she? Why were her eyes so heavy? Who had whispered those words of love to her? Her head pounded unmercifully. Was she having another one of her sick headaches? She tried to sit up, but a terrible pain ripped through her side.

"You'd better lie still," a woman's soothing voice said.

Miriam squinted against the invading light as her eyes came open. "Where—where am I?"

The woman, dressed in a white uniform, placed a gentle hand on Miriam's arm. "You're in the hospital. You were brought here when your buggy turned over in the storm."

Miriam frowned as the memory of the frightening ordeal rushed back to her. "I—I was so scared. The wind was howling, and the icy road must have spooked my horse. I knew I would be late picking up my daughter, and—"

Her daughter? Had she just referred to Mary Ellen as her daughter? Perhaps she was just a stepchild, but she was the only child Miriam would ever have, and she had come to love her as a daughter.

Miriam tried to sit up again. "Mary Ellen. Is my little girl all right?"

The nurse placed a firm but caring hand on Miriam's shoulder. "Your daughter's just fine. She and your husband are waiting in the visitor's lounge, and they are anxious to see you. Your family must love you very much."

The words *"I love you"* came back to Miriam. Maybe Mary Ellen had said them. But if that were so, then why had Mary Ellen called her *"Miriam"* and not *"Mama Mim"*?

Miriam remembered being trapped inside the buggy. She heard Amos call out to her and say that he was going for help. Maybe she'd fallen asleep and dreamed the endearing words about love. Her heart was so full of questions.

"How did I get here?" she asked the nurse.

"You were brought in an ambulance."

"When can I go home?"

"Probably in a day or so. You have a concussion, and the doctor wants to monitor you for a few days."

Miriam moaned. "What other injuries do I have?"

"Some cuts and bruises, and a few of your ribs are broken. You're fortunate, though. Your injuries could have been much worse in an accident of that sort."

Miriam nodded. "I—I'd like to see my family now."

"Of course. I'll tell them you're awake." The nurse moved away from the bed and left the room.

Tears slipped between Miriam's lashes and rolled onto her cheeks. She had referred to Amos and Mary Ellen as her family, but she reminded herself that Amos was her husband in name only.

The door opened, and Amos and Mary Ellen stepped into the room.

"Mama Mim!" Mary Ellen cried. "Are you all right?"

"I'll be fine," she answered as the child rushed to her bedside.

"You're crying, Mama Mim. Does your head hurt bad?"

"A little." Miriam couldn't explain to Mary Ellen the real reason for her tears.

"We were awful worried; you gave us quite a scare," Amos said in a serious tone as he drew near the bed.

Miriam studied his face. He did seem to be concerned.

"How—how did you find me?"

"I was a bit anxious when the snowstorm got so bad, and when you didn't return home with Mary Ellen on schedule, I began to worry. So I hitched up my rig and started for the schoolhouse. On the way there, I came across your carriage lying on its side. I stopped to see if you were okay; then I went to call for help."

"I do remember hearing your voice," Miriam murmured. "I must have dozed off, because I don't remember much after that."

Mary Ellen's chin trembled, and her eyes filled with tears. "I waited in the school yard for a long time. When you didn't come, I got real scared."

Miriam reached for the child's hand. "I'm sorry you were frightened, Mary Ellen."

Tears slid down the child's cheek. "When Pappy

sent Uncle Lewis to get me, he said you'd been in an accident. I thought you were gonna die and leave me like my first mamm did." She gripped Miriam's fingers. "Losin' you would make me feel so sad."

"I'm going to be fine," Miriam murmured. "Jah, just fine."

Mary Ellen leaned over and pressed her damp cheek against Miriam's face. "I love you, Mama Mim."

"I love you, too, daughter."

CHAPTER 30

Miriam spent three days in the hospital, and during that time, she did a lot of thinking, praying, and soul-searching.

Amos hired a driver and came to visit her twice a day. His daytime visits were after he'd dropped Mary Ellen off at school, but in the evenings, he brought Mary Ellen along. Miriam knew he must be getting behind on his work, but she looked forward to each of his visits.

The pain in Miriam's ribs and head was beginning to lessen, but her last night in the hospital was the worst, as every muscle in her body felt rigid. She had trouble falling asleep and asked for a sleeping pill. While waiting for it to take effect, Miriam stared at the ceiling and thought about her life with Amos and Mary Ellen.

She finally drifted off, only to fall prey to a terrible nightmare. In the dream, Amos was driving the same buggy she'd ridden the day of her accident. Miriam stood helplessly by the side of the road and watched in horror as the horse reared up and the buggy rolled onto its side. When she'd called out to Amos and he didn't answer, her heart was gripped with fear that he might be dead. "Amos! Amos!" she shouted. "Come back to me, Amos."

"Wake up, Miriam. You're having a bad dream."

Miriam opened her eyes and saw the night nurse standing over her.

"I—I was only dreaming?"

The nurse nodded. "The medication you took earlier probably caused that. Here, take a drink of water and try to go back to sleep."

Miriam's throat felt dry, and her sheets were wet with perspiration. She drank the water gratefully, thankful that she had only been dreaming. The thought of losing Amos bothered her more than she cared to admit.

When Amos heard the patter of little feet outside his room, he set his Bible on the nightstand and rolled over in bed. A few seconds later, a soft knock sounded on the door.

"Pappy, are you awake?"

"Jah, Mary Ellen. Come in."

As the child entered his room, the hem of her long white nightgown swished across the hardwood floor.

"I miss Mama Mim, and I couldn't sleep for worryin' about her."

He patted the patchwork quilt that covered his bed. "Lie down here awhile, and I'll take you back to your room after you're asleep."

"Really, Pappy? You wouldn't mind?"

He smiled and stretched his hand out to her. "Not at all. I would enjoy your company."

Mary Ellen settled herself against the pillows and released a sigh. "I wonder if Mama Mim's lonely there at the hospital without us."

"I'll bet she's as eager to come home as you are to have her back."

"How about you, Pappy? Aren't you lookin' forward to her comin' home?"

"Jah. Things haven't been the same around here without Miriam," he answered honestly. The truth was, Amos missed his wife more than he cared to admit, and if nothing but friendship ever grew between them, he knew he would always love her.

"If Mama Mim stays away much longer, I'm afraid the kinner at school will start makin' fun of my lunches again."

His eyebrows shot up. "What's wrong with your lunches? Aren't you getting enough to eat?"

"I get plenty. It's just that the lunches you make aren't near as tasty as what Mama Mim puts together for me."

Amos couldn't argue with that. He'd been the recipient of Miriam's lunches himself, and she had always fixed flavorful, healthy fare that would please any man's palate. "I'll try harder to make you better lunches," he said, gently squeezing the child's arm.

"That's fine, but will Mama Mim be comin' home soon?"

"Tomorrow, if the doctor says it's okay."

"Oh, I'm so glad!" Mary Ellen closed her eyes. "Gut nacht, Pappy."

"Good night, daughter of mine."

Miriam awoke the following morning, knowing it was the day she would be leaving the hospital. She was anxious to go home but felt confused as she continued to ponder the strange, frightening dream about Amos that she'd had the night before.

She could feel the beginning of another headache coming on, and her hands trembled. "What's wrong with me, Lord?" she cried, turning her head into the pillow and giving in to the threatening tears despite her desire to remain in control of her emotions.

Finally, when Miriam had cried until no more tears would come, she dried her eyes and sat up. Amos would be here soon, and she didn't want him to know she'd been crying.

Miriam was dressed and sitting on the edge of her bed, reading the Bible she'd found in the drawer of her bedside table, when Amos entered the room carrying a pot of purple pansies. He took a seat next to her on the bed, and she self-consciously averted her gaze, knowing she must look a sight. Her eyes were swollen and sore from loosing pent-up emotions that had been long overdue for release.

"Miriam, these are for you." Amos placed the flowers on the nightstand beside her bed.

"Danki. They're beautiful."

"Before we go, I want to discuss something with you," he said in a most serious tone.

Miriam forced herself to look into his eyes. "Oh?"

With a hesitant look, Amos reached for her hand, and he smiled when she didn't pull away from him. "I—I've been wondering if you've thought about what I said to you the other day."

"What day was that?"

"The day of the accident—right before I left to get you some help." Amos cleared his throat. "I—I've been wanting to tell you the truth for some time, but I didn't know how to say it, and I wasn't sure you would believe me or how you would take it."

"The truth about what?"

"The way I feel about you. Until the day of your accident, I was afraid to say anything. But when I saw your buggy toppled over on the side of the road, I was scared I might lose you, so I blurted out the truth—that I love you and have ever since we were kinner."

Miriam gasped. "I do remember hearing those words, but I thought I had only dreamed them, and I wasn't sure who had spoken the words to me." A film of tears obscured her vision as she stared at his somber face. "I had no idea you cared for me when we were kinner, Amos."

"How could you know when William never kept his word?"

"William? What's William got to do with this?"

"He knew I cared for you and that I was too shy to say anything. When I gave him some pansies to give to you, he promised he would put in a good word for me."

"You—you were going to give me flowers?"

"Jah." Amos groaned. "William, my so-called friend, let you think the pansies had come from him, and he never said a word on my behalf."

Miriam opened her mouth, then closed it again. She could hardly believe William would have done something so deceitful. But then he had led her to believe he loved her and wanted to make her his wife, only to run off to Ohio and marry someone else. "Amos, I—I don't know what to say," she stammered.

He placed one finger against her lips. "It's all right. You don't have to say anything. I know you don't return my feelings, but I had to tell you anyhow. When I saw you injured, I was afraid that I'd never have the chance to tell you what I would have told you years ago if I hadn't been so shy."

"You must have gotten over your shyness," Miriam pointed out. "Otherwise, you wouldn't have asked Ruth to marry you."

He nodded. "That's true. I did."

"Did you love her, Amos?" Miriam hated to think that Amos had married another woman while he was still in love with her.

"Jah, I loved her," he said in a voice barely above a whisper. "But not in the same way I've always loved you."

She stared down at her hands clenched tightly in her lap. "I—I don't see how you could love me when I've had such a bitter spirit. I've wasted a lot of time feeling sorry for myself because of William, and I'm afraid it's made me anything but lovable."

"I saw the old Miriam—the one I fell in love with when I was a boy." Amos took both her hands and pressed them gently against his lips. "Knowing the woman you were capable of being kept me loving you."

Miriam couldn't speak around the lump lodged in her throat.

"Are you angry with me for speaking the truth?"

"No, Amos, I'm not angry. I only wish that—"

"It's all right. I need you, Miriam, and so does Mary Ellen, but I've asked God to help me be patient, and if He wants us to be together as man and wife, then He will soften your heart toward me."

Miriam swallowed hard. "God is dealing with me, Amos, but I'm not ready to make a confession of love yet."

"I understand."

"No, I don't believe you do understand. Real love means a yielding of the heart to another person. It means commitment, loyalty, and trust. Since William's betrayal, it's been difficult for me to trust a man—or even God. My heart's been filled with bitterness because of William's betrayal."

Amos nodded. "I know, but you've kept your promise and not let it show to Mary Ellen. I thank you for that."

She sniffed. "I really do love her, Amos."

"Jah, I can tell. I also know that you and your family have been through a lot over the last few years. You've suffered a great hurt losing your daed, and then Rebekah's accident happened not long after that."

"Everyone in the family seems to have dealt with these things. Everyone—except for me." She leaned her head against Amos's shoulder and released a shuddering sob.

Amos lifted her chin and looked into her eyes with such love and compassion that she felt as if she could melt into his arms. "I understand your pain, Miriam. When Ruth died, I felt as if my world had been shattered. I even felt betrayed by Ruth for leaving me alone to raise our child. I blamed God for taking her. I was bitter and angry, and I didn't know if I could trust Him anymore. But I was reminded that His Word says, 'I will never leave thee, nor forsake thee.' I clung to the promise of that scripture verse, and one day I woke up and realized how much Mary Ellen needed me, and that I needed her."

Amos slipped his arm around Miriam's shoulders. "Life goes on, whether our hearts are filled with bitterness or love. Each of us must make the choice. We either choose to love, or we choose to harbor bitter, angry feelings. Hatred, anger, and bitterness are negative feelings that can make us ill. That's why the Bible says, 'A merry heart—' "

" 'Doeth good like a medicine,' " Miriam said, completing the verse. "Mom has quoted that passage of scripture to me many times. I'm ashamed to admit it, but I've chosen to ignore God's desire for my heart. Lying here in the hospital these past few days has given me time to think and pray. I want to yield to God's will, but I'm not sure I can. I'm afraid of failing and never finding happiness."

Amos ran his finger down Miriam's cheek, tracing a pattern where her tears had fallen. "I'm afraid, too, Miriam—afraid of being happy again. But I do love you, and I want to make you feel happy and loved, as well. I want you to be my wife in every way. I want us to have kinner and raise them in a way so they'll come to know God and trust in His Son as their Savior. I want our family to be full of God's love."

Miriam gulped on a sob. "I—I want those things, too, but I'm not sure I'm ready to have any kinner with you."

"I understand."

"Earlier this morning, I was reading in the Bible, and John 5:42 caught my attention. It said: 'But I know you, that ye have not the love of God in you.' That verse hit close to home, because I don't have God's love in my heart. You see, I've never completely yielded to Him—not even when I was baptized and taken into church membership. I did it because it was expected of me, not because I truly had faith in God or His Son, Jesus."

She paused and drew in a shaky breath. "I—I've struggled and tried to do things on my own far too long, and I know that I need God's love in my heart in order to find peace and happiness for my troubled soul."

"If you'd like to speak to Him about that now, I'll sit here quietly with you."

Miriam nodded and bowed her head. "Heavenly Father, forgive me for the hate and bitterness I've allowed to take over my heart. I thank You for sending Jesus to die for my sins. I accept His gift of forgiveness right now. Amen."

When Miriam finished praying, she opened her eyes and looked at Amos. He smiled, but she noticed tears in his eyes, which let her know he must have felt the emotion of the moment as much as she had. He blinked, and as the wateriness cleared, his lips lifted in a smile that warmed the last frozen place in her heart. "What God doeth is well done," he murmured.

It was then that a new realization came to Miriam. Amos wasn't William Graber or Nick McCormick. He was a kind, caring man, and he loved her. She knew without reservation that with God's help, her yielded heart could now become a loving heart.

CHAPTER 31

Miriam took a seat at the kitchen table and took a bite of the scrambled eggs Amos had set before her. For the first time in a long while, she actually enjoyed eating. Her whole world had taken on a special glow. She felt like a freed prisoner must feel after years of confinement.

"Danki for fixing breakfast," she said as Amos took a seat beside Mary Ellen, who sat across the table from her. "You shouldn't have let me sleep so long. I'm perfectly capable of cooking, you know."

Amos grinned. "I rather enjoyed fixing the eggs. I haven't done much in the kitchen since we got married. Besides, I want you to get as much rest as possible for the next few days. The doctor's orders, you know."

Miriam smiled in return. "These eggs are *appeditlich*. My compliments to the cook on their delicious flavor."

"Can we have pancakes tomorrow, Pappy?" Mary Ellen asked. "Pancakes with maple syrup are my favorite thing for breakfast, and since tomorrow's an off-Sunday and there's no preaching, we'll have plenty of time to make pancakes."

Amos laughed. "We'll see, Mary Ellen."

When breakfast was over, Amos excused himself to go outside and finish the morning chores, reminding Miriam not to do anything strenuous.

"I won't," she promised as she took a seat at the table and opened her Bible. Having decided to have a personal time with God each day, she turned to 1 John, chapter 4: "There is no fear in love; but perfect love casteth out fear: because fear hath torment. He that feareth is not made perfect in love."

Miriam was glad she'd decided to quit fearing love and stop trying to be in control of everything. She could love and be loved in return. She had nothing to fear anymore because she had God's love, as well as Amos's. The storm that had caused her buggy accident might have battered her body, but the storm that had been in her soul for too long had battered her heart. She had sought God's forgiveness and found the peace that only He could give.

Miriam turned the pages in her Bible and read from Philippians, chapter 4, which said, "Rejoice in the Lord always: and again I say, Rejoice." Further down the page, she read verse 8: "Finally, brethren, whatsoever things are true, whatsoever things are honest, whatsoever things are just, whatsoever things are pure, whatsoever things are lovely, whatsoever things are of good report; if there be any virtue, and if there be any praise, think on these things."

"I've wasted so much time thinking about all the bad things that have happened to me that I couldn't see all the good things You've done for me," she murmured.

"Who are you talking to, Mama Mim?"

Miriam turned to see Mary Ellen standing in the

kitchen doorway. The child had put on her coat and boots after breakfast, saying she was going out to play in the snow, but apparently she'd changed her mind.

Miriam reached her hand out to Mary Ellen and pulled her onto her lap. "I was talking to God."

"But your eyes were open, and you were praying out loud."

Miriam chuckled. "I suppose they were open."

"I'm glad today's Saturday and there's no school," Mary Ellen said eagerly. "I get to spend the whole day with my mamm and my daed!"

"Should we do something fun together?"

"Let's bake cookies; then we can go to the Country Store; and after that, we can go out to the barn and play with Pappy's new piglets; and—"

"Whoa! Slow down some, daughter!" Amos called as he entered the room. "Mama Mim has only been out of the hospital a short time and needs to take it easy. If we do all those things in one day, we'll wear her clean out."

Miriam looked up at Amos and smiled. "I'm fine, really."

"You may feel fine, but I don't want you to overdo."

"I appreciate that, and I will be sure to get enough rest," Miriam promised. "But I'll rest after Mary Ellen and I bake some chunky chocolate peanut butter cookies."

Mary Ellen's face lit up. "Yum! They're my favorite kind."

Amos laughed. "I think all cookies are your favorite." He took a seat next to Miriam. "May I help, too?"

"Pappy, do you know how to bake cookies now?"

"Sure he does," Miriam teased. "He knows how to lick the bowl, and he's an expert at eating the cookies." She poked Amos playfully in the stomach.

He gave her a crooked grin. "It's good to have you home, Mim."

"It's good to be home." Her forehead wrinkled. "Say, what are you doing back in the house? I thought you had chores to do outside."

"That's true, but I got to thinking about you and thought I'd pop back inside to see how you were doing."

"I'm doing just fine."

Amos grinned and pushed away from the table. "Okay then. Guess I'll head back out to the barn, but I'll be back soon to try out a few of those cookies."

Miriam smiled as he left the room. She knew her physical injuries were not the only injuries that were healing. So was her heart. Since love was a choice and not just an emotion, she could choose to love Amos in the way a wife should love her husband.

She reached for the most recent copy of *The Budget*, which had been lying on one end of the table, and opened it, hoping to find her mother's most recent article. As she scanned the pages, she noticed the CARDS OF THANKS heading and decided to read a few submissions.

A sincere thank you for the cards, letters, visits, and money I received after my recent knee surgery.
—Abe Byler, Strasburg, Pennsylvania

Thank you to all my friends and neighbors who brought me cards, cookies, and came by for a visit on my birthday last week.
—Carolyn Kuhns, Seymour, Missouri

A heartfelt thanks to the special woman I liked to call "fair lady" for her friendship and for helping me to realize that I could find happiness with a woman. In fact, I've met another very special lady, and she's even talked me into going to church with her a few times. So maybe there's some hope for this stubborn man yet. Be happy, fair lady.
—Knight in Shining Armor, Columbus, Ohio

Miriam gasped as tears slipped under her lashes and rolled down her cheeks. That message was from Nick, she was certain of it, and he'd found happiness and wanted her to know it.

She squeezed her eyes shut and offered a silent prayer on her friend's behalf, asking God to bless Nick, and thanking Him for the happiness that she, too, had found.

Amos whistled as he did his chores in the barn. He couldn't help himself, for he was happier than he'd been in a very long time. Miriam was home from the hospital and recovering nicely, and she seemed more peaceful now that she'd committed her life to God.

"Maybe there's some hope that she will come to love me," he said aloud as he spread clean straw in one of the horse's stalls. "She's been friendlier toward me since I admitted that I'm in love with her." He shook his head. "Of course that doesn't mean she loves me."

"You talkin' to yourself or one of the horses?"

At the sound of a man's voice, Amos nearly dropped his pitchfork, and when he whirled around, he saw Miriam's youngest brother standing a few feet away. "Lewis, you about scared the wits out of me. I didn't hear your horse and buggy. What'd you do, walk over to our place?"

"Nope. Parked my rig down by your blacksmith shop, figuring I'd find you there."

"Not today." Amos leaned the pitchfork against the wall and stepped out of the stall. "Miriam came home from the hospital yesterday."

"Jah, I heard the doctor might be lettin' her go soon. Mom will be happy to hear that news."

Amos nodded. "I figured it would be best if I stuck around the house, at least through the weekend, just to be sure Miriam doesn't do anything she shouldn't be doin'."

"Makes sense to me. My big sister has always been a hard worker, and she's not likely to let a little thing like a bump on the head and a few broken ribs keep her down for long."

"Which is why I'm not working today."

Lewis motioned to the bales of straw stacked along one side of the barn. "Looks like you're workin' to me."

Amos chuckled. "Well, the horses needed some clean bedding, and I hadn't planned on being out here that long." He motioned to the barn door. "Why don't we go inside so you can say hello to Miriam? That will give me another chance to make sure she's not overdoing."

"Sounds like a good idea." Lewis opened the barn door and stepped outside. Amos followed.

When they entered the house a few minutes later, they found Miriam and Mary Ellen in the kitchen, baking cookies.

"Umm . . . smells mighty good in here," Lewis said, stepping up to Miriam and giving her a pat on the arm. "Welcome home, sister. I'd hug you real good, but I know your ribs are probably still pretty sore."

"They aren't so bad." She held a cookie out to him. "Try one of these."

"Hey, where's my cookie?" Amos asked with a mock frown.

Miriam smiled and handed him three cookies. "Is that enough?"

He wiggled his eyebrows. "I think that will tide me over for a while."

Mary Ellen giggled. "Pappy, you're so *eefeldich*."

"Oh, you think I'm silly, do you? Why, I'll show you silly!" Amos chased his daughter around the table, laughing like a schoolboy and tickling her as he went.

Lewis and Miriam stood off to one side, shaking their heads. “Maybe I need a couple more cookies,” Lewis said. “Then I’ll be smiling like your high-spirited husband.”

Amos scooped Mary Ellen into his arms and gave her a hug. He wouldn’t admit this to Lewis, but the reason he was so happy had little to do with the cookies he’d eaten and everything to do with the woman who had baked them.

Miriam had been home from the hospital for several days, and even though she said she was feeling stronger, Amos wouldn’t allow her to drive the buggy yet. So every morning, he drove Mary Ellen to school and picked her up again each afternoon. One morning when he returned from the schoolhouse, he entered the kitchen and found Miriam making a pot of coffee.

“I was wondering if you’d have time for a little talk,” she said as he slipped out of his jacket and hung it on the wall peg.

He rubbed his hands briskly together. “That sounds good if a cup of hot coffee goes with the talk. It’s pretty cold out there this morning.”

Miriam smiled. “I’ll even throw in a few slices of gingerbread. How’s that sound?”

“Real good.” Amos smacked his lips in anticipation and pulled out a chair at the table.

“I’ve been thinking,” Miriam began. “That is, I was

wondering if it would be all right if I moved my things out of my room and into yours."

"Are you saying what I think you are?" Amos asked as hope welled in his chest.

She nodded. "I want to be your wife in every way as God intended it should be."

Amos pushed away from the table and crossed the room to where she stood at the cupboard cutting the gingerbread. He placed his hands on her shoulders and turned her around to face him. Miriam's eyes held a look of tenderness and something more, too. Did he dare believe she might actually love him?

"Are—are you certain about this? I don't want to pressure you in any way. I know we're getting closer, but—"

Miriam placed a finger against his lips. "I want to be your wife, Amos. With God's help, I want to love you as a wife should love her husband."

Amos wrapped his arms around her as every nerve in his body tingled with the joy of holding her. "I love you so much, Miriam."

She pressed her head against his chest, and he inhaled the sweet scent of her freshly washed hair. "I love you, too, Amos," she murmured.

"Really?"

"Jah, it's true."

The words Amos had so longed to hear poured over him like healing balm, and he lifted Miriam's face toward his and placed a gentle kiss against her lips.

She responded with a sigh, and he felt her relax against him as they kissed again. It was a kiss that told Amos how full of love his wife's heart truly was. It was an answer to his prayers.

Chapter 32

If love was a choice, then Miriam had made the right choice, for she found the love she felt for Amos seemed to grow more with each passing day. His tender, gentle way had always been there, but before, she'd chosen to ignore it. Now she thanked the Lord daily for helping her see the truth.

Miriam hardly missed teaching anymore. Her days were filled with household duties she now did out of love. When Amos wasn't busy with his blacksmith duties, he helped her with some of the heavier housecleaning. They took time to read the Bible and pray together, which Miriam knew was the main reason they were drawing closer to one another and to God. Their evening hours were spent with Mary Ellen playing games, putting puzzles together, reading, or just visiting.

Miriam had a special project she was working on, and whenever she had a free moment, she would get out her cross-stitching, just as she had done tonight after she'd tucked Mary Ellen into bed.

"What are you making?" Amos asked as he stepped into the living room.

"It's a surprise for Mom." She patted the sofa cushion. "Have a seat. You look tired."

He sank down beside her with a groan. "*Ich bin mied wie en hund*—I'm tired as a dog."

She reached over and took his hand. "I don't know of any dog that works as hard as you do, Amos."

He smiled. "I think you're right about that. I've had so much business in my blacksmith shop lately that I'm plumb wore out. If things keep on the way they are, I might have to hire an apprentice."

"Might not be a bad idea; I hate to see you working so hard."

He leaned over and kissed her cheek. "It's nice to know you care about me."

"Of course I care." She needled him in the ribs with her elbow. "If you wear yourself out, who's going to brush my hair for me every night?"

"Oh, so that's how it is, huh?" Amos tickled her in the ribs. "I'm just a convenience to have around whenever you need something, jah?"

"Be careful, or you might get stuck with this needle," she scolded, holding her handwork out of his reach.

He took the sampler from her and placed it on the coffee table. Then he pulled her into his arms and kissed her gently on the lips.

One Saturday afternoon, Miriam suggested they go for a buggy ride.

"Where would you like to go?" Amos asked.

"I think it's time to pay my family a visit. Let's stop and see Lewis and Grace first. Then we can go over to Crystal and Jonas's, and finally, we'll call on Mom at Andrew and Sarah's. I want to give her the gift I've been working on."

Amos raised his eyebrows. "A little ride, I thought you said. It sounds to me like you're planning to cover the whole of Lancaster County." He smiled at Miriam and gave his daughter a playful wink.

Mary Ellen, who had been coloring a picture at the kitchen table, jumped up immediately. "Can I go, too?"

Amos bent down and lifted the child into his arms. "Of course, you may. It'll be a fun outing for the three of us."

Miriam gathered up the chunky chocolate peanut butter cookies she had made the day before and placed some into the plastic containers she'd set out. She planned to give one package to each of the families they visited.

The buggy ride was exhilarating, and the trees, budding with spring, were breathtaking. It felt good for Miriam to be out enjoying God's majestic handiwork again.

Mary Ellen, who sat in the seat behind Miriam and Amos, called out, "Oh, look—there goes a mother deer and her boppli. Isn't it lieblich?"

"Jah, Mary Ellen. All babies are adorable," Miriam answered.

"I wish I had a boppli of my own to play with," Mary Ellen said in a wistful tone.

"Someday when you're grown-up and married, maybe you will," her daed answered.

"But I'm still a little girl, and that's a long time off."

"Maybe Uncle Lewis still has some of those baby bunnies left."

"Really, Pappy? Can I have a baby bunny for my own?"

"If it's all right with Mama Mim, it's all right with me."

Miriam smiled. She rather liked the nickname Mary Ellen had begun when they were first married. "If Uncle Lewis still has some bunnies left, you may have one, but only on one condition."

"What condition?"

"That you promise to help care for the bunny."

"Oh, I will. I promise!"

Mary Ellen knelt in the hay next to her father. Uncle Lewis had taken all of the bunnies out of their cages so she could have a better look and could choose which one she wanted.

The rabbit Mary Ellen finally selected was the smallest of the litter, but it looked healthy and bright-eyed and was certainly playful. As they left Lewis's place and headed to Crystal and Jonas's house, Mary Ellen had quite a time keeping the bunny inside the box she'd been given.

Crystal and the twins were out in the yard when Amos pulled their buggy near the barn. The boys jumped up and down, obviously happy to see their cousin.

"I have a surprise!" Mary Ellen called to John and Jacob.

When Amos lifted Mary Ellen down from the buggy, she and the twins rushed off toward the barn.

"Jonas is in the barn working on his old plow," Crystal told Amos. "I'm sure he could use a friendly face about now."

Amos laughed. "Maybe it's time to retire that aged thing. Floyd Mast has some good buys on the new ones he sells."

"I know he probably should buy a new one," Crystal agreed, "but Jonas is rather partial to the old one. It belonged to his daed, you know."

The mention of Papa caused a sharp pain in Miriam's heart. She still missed her father and probably always would. He'd been a devout Christian man, and someday she was sure she would see him in heaven.

"I'll go see Jonas and leave you two ladies to yourselves. I'm sure you both have plenty to talk about. Women usually do." Amos winked at Miriam and poked her playfully on the arm.

She lunged for him, but he was too quick. His long legs took him quickly out of reach, and soon, he disappeared inside the barn.

"It's good to see you looking so happy," Crystal said as she steered Miriam toward the house.

"I am happy—more than I ever thought possible."

"I'm glad to hear it."

"I brought you some chunky chocolate peanut butter

cookies, and I'll tell you about my reason for being so happy over a cup of your great-tasting cider."

"You're lookin' a mite tired today," Jonas said soon after Amos stepped into the barn. "Is that sister of mine workin' you too hard?"

Amos chuckled and shook his head. "It's that business of mine that's wearing me out. I might have to find an apprentice."

Jonas grabbed a piece of straw from a bale nearby and stuck it between his teeth. "I'll spread the word if you want me to."

"I'd appreciate that."

"Other than being tired, how are things going?"

"Real well. Things are much better between Mary Ellen and the other kinner at school, and Miriam and I are happier than I ever thought possible."

Jonas thumped Amos on the back. "I'm glad to hear that, because you've both been through your share of trials, and you deserve all the happiness you can get."

The last stop of the day was at Sarah and Andrew's place. While Miriam was looking forward to seeing her brother and his family, she was most anxious to see Mom and give her the gift she had made.

The sun had been shining all morning, but now, as a light rain began to fall, it slipped behind the clouds. Amos hurried Mary Ellen out of the buggy.

"Wait, Pappy. My bunny's still in the box. I want to take Dinky in to show Rebekah."

"Oh, it's Dinky, is it?"

"Jah, I like that name."

"Okay then. I'll get Dinky for you." Amos grinned at his daughter. "You go on ahead with Mama Mim."

The warmth of the kitchen was welcoming, but the heat from the stove didn't warm Miriam nearly as much as the welcome she and Mary Ellen received from her family.

"What brings you by today?" Andrew asked.

"Jah, to what do we owe this pleasant surprise?" Mom questioned.

"Amos and I thought it would be nice to take Mary Ellen for ride."

"And I've got a surprise!" Mary Ellen hopped up and down in front of Rebekah, who had been wheeled into the room by her mother. "Pappy's gone out to the buggy to get it."

"What's the surprise?" asked Rebekah. "I love surprises."

"I think nearly everyone loves surprises," Miriam said, smiling down at her daughter. "I have one for Mom, too."

"Who wants to be the first to share their surprise?" Sarah asked as she pushed her daughter up to the kitchen table.

Miriam touched Mary Ellen's shoulder. "I'd better let you go first, since you can't seem to stand still."

"But Pappy isn't here yet."

Just then the door opened, and Amos stepped into the room with Dinky in his hands.

"En gleener Haas!" Rebekah squealed. "May I hold it, please?"

Mary Ellen reached for the small bunny. With a huge smile on her face, she sashayed across the room and placed the furry critter in Rebekah's lap.

Dinky's nose twitched as Rebekah stroked its floppy ear. "He's awfully cute. Where'd you get him?"

"From Uncle Lewis, and he still has three more, so maybe you'd like a bunny, too."

With an expectant expression, Rebekah looked first at her mother and then over at her father.

Andrew smiled. "If it's okay with your mamm, it's fine by me."

Sarah nodded. "I think it's a good idea, but you must help care for the bunny."

"Jah, of course I will."

"And you must share the bunny with your younger brother and sister," her daed reminded.

"I promise, Papa."

"Come, everyone. Sit awhile." Miriam's mamm motioned to the table. "I'll put water on the stove to heat, and we can have some hot chocolate."

"And I've brought along some chunky chocolate peanut butter cookies," Miriam said as Amos pulled out a chair for her.

When everyone was seated and the hot chocolate and cookies had been passed around, Miriam lifted the canvas tote bag from the back of her chair and reached inside.

“What’s this?” Mom asked as Miriam pulled out a small package wrapped in tissue paper and handed it to her.

“I made this for you—to let you know how much I love you.”

Mom took the gift, and she emitted a sob when she opened it. “Oh, Miriam, it’s lieblich.”

“What’s lovely?” Sarah asked, craning her neck to see.

Mom held up the beautiful cross-stitched wall hanging Miriam had made. It read: “A merry heart doeth good like a medicine.”

Miriam gave her mother a hug. “Those words from the Bible are true, Mom. You’ve been right all along, and I just couldn’t see it. God wants His children to have merry hearts. It’s my hope that anyone in our future generations who see this sampler will know that the only way to be truly healthy spiritually is to have a merry heart.”

“This is a blessed surprise,” Mom said tearfully. “And it’s certainly an answer to my prayers to know that you finally understand the importance of having a merry heart.”

“God had been calling to me for a long time. I only wish I had listened to Him sooner.” Miriam looked over at Amos and smiled. “Would you like to tell them our other surprise?”

He shook his head. “I think we should let Mary Ellen tell ’em, don’t you?”

Miriam nodded. “That’s a fine idea. Mary Ellen, please tell everyone our other surprise.”

Mary Ellen giggled; then in her most grown-up voice, she announced, "On the way here, Mama Mim and Pappy told me that I'm gonna be a big sister."

"Miriam, is she saying what I think she's saying?" Mom asked breathlessly.

Miriam nodded. "I'm expecting a boppli."

"Now that's wunderbaar news," Sarah exclaimed.

"I'm so happy for you." Mom gave Miriam a hug. "Oh, I wish the rest of our family were here for this joyful news."

"We've already seen Lewis and Grace, as well as Jonas and Crystal, so they've been told," Amos was quick to say.

"Congratulations!" Andrew said, thumping Amos on the back, then hugging Miriam.

Mom dabbed the corners of her eyes with a hankie. "If only my Henry could be here. He would be so pleased to see how happy our Miriam is now."

"Someday, we'll be reunited with Papa, but until then, he'll always be with us—right here." Miriam placed her hand against her chest. "I hope my own kinner and future *kinskinner* will grow up to love the Lord and have merry hearts, too."

Miriam's Chunky Chocolate Peanut Butter Cookies

Ingredients:

- ¾ cup margarine
- 1 cup white sugar
- 1 cup brown sugar
- ½ cup peanut butter
- 2 eggs
- 2 teaspoons vanilla
- 2½ cups flour
- 1 teaspoon baking soda
- ½ teaspoon salt
- 1 (8 oz.) chocolate candy bar, chopped

Preheat oven to 350 degrees. Beat margarine, sugars, and peanut butter until light and fluffy. Blend in eggs and vanilla. Add the dry ingredients and mix well. Stir in chocolate pieces. Drop rounded tablespoons of dough onto ungreased cookie sheet. Bake 10–12 minutes or until lightly browned. Let stand a few minutes before removing from cookie sheet. Makes four dozen cookies.

Center Point Publishing
600 Brooks Road • PO Box 1
Thorndike ME 04986-0001 USA

(207) 568-3717

US & Canada:
1 800 929-9108
www.centerpointlargeprint.com